ROBERT B. PARKER'S
PAYBACK

A SUNNY RANDALL NOVEL

ROBERT B. PARKER'S PAYBACK

MIKE LUPICA

THORNDIKE PRESS
A part of Gale, a Cengage Company

Copyright © 2021 by The Estate of Robert B. Parker.
Thorndike Press, a part of Gale, a Cengage Company.

Thorndike Press® Large Print Core.
The text of this Large Print edition is unabridged.
Other aspects of the book may vary from the original edition.
Set in 16 pt. Plantin.

**LIBRARY OF CONGRESS CIP DATA ON FILE.
CATALOGUING IN PUBLICATION FOR THIS BOOK
IS AVAILABLE FROM THE LIBRARY OF CONGRESS.**

ISBN-13: 978-1-4328-8678-3 (hardcover alk. paper)

Published in 2021 by arrangement with G.P. Putnam's Sons, an imprint
of Penguin Publishing Group, a division of Penguin Random House LLC.

Printed in Mexico
Print Number: 01   Print Year: 2021

*This book is for
John (Ziggy) Alderman.*

ONE

I was in my brand-new office over the
P. F. Chang's at Park Plaza, around the
corner from the Four Seasons and a block
from the Public Garden, feeling almost as
cool as Tina Fey.

I'd just walked through the door that had
SUNNY RANDALL INVESTIGATIONS written
on the outside, put on some coffee, sat
down behind my rustic wood Pottery Barn
desk. All in all, I was everything a professional woman should be, if you didn't count
the Glock in the top right-hand drawer of
my desk.

There were two chairs on the client side
of the desk, a small couch against one wall,
and a table on the other side of the room
that I used for painting when I needed to
take a break from world-class detecting. It
housed my pads and boards and a palette
and all the other tools of a world-class
watercolorist's trade.

"Forget about the gun," Jesse Stone said. "If somebody shows up and threatens you, just pull a paintbrush on them."

"What about the boxing classes you made me take?" I said. "You should see how good my right hand has gotten."

I had signed up for a half-dozen at the gym an old boxer named Henry Cimoli owned over near the harbor.

"Here's hoping you never need to throw it," he said.

Jesse. Chief of police, Paradise, Massachusetts. On-again, off-again boyfriend. Mostly on over the past year. I had given in and started calling him that, my boyfriend, just because I hadn't found a better way to describe his role in my life. We were still together, anyway, even though we were mostly apart, our relationship having survived the virus. We were official, as the kids liked to say, even if we hadn't announced it on Instagram, or wherever kids announced such things these days, in a world where they found everything that happened to them completely fascinating. Jesse and I had been as close as we'd ever been before the virus caused the world to collapse on itself. Now we'd once again grown more used to our own social distancing, and for longer and longer periods of time, him up in

8

Paradise, me in Boston.

But still official, at least in our own unofficial way.

"I feel like Jesse and I are happy," I said to Spike the night before, over drinks at Spike's.

"Low bar," he said. "For both of you."

"Come on," I said. "I've got a stress-free relationship going, money in the bank, my own office, I've still got Rosie the dog, I've even lost five pounds, not that you seem to have noticed."

"Just like a big girl," Spike said.

"Not as big as I was five pounds ago," I said.

"You also still have ex-husband issues," he said, referring to Richie Burke, still in Boston, still in my life as he raised his son from his second marriage.

"Do not," I said.

"Do so," Spike said.

"You sound childish," I said.

"Do not," he said. "Do not, do not, do not."

Spike and I had been celebrating the fact that I'd finally gotten paid by Robert Magowan, who owned the second-biggest insurance company in Boston. Magowan had hired me to prove that his wife had been cheating on him. This I did, well over two months ago. Then he refused to pay, and kept refusing, until Spike and I had finally shown up at his office and Spike threatened to shut a drawer with Magowan's head inside it. That was right before I handed Mr. Magowan my phone and showed him the images of him in bed in a suite at the Four Seasons, park view, with Lurleen from accounting, and wondered out loud who'd win the race to the divorce lawyers, him or the missus, once the missus got a load of what I thought were some very artsy photographs.

"You were only supposed to follow *her*," he said.

"Well," I said, "to put it in language you can understand, I thought I might need additional coverage."

He'd proceeded to transfer the money over speakerphone from an L.A. branch of Wells Fargo while Spike and I watched and listened.

On our way out of the office Magowan had said to me, "They told me you were a ballbreaker."

"Not like Lurleen," Spike had said.

I knew I could have handled Magowan myself. I'd brought Spike along just for fun. His, mostly. He'd gone through a bad time during the pandemic, nearly having lost

Spike's at the worst of it. But he'd come up with the money he needed at the last minute, thanks to a loan from one of his best customers, a young hedge-fund guy named Alex Drysdale, who spent almost as much time in the place as I did.

Spike still wasn't back to being his old self, but threatening to kick the shit out of Robert Magowan, even if it hadn't come to that, had made him seem happier than he'd been in a year. And more like his old self.

He was about to pay off his loan this morning, having invited Drysdale to the restaurant so he could hand him the check in person. The thought of that made me smile, just not quite as much as the memory of the ashen look on Magowan's face when I showed him the pictures of him and Lurleen in one particular position that should have had its own name, like a new yoga move:

Downward dogs in heat.

The sound of my cell phone jolted me out of my reverie.

The screen said *Spike.*

"Sunny Randall Investigations," I said brightly. "Sunny Randall speaking. How may I help you?"

"I need to see you right away," he said.

His voice sounded like a guitar string

11

about to snap. I realized I was standing.

"What's the matter?" I said. "Something's the matter. I can always tell."

"I just knocked Alex Drysdale on his ass, is what's the matter," he said.

"The guy who loaned you the money?" I said. "*That* Alex Drysdale?"

"I wanted to kill him," Spike said. "But I stopped after breaking his fucking nose."

"Spike," I said. "What the hell happened?"

"He stole my restaurant."

There was a pause.

"Wait, let me amend that," Spike said. "I mean *his* restaurant."

I told him I was on my way, ended the call, grabbed my leather shoulder bag, remembered to turn off the coffee machine, locked the door behind me, ran down the stairs.

I had started to believe that maybe God, at long last, had stopped being pissed off at everybody.

Obviously She hadn't.

TWO

"Payback really is a bitch," Spike said. "Only it turns out Drysdale's the bitch."

We were seated at the bar. Spike had a Bloody Mary in front of him so big it looked like a fire hydrant. He also had a glass filled with ice next to it, and would occasionally pluck out a cube and press it to his cheek. Spike said that after he hit Drysdale, the two guys with him — neither of whom, he said, looked like fund managers — hit him back. I knew how hard it was to get the better of Spike in a fight, even when it was two against one. But they'd managed.

"At least you got your shot in," I said.

"I even managed to get some good ones in on the extras from *The Sopranos*," he said, "before one of them kicked my legs out from underneath me and the other just kicked the shit out of me."

"Literally kicking you while you were down," I said.

"My upper body is already starting to look more colorful than Pride month," he said.

Drysdale, he said, finally told them to stop; he didn't want Spike scaring the customers.

"Called them *our* customers," Spike said, and drank.

I asked then how Drysdale had done it, if he could explain it to me without trying to sound like Warren Buffett.

"I'm too stupid to sound like Warren Buffett," he said. "I'm the one who let him pick my fucking pocket in broad daylight."

Drysdale had been a regular at Spike's from the time he turned it from a sawdust-on-the-floor to an upscale restaurant on Marshall Street that had become one of the hottest places in town, not just because of the food, but because of the bar crowd, which could include professional athletes and local TV personalities and politicians and the lead singer from Dropkick Murphys and young women from the modeling agency that had opened around the corner. Drysdale was good-looking, a big tipper, often came in with a beautiful woman or left with one. And was rich as shit. He finally became aware that Spike, even with the government loans and takeout business and furloughing of a lot of the staff, was

14

about to shutter the place. So he offered Spike the loan that he needed at a two percent rate, on one condition:

He didn't tell anybody about the terms.

"I'm a one-percenter," he joked to Spike, "but let's keep that two percent between us."

Spike had been a business major at UMass. When Drysdale presented him with the document, he told Spike to ignore all the bullshit language about floating rates and warrants and even what would happen if Spike somehow still had to declare bankruptcy down the road, that it was all boilerplate stuff and would never come into play until maybe the next pandemic in another hundred years or so.

"We're friends," Drysdale said. "We could have done this on a handshake. But my lawyers are making me."

Spike was one of the smartest people I knew, on every subject except maybe the periodic table. But desperation made him careless, and so did trust in what he considered a real friendship. The wolf was at the door and he needed his money, as he said, right fucking now.

"Stay with me," he said, knowing I was often challenged doing the math on a dinner check with girlfriends.

I stayed with him, but barely, as he began to speak of floating rates and cash positions that Spike said he never could have met, the ones Drysdale had assured him he didn't need to worry about. And interest coverage. And revenue targets for a business that had no chance to meet those until the pandemic was over. Spike never knew it, but by the time Spike's started making money again, by the time he could finally see some daylight, it was too late.

"But the only one who knew that, from the start, was my pal Alex Drysdale," he said.

Then Drysdale came through the door a couple hours ago with his bruisers and handed Spike his check back as soon as Spike handed it to him, saying he could keep it, he'd basically been in default on the loan from the beginning.

I said, "Are we getting anywhere near the bottom line?"

"He now owns Spike's is the bottom line," he said. "He even showed me the part of the agreement where he was entitled to a special dividend for what he called his 'consulting' services."

Spike put air quotes around *consulting.*

"Consulting on what?" I said.

"Fucking me over," Spike said. "It was at

16

that point that I dropped him. Cost me a bunch of my new Doppio napkins because of all the blood. I was actually hoping he might bleed out and my problems would be solved."

Spike drank more of his Bloody Mary. I idly wondered if it was his first of the day. He rarely drank this early. But these were special circumstances. I was starting to think about asking him to build a Bloody for me.

"You know what he said when I asked him why?" Spike said. "He said it was for the same reason dogs lick their balls. Because they can."

At that point, Spike said, Drysdale turned and walked out.

"What am I going to do?" he said.

"I believe you mean what are *we* going to do?"

There was a flicker of light then in his eyes, for the first time since I'd arrived. Not much. A little. I was telling him what we both knew in that moment, that I was here for him the way he had always been for me. I was his wingman now. Just far cuter.

"Have it your way," he said. "What are *we* going to do?"

I smiled at him. It was as big as I had. Trying to tell him that things were going to be all right, even if I had no idea how.

"What the horny insurance guy said I did to him," I said. "We're going to *break* this dog's balls."

THREE

Before I left I told Spike not to do anything stupid.

"Don't you mean more stupid than I already did?" he said. "It would make me as dumb as a hamster."

I told him I would call him later. He said if I couldn't reach him that would mean he was passed-out drunk. I kissed him and told him we'd figure a way out of this. He said I was full of it, but that he still loved me. I told him I loved him more.

I was supposed to have lunch with Lee Farrell at the Legal Sea Foods across from my office. I hadn't seen him for a few weeks, not since he'd caught the disappearance of a local social media sensation named Carly Meme that the cops were treating as a possible homicide. Carly had made a huge name for herself as an influencer, pushing products and places to people her age and getting paid handsomely to do it. It was just

19

one more thing that made me feel old. I used to think influencers were guys like my friend Wayne Cosgrove at *The Boston Globe*.

To make things far racier in all media, it turned out that Carly Meme — real name Carlotta Espinoza — had been the girl-on-the-side for Jack Norman, the most powerful political consultant in the state and right-hand man and fixer for Carlton Miller, who owned half of downtown Boston and was in line to be the next treasury secretary, if you could believe what you read. Of course, Norman had been extremely married for the past hundred years or so. He hadn't graduated to suspect yet, remaining the ever-popular person of interest, swearing that he had nothing to do with Carly's disappearance, that he'd been nothing more than a mentor to her. I told Lee one day that I'd never heard not being able to keep it in your pants described as "mentoring."

But when I called to make sure Lee and I were still on, I went straight to his voicemail. Got no immediate reply to my text. He had either forgotten or was too jammed up with the case.

With lunch taken out of play, and not feeling particularly hungry, I decided to do what I often did in moments of great uncertainty.

Go annoy someone.

The someone was Alex Drysdale, whom I suspected was enough of an arrogant asshat to meet with me, even knowing how close I was to Spike.

Drysdale had asked Spike, when he first became a regular, if it was worth taking a shot at me.

"You can go ahead and fire," Spike told him. "But you'd miss."

Alex Drysdale, at least for a few months, remained undeterred. He'd never pushed too hard, never made me feel uncomfortable or too close to being Me Tooey. Maybe it was because Spike was always close by. Or me having told him, when asked, that I did indeed have a gun in my purse and so knew how to use it. He'd finally given up, still acting shocked that someone he found attractive didn't return the feeling.

One night, when it was just Spike and me and him at last call, Drysdale had said, "Well, at least you let me down easy."

"Dude," Spike said, "how can you be down if you were never up?"

I still had Drysdale's office number in my phone to go with his cell number, because he'd given me both. I called the office number, told his assistant who I was. She put me right through. I asked if I could come by his office. He said to come ahead. There was no point in him asking why I wanted to see him or me telling him.

"You're not going to finally shoot me, are you?" he said.

"To be determined," I said, and he reminded me that his office was at One Financial Center.

"Where else?" I said.

FOUR

One Financial Center was a glass-and-steel monstrosity next to Dewey Square. It advertised itself, for some bizarre reason, as the ninth-tallest building in town, but only if you measured by its "pinnacle" height, as if there were any other measure for the eight taller buildings in Boston.

The Sale Riche Group had a small suite of offices on the fortieth floor. Out of forty-six. I knew enough French to know that "sale riche" meant filthy rich. I was surprised at how few people I saw when I got off the elevator. Maybe I'd seen too many Wall Street movies. I spotted Drysdale's name on the door, big letters, straight ahead of me.

The nameplate on his assistant's desk said GINA PATARELLI. She had a lot of thick black hair, dark eyes, olive skin, lot of eye makeup. A little done for my taste. But still pretty. I told her I had an appointment.

"Aren't you the lucky girl," she said, in a North End accent, fun in her dark eyes.

"Relative to what?" I said.

She lowered her voice and grinned. "Just don't make any sudden moves."

"You been with Alex long?" I said.

"Only in Alex years," she said.

"Like dog years?"

"Woof," Gina Patarelli said. "Woof."

"What would he do if he heard you talking about him like that?" I said.

"Not one freakin' thing," she said.

"Are you sure you're working for him and not the other way around?" I said.

"Nah," she said. "He just knows that I know enough to be dangerous. Between us girls."

"Everything he knows?" I said.

Her answer to that was a flamboyant wink.

She buzzed him then, told him I was here, showed me into his office. Drysdale was behind his desk and didn't get up. He wore a white shirt rolled up at the sleeves and a matching bandage across the bridge of his currently less-than-perfect nose.

"Look on the bright side," I said. "If we were all still wearing masks no one would know you lost the fight."

"I lose the early rounds sometimes," he said. "But never the fight." He cocked his

24

head slightly. "Was that supposed to be funny, by the way?"

"Apparently not," I said.

It was always my default position in a mirth-free zone, which this clearly was.

"I've got no beef with you, Sunny," he said after motioning me into the one chair across from him. "But I'm not changing my mind, if that's what you're here for." He grinned. "No matter how hard you try to persuade me."

"You wish," I said.

I'd worn a short, cream-colored skirt to go with a black sweater not as tight as it had been five pounds ago. I crossed my legs. Eat your heart out.

"I'm not here to change your mind," I said. "I just want to hear for myself why you'd do something this lousy to this good a guy. And, additionally, why you waited this long to do it."

"Nobody's stopping him from paying back the money," Drysdale said. "I'd told him that right before he sucker-punched me."

"He was about to pay you back," I said, "just at the original interest rate."

"Not to use a cliché," Drysdale said, "but he didn't read the fine print."

"You're the cliché, Alex," I said.

He leaned forward now. It was problem-

25

atic, at best, trying to smirk around a bandaged nose, but Drysdale gave it the old college try. Stanford, as I recall him telling me when I first met him, without being asked, before getting his MBA at Wharton.

"He made a monumentally bad deal," he said. "And that's not on me. That's on him. If he'd read the agreement properly, he would have understood that he'd practically breached most of the covenants as soon as the ink was dry. But when you're about to go under, you don't bitch that the life preserver is too tight."

"I imagine loan sharks say pretty much the same thing," I said.

He shrugged. "I am who I am," he said.

"You can't possibly need his restaurant."

"I don't need it," he said. "I just happened to want it."

He leaned back and folded his arms in front of him. Behind him was a view of just about everything except the northern coast of Maine.

"I'd like you to reconsider," I said.

He laughed now.

"Yeah, well, that would be a no," he said.

"You're sure," I said.

"I am," he said. "Imagine how much I'm going to save in bar bills alone."

I stood up.

26

"Well," I said, "it's not like I didn't give you a chance."

"A chance to do what?"

"The right thing, mostly."

"Oh, get the fuck out of here," he said. "And then give this up. There's nothing you can do about it."

"Now, see, that is where you're wrong," I said.

"Really?" Drysdale said. "What do you *think* you can do about it?"

I smiled and came around his desk and sat on the edge of it, close enough that I knew I'd made him uncomfortable, even though I knew he considered himself too much of a guy's guy to act as if he were afraid of me. On top of that, I was showing a *lot* of leg.

"Not *think*," I said. "What I *know* I can do. Which means, Alex, that I am about to get up into your shit and never get out."

Then, before he could get his head out of the way, I leaned over and pinched his nose hard enough to make him cry out in pain. I would have told him he sounded like a girl, but why insult the sisterhood?

As I walked out the door, leaving it open behind me, he was yelling at me that I didn't want to fuck with him. Over my shoulder, I told him that I just had.

As I walked by Gina Patarelli she whispered, "I think I may be in love with you."

FIVE

I had walked to One Financial Center from Spike's and decided to walk back to my office from there. I tried Lee again, but got no answer. No surprise. Carly Meme's disappearance, if it did turn out to be murder, might end up being the most prominent case of his career, and would give him even more standing in Homicide than he already had. It hadn't been easy for him as a gay cop, especially at the time he'd gotten his badge, with the BPD about as enlightened on the subject as Falwell Jr. It still wasn't easy. A good arrest on this case, after all the media face time he was getting already, would officially make him a star.

He was Spike's friend, too. Despite my best efforts, I had never been able to make it more than friendship between the two of them. But I wanted him to know what had happened, even as he was working his case and I was just beginning to work mine. It

29

was a shitty thing that had happened to Spike. A chance to help him — and take down Alex Drysdale in the process — made me feel the kind of rush of cop adrenaline that Jesse so often talked about, and I was sure Lee himself was feeling right now. It was a good thing. Catching people like the frisky Mr. and Mrs. Robert Magowan in the act was something I occasionally did to pay the bills. But something like this, making things right for Spike, or at least trying, was why I wanted to be a detective in the first place.

"Your work doesn't define you," my therapist, Dr. Susan Silverman, said to me once. "It *is* you."

"I am capable of committed relationships," I said, sounding like a defense attorney and not a patient.

"Not like the one with your chosen career, Sunny," she said. "You can feel passionately committed to it and still be alone."

I took my time making my way back to Park Plaza, choosing not to turn this into a power walk, not while wearing my new Stuart Weitzman ankle boots. They were officially known as booties. I still couldn't say that out loud without giggling. It was the second half of October by now, the temperature in the fifties today, one of those

30

October days when you started to feel summer finally letting go.

As I was making the turn off Stuart I pulled out my phone and called my father.

He asked what I needed.

"Can't a girl just call her pops to say hello?"

"Even in retirement," he said, "I still look for tendencies," then asked where I was. I told him. He said he'd just finished a dentist's appointment on Chauncy Street and hadn't had lunch yet.

Half an hour later we were seated across from each other at the Legal Sea Foods near my office, and I was telling him what had happened to Spike, and how I'd left things with Drysdale, and what I'd done to him before I left his office.

"My girl," he said.

"It was awfully immature of me," I said.

"But how did it feel?"

"Fucking awesome," I said.

"The mouth on you," he said.

He wore a tweed jacket that I knew was nearly as old as the Old North Church, a zippered sweater that I'd given him for his birthday, tattersall shirt underneath the sweater. His hair had gotten a lot whiter in the last year and his step a little slower, even though he swore he was still walking his

31

three miles a day. But he still woke up every morning thinking his day was somehow going to be full of adventure.

"You need to talk to a lawyer," he said. "What about the redhead you don't like from Cone, Oakes?"

He was referring to Rita Fiore, still the best criminal attorney in town.

"I don't not like her," I said.

"Not what you said when you found out she'd had a little fling with Jesse back in the day," he said.

"That was another immature reaction," I said. "But I've evolved since then."

"Sure you have."

"The problem is," I said, "Spike thinks it's all legal."

"I'm sorry," Phil Randall said. "Is he now practicing law at Cone, Oakes?"

He took his spoon and dabbed some cocktail sauce on one of his oysters and then added just a drop of Tabasco sauce and somehow managed to look elegant as he ignored his tiny fork and just slurped the thing down.

"Even if he wanted it, it's not as if Spike can currently afford high-priced legal talent," I said.

"You could always call your former client the gangster," he said.

He was referring to Tony Marcus. Tony hadn't actually been a client when he'd asked me to find his missing girlfriend, and ultimately no money ever changed hands between us. Phil Randall still maintained it was a tomato-and-to*mah*to type thing.

He ate another oyster, and smiled.

"A couple pimps, him and this Drysdale," Phil Randall said. "Even though Drysdale frankly sounds like more of a bunco artist."

"No offense, Dad," I said, "but you don't hear a lot of talk about bunco anymore."

"The definition nevertheless remains the same," he said. "A confidence trickster." He looked down at the Caesar salad I'd ordered but had barely touched. "Can I have your anchovies?" he said.

For those he used the tiny fork.

"So what are you going to do, and how can I help?" he said.

As much as I prided myself on being a modern and independent woman, I was also aware how many smart men I had in my life, and how often I leaned on them when there was trouble. Spike was always my first call, only now he was the one in trouble. I knew Jesse was always there for me. Richie, too.

And Phil Randall, forever.

"I'm going to find out everything I can

about this jamoke until I can find something I can use," I said.

"Jamoke," he said, and smiled another elf smile.

"I'm not saying that all money guys are like him, because I'm smart enough to know they're not," I said. "But Drysdale acts like he gets to use another rule book."

"I believe it's known as the tax code," my father said.

He'd long since finished his oysters. Now he just reached over and slid my plate across to him.

"I saw something in him today that I'd missed when we were all hanging around Spike's," I said. "Maybe he just wasn't important enough for me to notice. But he likes this. He *likes* wiping the floor with Spike this way. I felt like I was listening to a banker laugh his ass off about a foreclosure."

"He does sound like one of your gangster friends," Phil Randall said. "You're coming at this in the right lane, kiddo. You treat him like a thief. A perp. He stole from Spike, whatever that piece of paper says."

"All he cares about is money," I said.

"Find out about how he made his."

"I'm not even good balancing a checkbook," I said. "No one knows that better than you."

He reached over and patted my hand. "But you've always been a fast learner, kid."

He waved for the check then. I told him I wanted to pay, I'd just made a big score. He said I could get the next one, even though there never seemed to be a next one for me to get.

"Find his secrets," Phil Randall said.

"You're sure he has some."

"Everybody has them," he said. "You just have to know where to look. And you will."

"You sound pretty certain."

He smiled the elf smile again.

"Genetically determined trait," he said.

SIX

This had quickly turned into one of those days when I longed for the old times about which my father constantly romanticized, when investigating bad guys involved walking up stairs and knocking on doors, not search engines and Google searches.

"If I had ever known that a mousepad would be one of the tools of the trade," Phil Randall had once told me, "I would have reconsidered the priesthood as a vocation."

"Not what Mom says," I told him.

But by the end of the afternoon, I knew a lot more about Alex "Ace" Drysdale and what a repellent financial whiz boy he was than I'd known before Spike's phone call.

He'd grown up in Sausalito, played football in high school and then at Stanford, before coming east for the MBA. In one of the interviews he'd done, with the *Financial Times,* he said he might not have been the best student in his class at Wharton, but he'd gotten straight A's in connections.

"You know how you show how smart you are?" he said. "By realizing there are people smarter."

He was consistently vague about how much of his start-up money he'd gotten from his late father, a real estate mogul type in San Francisco, and how much of it came from those grad school connections. But five years after Wharton — a place he mentioned in just about every interview he gave, almost as some kind of validation, or badge of honor, as if it were far more meaningful to him than having gone to Stanford — he had started his first fund with his Stanford roommate, Christopher Lawton, who'd gone on to get his own MBA at Harvard Business. They were among the whiz boys who had absolutely nailed the financial crisis at the end of George W. Bush's second administration by shorting mortgage securities, a couple "Big Short" players about whom books had been written and movies made. I had watched one of the movies recently, with Christian Bale, not so much for the subject matter, just because I wanted to look at Christian Bale for a couple hours.

A lot of what I read about Drysdale made about as much sense to me as when Spike would begin to rhapsodize about the intricacies of baseball. But I understood the basic premise of Drysdale and Lawton being among those who identified the fact that the housing bubble was about to explode in 2008 like a water balloon dropped out of a window.

And just like that, they were both rich.

To this day, no one was quite sure about what caused their separation, but separate they eventually did. The most Drysdale had ever said about it publicly was that they had different visions of the future. Lawton? He never said anything, because of the nondisclosure agreement he had reportedly signed on his way out the door.

At this point, Alex Drysdale was on his own. And, according to a very long piece about him in *The Wall Street Journal,* he proceeded to lose everything except his Turnbull & Asser shirts. According to the *Journal,* he lost and lost big, mostly because of disastrously bad bets on "emerging market debt," whatever *that* was.

Drysdale survived, though. "Like one of those cockroaches that would survive a nuclear attack," one unnamed source said in the *Journal.* He continued to maintain, up to the present, that his comeback was simply the by-product of "good luck and good looks and day-trading." He got rich again on tech stocks after Donald Trump was elected. Somehow, even after the virus hit the world like a meteor and after another well-documented slump, Sale Riche flourished while other funds went belly-up.

And even though there were always rumors about sketchy methods and even sketchier investors, he had never been fined by the SEC, had never even been investigated. Another source, in a *Crain's,* described Drysdale as the kind of shark who made other sharks swim in the opposite direction, mostly out of respect.

Now he'd eaten Spike's, whole. It made me wonder how many other businesses, small or large, he might have eaten alive after COVID brought them low.

Before I closed my laptop and headed home to Rosie, I Googled Christopher Lawton and happily discovered he was still in Boston, running a new boutique hotel, The Carmody, that had gone up the year before in Brookline. He was also majority owner in the place.

Tomorrow I'd do things the old-time way and go knock on his door, see if I could get him to fold his NDA with Alex Drysdale into a party hat.

SEVEN

I was alone tonight with Rosie, not entirely by choice. I had called Jesse and asked if he wanted to come down for dinner, telling him I was prepared to cook him my specialty.

"Wasn't aware you *had* an official specialty," he said.

"I have many."

"And don't I know it."

"And what would you consider my specialties, as I believe we're clearly no longer talking about food?"

"Too many to list," he said, and then told me he had to take a rain check, he was having dinner with his son, Cole.

"Do you miss me?" I said.

"Intensely."

"You're intense about everything," I said.

"Missing you is *my* specialty," he said.

Dr. Silverman had spoken more than once about how I was still my most authentic self

40

when I was alone, whether I was in a relationship or not. There had been other men in my life besides Richie and Jesse. Just not like Richie, and not the way I was with Jesse now, intensely, even with him living in Paradise and me here.

But then came the virus, and I was once again alone more than ever. I managed to continue meeting with clients, thanks to the weird magic of Zoom. I painted more than I had in the past couple years. I was terrified, especially in the early days when testing was still problematic at best, of seeing my parents because of their age. Richie was fiercely vigilant about protecting his son, so I hardly ever saw them. Once Jesse and I had both tested negative, I could at least go up there occasionally, or he would come to Boston, Jesse finally saying, "If we die, we die." I took long walks with Spike, and occasionally we went on long runs.

I saw Dr. Silverman over Zoom and told her, often, that I didn't feel isolated at a time when others did.

"You were social distancing before it was a thing," she said.

"But is that a *good* thing?" I said.

She had given me her Mona Lisa smile on my laptop screen and said, "You tell me."

"Here we go," I'd said.

Today when I was back at River Street Place I went straight upstairs to my studio and got back to work on one of my favorite pieces in a while, working off a picture of the lighthouse in Paradise. I'd taken the photo on a beach walk one day with Molly Crane, Jesse's deputy, when we were working a case together.

"Jesse's like your lighthouse," she said. "And you his. You both know you're there when you need each other."

"Just not all the time," I said.

"Oh, God, no," she said. "What would be the fun in that?"

Then I had taken the picture, with that amazing quality you could get now on your phone, on another one of those days the color of slate when you couldn't decide where the water ended and the sky began.

I painted until my back started to hurt, the way it did sometimes when I kept leaning over to get closer and closer to my board, as if trying to lose myself in the place and moment I was trying to recapture.

It was a way to turn off my brain and stop thinking about what Alex Drysdale had done to Spike, and getting angry enough to do a lot more than squeeze a nose that really did look as if it had taken years of genetic engineering to produce. Spike was as strong as any man I knew, strong as my father or Jesse or Richie or anybody. And this creep had come along and made him feel weak. And small.

"Fuck Alex Drysdale," I said to Rosie.

She looked up, instantly at high alert, as if what I'd just said sounded exactly like "Want a treat?"

I cleaned my brushes, took a shower, got into sweatpants and my IT WON'T ALWAYS BE LIKE THIS T-shirt, and made myself a western omelet, first cooking up tomatoes and red bell peppers and green bell peppers and onions in olive oil. That would show Jesse Stone. No garlic bread on the side. I had made a vow that last year's jeans were going to fit forever. I cleaned up after myself and went into the living room with the one glass of rosé I was allowing myself these days, at least when it hadn't been a martini night at Spike's.

I put on Sonny Rollins's *Saxophone Colossus* and sat on the couch with Rosie next to me and read the notes I'd taken as I'd done my research on Alex Drysdale. I had read somewhere that some people in New York wanted to rename the Williamsburg Bridge after Sonny. Maybe it would start a movement. Maybe next we could rename the Tobin Bridge here after Miles.

I finally took Rosie out for her final walk of the night, relied on iron will not to have a Jameson before bed. Tomorrow I would begin to figure out a way to do to Drysdale what he'd just done to Spike. That was the job now. When I needed help on a case, Spike would drop everything. I was now returning the favor. He was the case now.

Until Lee Farrell showed up the next morning to tell me what had happened to his niece.

EIGHT

We were at my kitchen table a little after eight. He looked as if he'd been up all night because he had, starting at the Emergency Room at the new medical center at Taft University, west of town, in Walford, a night that really wouldn't end for him until he drove her back to his new apartment on Summer Street in Fort Point, not far from where Rosie and I used to live.

Emily Barnes, the only child of Lee's sister, had been walking around the reservoir at Taft late the previous evening, the way a lot of kids did there, when she had been assaulted. I knew the reservoir because Lee and I had walked it with her the previous year, when we'd been her substitutes for Parents Weekend. Her mother, divorced, lived in Hawaii now. Her father, a lawyer, had moved to Los Angeles and generally didn't give a shit beyond tuition checks. He had also cheated, and copiously, on Emily's mom, for which the kid had vowed never to forgive him.

"Not sexually," Lee said before I even got the chance to ask.

"They do a rape kit?"

"She told them she'd know whether she got raped or not, she didn't need one," he said.

"They let it be her call?"

"She said she was leaving if they even tried," Lee said. "She said she knew how long the process took from one of her friends and she didn't need one and why bother."

"Did her attacker even try?"

"Until she started yelling her head off according to Emily," Lee said. "For some reason he decided to hang around long enough to punch her around instead, the asshole."

"She get a look at him?"

"Says he was wearing the kind of black gaiter we wore during the virus, and a ball cap," Lee said. "Says all she could see were his eyes."

"She try to fight back?"

"The self-defense course I made her take paid off, until it didn't," he said. "He finally ran one way and she ran another, out of the woods and to the walking path. She would have gone straight home except she ran into a friend who insisted she go to the Emergency Room. Em didn't even want to give them a contact at first, but they insisted, and she finally called me."

He rubbed his forehead hard.

"What the hell?" he said.

He still looked younger than he actually was, as if he could have been the cool professor at Taft, dressed as if the Brooks Brothers on Newbury had opened early for him, blazer and white shirt with the roll in the collar and silk tie and khakis.

"She talk to the Walford Police or just the campus police?"

"She told them at the ER the only cop she was going to talk to was me," Lee said, "and to stop treating her like some kind of victim."

"She *is* a victim," I said. "And *could* have gotten raped." I drank some coffee. So did he. "Is there any chance this is somebody she knows, and was waiting for her?"

"She says no," Lee said.

"Is it worth talking to her roommate?"

"Doing the semester abroad thing in Copenhagen," he said. "Or maybe it's Stockholm."

"How can I help?" I said.

"Find out who did this to her," he said. "I

just feel as if there's more here than she's telling. She might tell a woman more than she's willing to tell me."

"But it sounds as if she just wants it all to go away," I said.

"Wishing doesn't make it so," he said. "And you have connected to girls in trouble before."

I smiled. "Young women."

Lee almost managed a smile. "And me the sensitive one," he said.

I got up and walked over to the coffee-maker and came back with the pot and topped off our mugs. When I sat back down it occurred to me that there had been times when we'd sat at this same table and Lee had questioned me after a case he was working on and I was working on had intersected. Or collided.

"The last thing she said before she got into the bed in my guest room was that I just needed to leave this alone," Lee said.

"But you don't leave things alone."

"Look who's talking."

"You tell your sister?"

"Em made me promise not to."

We sat there in silence. I asked again if he wanted something to eat. Usually when I felt maternal instincts coming on, I found a place to lie down until they passed.

"I'll be happy to talk to her," I said.

"I want to hire you," he said.

"Friends don't hire friends," I said.

"I'm asking you, as a friend, Sunny, to let me hire you."

"Okay."

"I would find out who did this to her myself," he said, "but I am up to my ass in alligators with this Carly Meme shit."

I told him he didn't have to say anything more, and put my hand across the table for him to shake.

"I didn't even ask if you have anything going yourself," he said.

I told him about Spike then.

"But as you know, I can multitask with the best of them," I said.

He smiled again. "Look at how well you're doing with Jesse and Richie."

"Don't take this the wrong way, but I'm currently only tasking Jesse."

Lee said, "Not sure I've heard that word used quite that way."

"Dirty mind," I said.

"Why we get along," he said. "I can afford this, Sunny. My father left me more money than you think. It was guilt, mostly, once he finally decided that me being gay didn't make me the devil's spawn."

"Better late than never."

I walked him out to his car. He said he'd call Emily when she was awake and tell her I was going to stop by. For now, he said, he was off to fight crime. I told him I felt as if I were doing the same with Alex Drysdale.

"Same church," Lee said. "Different pew."

Then I watched him get into his car and head up River Street Place toward Charles, not able to help myself from thinking that this showed all signs of being a particularly shitty week.

NINE

Christopher Lawton, who'd had a Massachusetts Lodging Association meeting a couple blocks away, sat next to me on a bench behind the Marriott Long Wharf, each of us holding coffee we'd bought at the Starbucks inside the hotel. We stared out at the water on one of those perfect days that made you remember what it was like when you actually felt like the world was on the right course, and not headed straight for the iceberg.

Even though he and Drysdale had to be the same age, Lawton looked older. He was trim, not much taller than me, his hair a salt-and-pepper color that I described as George Clooney.

"I couldn't resist seeing you," he said, "after what you told me on the phone."

"That I wanted to string Alex Drysdale up by his balls and hang him over a railing on Old Ironsides?" I said.

51

"Very powerful imagery," he said. "It was like having me at hello."

"I was a fine arts major," I said.

He had a nice smile. Definitely cute. Maybe I had been spending too much time alone after all, whatever Susan Silverman said.

"I read up on you before I came over here," Lawton said.

"Then we're even," I said.

He grinned. "So, as a trained detective," he said, "I'm sure you're aware that I signed an NDA with Alex after we dissolved our partnership."

"Whose idea was that?" I said.

"His," he said.

"Why did he need one?" I said. "Unless he was worried about some really bad juju you had on him."

"There are all sorts of reasons for nondisclosures," he said.

"Almost all of them involving having bad juju on someone," I said.

I looked out at the seagulls over the water, struck again by how many different kinds there were, black-backed and black-tailed and the white-and-gray common gulls. My dad knew a lot about gulls. He knew a lot about a lot of things. Most of which he had taught me. But, as he constantly reminded me, not all.

"So why the NDA?" I said.

Lawton turned to face me. "Other than him being a paranoid narcissist?" he said.

"I thought for a narcissist paranoia only came into play in intimate relationships," I said.

"With Alex Drysdale," Christopher Lawton said, "there is nothing more intimate than his relationship with his money."

"Were you any different?"

"No," he said, "I was not. Once you start making it the way we were making it, it's like a drug. I was never into drugs, not even in college, but it was like whatever the guy was making in *Breaking Bad*. The more money we made, the more we wanted. And as hard as he was pushing at the time, I was pushing just as hard."

It was as if he were talking to the water now.

"But over time," he continued, "I came to hate myself, and what I'd become. And came to hate *us* in the process. I finally decided I didn't want to spend every single one of my waking hours running with the big dogs. I told Alex I wanted out, and I got out. Took a year off. Got divorced, after my wife left me. Hell, I could have taken the rest of my *life* off. Now I'm back in the game, building something on my own from scratch again. We're hopeful that The Carmody is going to be the first of a chain."

"Good luck with it," I said, resisting the urge to say that it was what the world needed, another high-end hotel chain.

"At least I don't feel like a robber baron any longer," he said, "like my old friend Alex."

"Explain to me again why you'd sign an NDA," I said.

"Because it got me better parting gifts," he said.

"That only explains why you'd sign one," I said. "But what did you know that he didn't want everybody else to know?"

Lawton shook his head.

"I'd like to help you and I'd like to help your friend, because it sounds like he got royally fucked," Lawton said. "But if I even come close to violating our deal, his lawyers will be coming over the hill like the First Army. I'll be the one hanging over the side of Old Ironsides by my balls."

"Narcissists are cruel, too," I said.

He took in a lot of sea air and let it out.

"Another reason I got out," he said.

"After you did, he pretty much lost everything," I said.

"Not everything. But close enough."

"But he came back."

"He sure did."

"I did a lot of reading on him yesterday," I said. "But it remains unclear how he managed to get whole again."

"You know what he always says," Lawton said. " 'Luck and day-trading.' "

"You believe that?"

"Not even a little bit," he said.

He stood. I stood. He shook my hand, almost in a courtly way.

"I wish I had been more helpful," he said.

"May I call you with further questions about him?"

"I'd rather you didn't," he said.

"Are you scared of him, Mr. Lawton?"

"Put it this way," he said. "I'm wary."

I thanked him for taking the time to talk to me. Told him he'd probably be hearing from me again, whether he liked it or not.

"I can't be your Deep Throat," he said.

"Follow the money," I said.

TEN

Lee Farrell had used a lot of his inheritance money to buy his new apartment, a couple blocks over in Fort Point from where Rosie and I had lived.

It had two bedrooms and a large study that had once been a recording studio, soundproofed, for the drummer who had owned the place before him, where Lee could crank up his classic rock collection as loud as he wanted. He told me that even people next door couldn't hear Robert Plant wailing away when he was in a Led Zeppelin mood. He had lots of windows, lots of light, maple floors that gave me floor envy for the first time in my adult life, even one wall of red brick in the study, which was actually bigger than his living room.

When he'd shown me around the first night he'd moved in I'd said, "Do you ever worry you gay guys are getting a little *too* hip?"

56

"Getting?" he said.

He shared his new digs with his Scottish fold cat, Westley. I wasn't a cat person. But if Westley and I hadn't developed a friendship over time, I felt that we had at least achieved an understanding. I was in charge of feeding him and cleaning his litter when Lee was out of town, having a key to the place the way Spike had a key to my house when I needed him to look after Rosie.

"If only cats were more like dogs," I'd said to Lee once.

"He's like me that way," he'd said. "He didn't get to pick a lane."

When Emily opened the door she said, "I tried one last time to get him to tell you not to come."

"He's a little stubborn, your uncle," I said.

"Like a deer tick," she said.

"He just cares about you," I said.

"And I care about him. But right now I just want you and him and everybody else to just leave me alone."

But she stepped aside and reluctantly let me in, as if this were a dorm room and I were here for a spot inspection. I noticed her backpack next to the door, locked and loaded, some kind of vest on top of it.

"Going somewhere?" I said.

"Back to Taft."

"Would you like me to drive you?"

"A friend is picking me up in a few minutes."

She moved slowly and lowered herself with great care onto the couch. First Spike had gotten worked over this week. Now her. Every time you thought the universe had gotten as mean as it possibly could, it somehow got meaner.

Other than some slight bruising along the hairline next to her left eye, you wouldn't have known what had happened to her. She must have used the apartment before, or left clothes here, because everything she wore looked clean, plain white tee and distressed jeans. Her hair was wet, as if she'd just gotten out of the shower. She was very pretty, tall, sandy-colored hair, a Taylor Swift quality to her, great figure. You could learn to hate college girls if you spent enough time around them.

"I know Lee wants you to try to find out who did this," she said. "But I don't. It won't change anything even if you do."

She pulled up her knees in front of her.

"Obviously I won't do anything you don't want me to do," I said. "But before you go, do you mind if I ask you a few questions? That way I can at least tell your uncle I tried."

"Just tell him I'm fine," she said. "Try that."

"But you're not," I said. "Fine, I mean."

"I was just at the wrong place at the wrong time, is all."

I let it go, at least for now. But this wasn't a grand jury, and I didn't want it to sound like one.

"You're the victim here, Emily."

"I'm not a victim!" she said, with force that seemed to surprise her. "I'm just an idiot."

"Could your attacker have been somebody you know?"

"No."

She pulled out her phone and checked it. I hadn't even been there five minutes, but even going that long without checking her phone must have felt like a lifetime.

"I'd very much like to be left alone," she said. "You want to help? Help by doing that."

She gave me a sullen look that I wondered if I'd perfected at her age. Or maybe kids were getting more sullen these days, now that they saw the world turning into a dumpster fire.

"If you want to talk to someone," I said, "I know a good therapist."

"You're just going to make it worse!"

She looked as if she were about to cry. Drawing people out. Sometimes it was like a gift with me, like painting.

"Make what worse?" I said.

I heard her phone buzzing now. She looked at it again, nodded, stood, wincing again as she did, and stuck the phone in the back of her jeans, though I wondered where there might be room back there.

I stood as well, reached into the bag I'd dropped next to my chair, pulled out a pen and one of the business cards I'd had printed up to go with my new office, wrote my cell phone number on the back, handed it to her.

"You call me if you need anything," I said.

"I won't."

But she took the card, stuck it in the pocket of her T-shirt, put on her sleeveless vest, and picked up her backpack. She looked as if she might be about to say one more thing, but must have thought better of it, just gave me a quick wave of the hand and left before I could offer to walk out with her.

I walked over to one of the floor-to-ceiling windows and looked down to the street. Lee lived on the fourth floor. The elevator must have been waiting for her, because I saw her on the sidewalk a minute later. A tall young guy with long hair and wearing a navy vest of his own was waiting for her next to a red Mazda, motor running. But before they got in, they engaged in what was a very animated conversation. At one point, Emily started to walk away. He held her arm. She yanked it away.

As I wondered how quickly I could get down there, the standoff ended. She tossed her backpack into the backseat, got into the passenger seat. Her boyfriend, or whomever he was, was pulling into traffic before her door was closed. The Mazda was too far away and gone too quickly before I could even try to take a picture of the license plate.

The only thing left to do then was turn to Westley the cat, staring at me from across the room, and tell him I could show myself out.

ELEVEN

I was back in my office and had just opened the top right-hand drawer of my desk to get reading glasses that I wore only when alone when a guy came in without knocking. I left the drawer open, comforted by the sight of the Glock.

"Good afternoon!" he said, and sat down without invitation in the visitor's chair across from me.

I said nothing, just watched him with mild curiosity, as if having watched a fly pick a landing spot.

"Gun in that drawer?" he said, smiling.

"You bet," I said.

"You won't need it," he said.

"Thanks," I said. "But pretty sure I'll be the one to make that determination."

"The door *was* open," he said.

"Unlocked," I said. "There's a difference."

He wore an expensive-looking black suit, open-necked shirt the color of a robin's egg, one of those cuts where his hair was buzzed short on the side and longer on top, as if there were a couple floors of it. He crossed his legs, paying attention to the crease in his pants. No socks. That look. Men's fashion could wear my ass out when they tried too hard. He looked to be about my height. And maybe my new weight.

"Do you treat all potential clients this brusquely?" he said.

I smiled.

"Brusquely," I said.

"Something funny?"

"Just to me," I said. "Happens a lot."

He smiled back at me. I wanted to tell him that the whiteners were working.

"Do you have a name?" I said.

"I do," he said.

"But one you're unwilling to share?"

"No point," he said. "You've probably ascertained by now that I'm not really a potential client."

"I'm a trained detective," I said. "And an armed one. Now telling you that you need to leave."

"And you need to stop harassing Alex Drysdale," he said. "Jump ball."

Guys and their sports references. Like security blankets.

"I wasn't aware that I was harassing him," I said.

"But you're about to," he said. "It's why we need to get out in front of this now."

" 'We'?"

"You and me," he said.

"Not to make too fine a point of things," I said. "But there is no 'you and me.' "

He ignored that.

"Are you a business associate of his?" I said.

"In a manner of speaking," he said.

"Good to know," I said.

"Alex has made his business associates a lot of money in his current incarnation," he said. "And is in the process of making even more. So, as you might imagine, when he feels threatened, the *we* who are his business associates begin to feel threatened as well."

There was a clipped precision to his words, to his cadence, that made me wonder if English might be his second language, and he had gone to great lengths to bury his first, whatever it was.

"Something else good to know," I said.

"So, again, just in the interest *of* getting ahead of all this, I have come here to discourage you from continuing down that path and making trouble for all concerned," he said. "Mostly for yourself, truth be told."

"So you've come here to threaten me?" I said.

"I have come here to offer you friendly advice," he said. "Just walk away from this now."

"No," I said.

I casually reached over to the open drawer, showed him my phone as I pulled it out, stared down at it as if a message had just come in, tapped the camera icon, held it up, said, "Smile," and took his picture.

I placed the phone back in the drawer but left my hand there, my eyes on him the whole time. There was an expression I had once heard Dr. Silverman use, "affective presence," about an aura that a person could bring with them into a room, good or bad, but one you recognized on an instinctive level. The point she was making was that even charming psychopaths are still psychopaths. I had nothing more to go on at this point than the affective presence of the skinny suit across the desk from me. But all of my own clinical observations were telling me that this was a bad man.

He shook his head, sadly, and sighed, and stood.

"You have now been warned, in a civil way, to back off," he said.

"Or?"

"Or the next time we meet," he said, "I will be the one, as you put it to Alex, up in your shit, Ms. Randall. And as good as you think you might be, I am much better at it."

He gave me a one-fingered salute, turned, walked out the door, leaving it open behind him. I hadn't met all that many hedge-funders or investment bankers in my life. Or any kind of bankers, for that matter, or accountants. But if he were a legitimate businessman, I was one of those Real Housewives of Beverly Hills.

I closed my gun drawer, made sure the snub-nosed .38 was in my shoulder bag, set the alarm, and was careful not to touch the knob on the open door, not wanting to take the time to dust it until tomorrow. Then I used my key and locked the office from the outside, walked down the steps and across the Common, on my way to Charles Street and home, looking over my shoulder only a couple times. As always, not being paranoid. Just alert.

TWELVE

I told Spike he needed a new lawyer who was more like James Bond.

"Last time I checked," Spike said, "he was a British Secret Service agent."

"But licensed to kill," I said.

It is how I came to meet Rita Fiore of Cone, Oakes in the street bar at The Newbury. When I was a kid, the hotel was the Ritz, before it was sold and became Taj Boston. Even then I still thought of it as the Ritz, and called it the old Ritz the way my father did, only because there was a new Ritz-Carlton on the other side of Boston Common, on Avery Street. Now they had closed down the old one for a couple years and renovated it, and reimagined it, this time as The Newbury.

But they had been smart enough to mostly leave the bar alone, just because it was one of the great bars on the planet, everything a good bar should be, just dark enough, a perfect view of the Public Garden across Arlington Street if you could score a window table, generous pours from the bartenders, good appetizers if you wanted them, a great bar menu, just the right amount of noise. There was also a set of permanence to it, and timelessness, as if wanting you to imagine what it had been like to come here for a drink as far back as the 1930s.

Rita and I had managed to score a window table. From the greeting she'd gotten upon our arrival, I imagined the bar staff throwing people through plate glass to get us our table.

"When you called and said you wanted to meet for a drink," she said, "I assumed you'd killed somebody but had not yet been arrested."

"Because of our shared history?" I said.

"Well, not history," she said. "We just shared Jesse."

"Not to parse things with the best lawyer in town," I said, "but my recollection is that it wasn't as much 'history' with you and Chief Stone as a bit of a fling."

"But," she said, taking a healthy swallow of her martini, "extremely well flung."

I sipped some chardonnay. I wasn't in a martini mood. Maybe it was because my visitor had given me the creeps. By now I had emailed Rita a copy of Spike's contract with Drysdale, and she'd already had one of her corporate partners go over it.

"I'm always happy to have somebody else buy my vodka for me," she said, "but I could have told you over the phone that your friend is screwed."

"Did your partner know much about Drysdale?" I said.

"I asked," Rita said. "He does."

"What kind of reputation does he have?"

"Do you mind if I use a somewhat technical legal expression?"

"Have at it."

"He's a dick," Rita said.

"I was actually able to figure that out without benefit of a law diploma," I said.

"Aaron — that's the partner I showed the contract to — also said that your friend Spike isn't the only one Drysdale vultured in on during the virus," Rita said.

"Were there other restaurants?"

"A couple," she said. She named one in the North End, another in the seaport. "And a hair salon. And a gym."

"He ended up owning *their* businesses, too?"

She nodded.

"Aaron only heard this secondhand, from a friend of the gym owner," Rita said. "But when the owner threatened to beat the living shit out of Drysdale, he got a visit from a couple of Drysdale's 'friends.' "

She put air quotes around *friends.*

I told her then about my visitor earlier in the afternoon.

"Maybe Wharton is turning into a new crime family," she said.

She wore a short green dress that showed off her amazing figure and amazing legs. She had so much red hair I imagined a team of colorists working on it. I knew she had to be older than she looked. But, then, who wasn't? And if she'd had work done on that face, as I believed she had, it was the best since some of the legendary sculptors I'd studied at BU.

"Spike should have called our firm before he signed," Rita said. "Remember how in less-enlightened times these people used to say women didn't have a head for business? Maybe it's gay guys now."

"Wait, what about Geffen?" I said. "And the Apple guy."

"And Armani," Rita said. "Okay, you got me."

She waved at our waiter and pointed to our drinks.

"I'm fine," I said.

"You're about to turn this into a crusade,

aren't you?" Rita said.

"Spike would do the same for me."

"I have a friend in your business a lot like you," she said.

Now I smiled. I knew who she meant.

"How good a friend?" I said.

"Not the kind I wanted him to be, which means with unlimited benefits," she said. "Not even once, despite my very best efforts."

We sat there in silence for a minute or two, the room around us beginning to become more crowded, the way the bar area was. In an impermanent world, this bar really was forever.

Finally she said, "So how is the chief, if you don't mind me asking?"

"Kind of do mind," I said, "if you're seriously asking about us."

"So there's still an 'us'," she said. "Seriously?"

"In a manner of speaking."

"Damn," Rita said. "I was afraid of that."

But she toasted me with her glass and I toasted her back.

"So you want to take this guy down," Rita said.

"Big-time," I said.

"Dealing with these people really can be like dealing with the Mob," she said. "They end up with all this money. But it's almost as if as soon as they've got it, they start worrying about losing it. Or somebody taking it away from them. And it scares their things right off them."

I laughed. *"Things?"*

She threw back her head and laughed. "I sometimes think of them as accessories," she said.

"Not what I heard," I said, and then told her that I could handle myself around any kind of gangster, that over the past few years my interests had occasionally been aligned with Tony Marcus's. She said she'd heard about that.

"What about when your interests weren't aligned with Tony's?" Rita said.

"He'd talk about the balls on me," I said.

Rita sighed.

"Men always think that's a compliment," she said.

I offered to pay the check. Rita let me, telling me it was a lot cheaper than a billable hour. I asked her if she could ask her friend to get the name of the gym owner who wanted to put Alex Drysdale down and to call me with it in the morning. She said she would.

Her Uber was waiting on the street when we were back out on Arlington Street. Tom, one of the veteran bellmen who was still around, who had been out in front of the place since my father used to take me to the old Ritz for special-occasion lunches when I was a little girl, was already holding the door open for her.

"Give my best to Jesse," she said.

I told her that it sounded as if she already had.

I cut across the Public Garden and thought about picking up a small pie at Upper Crust Pizzeria on my way up Charles Street, but then changed my mind, mostly because of an iron will, deciding that if I got hungry later I would make myself a salad. When I got home I walked Rosie and got into my sweats and decided I wasn't hungry after all. I fixed myself a small Jameson and took it with me into the living room and called Jesse Stone and told him I'd just had drinks with Rita Fiore.

"How is old Rita?" he said.

"Old Rita seems to be just fine," I said. "By the way? She wanted to know how you were doing."

"What did you tell her?"

"That will have to stay between us girls," I said.

"I was hopeful it would, truth be told," he said.

He asked why I'd met with Rita. I told him, and took him through the whole story: what had happened to Spike, the guy who'd visited my office, what I'd learned about Alex Drysdale, and how I wanted to separate him from his thing.

" 'Thing'?" Jesse said.

"It's a word Rita used to describe the male organ."

"One of many words she has for it," Jesse said.

"Hey," I said.

"Where do you go next?"

"First thing I'm going to do is dust my doorknob when I get to my office. I didn't have time today to do it right because I was going to meet Rita."

"You have the kit?"

I told him I did.

"Then I'm going to visit a dear friend I have in law enforcement and ask him to have the state police run the prints for me," I said.

"Must be a really dear friend," he said.

"Maybe I just want an excuse to see you."

"You don't need an excuse," Jesse said. "It's in the benefits package."

He asked if I wanted to talk dirty for a while. I told him I did and that Rita Fiore could eat her heart out. When we finished talking dirty I neglected to mention before we ended the call that I was going to see my ex-husband in the morning, feeling it would spoil the mood.

When I got up in the morning to take Rosie outside, the unmarked envelope was on the mat in front of the door. When I opened it there was a photograph inside, clearly taken at Legal Sea Foods the day before.

It was a close-up of my father.

With a red dot superimposed on his forehead.

THIRTEEN

When I called Phil Randall and told him
about the picture, he said it made him feel
like a cop again, somebody trying to
threaten him this way, even though whomever it was clearly was trying to threaten
me.

"I can take care of myself," I said.

"And I can take care of *my*self," he said.

"You're not a cop anymore, Dad," I said.

"Once you were, you are," he said, and
then told me to call him if I needed him.

"Always have," I said.

When I got to the office in the morning I
called Lee Farrell first thing. When he actually picked up for a change I told him about
the picture. He asked who I thought had
left it. I told him about my visitor the day
before. He asked if I wanted him to dust for
prints and I told him I was about to do that
myself, I was a dusting fool today, but I
doubted I'd find any prints on the envelope

or the photograph.

Then I asked for an update on Emily. He said he hadn't heard from her since she'd left his place. Had tried calling, but always went straight to voicemail. I asked if he knew she was attending classes today. He said he knew more about where Carly the influencer was than he did about his niece's course load. She was a math major, he knew that, with a minor in econ. That was about it. He knew her campus address even if he hadn't been there yet this semester, and that the house in which she lived was within walking distance of the library.

"Is this your passive-aggressive way of getting me to take a ride over to Taft?" I said.

"Only passive," he said. "You called me, remember?"

I told him I might have someone I needed to see on Spike's case, and some laptop detecting to do at the office, but I would try to go out to Walford sometime in the afternoon.

"I know I keep saying this," he said, "but she's family."

"I feel the same way about you," I said.

I then set to work on dusting both the inside and outside knobs to my door. It was highly unlikely that anybody had tried the door since I'd left the day before. But even if someone had handled the outside knob, the last person to touch the one inside was Skinny Suit when he was leaving. A good thing. The cleaning woman had been here for the first time the previous Friday, and had polished everything except my gun. Including the knobs. It would make my job a lot easier.

I didn't know if every hotshot detective in town had their own dusting kit, the way I didn't know how many could pick a lock the way I could. But I had one, and there had been times in the past when finding a usable print had helped me more than somewhat.

Another fine art they had not taught at Boston University.

I used black fingerprint dust that came in a small container roughly the same size as a nail polish bottle. The brush I used resembled the one I used to apply blush, just smaller, and with even finer bristles.

I tapped some powder on white printer paper, lightly spinning the brush on it. Then I carefully walked across the room, set the paper down on the floor, and spun the brush again before lightly depositing the powder on the doorknob.

After that, and as gently as I could, I used the brush again to clear away the excess powder, clearly exposing a couple clear prints. One had to be mine.

The other had to be his.

The last part of the job was lifting the print. I liked to use what was called a hinge lifter. It basically looked like clear tape cut up into two-inch strips. I applied one strip to each print, then gently laid them into their own flat containers. Jesse said he couldn't get down to Boston in the next couple days, and I'd told him I wasn't sure I could get up to Paradise. I offered to overnight the prints to Brian Lundquist at the state police, but Jesse said that it would be better if he dropped them off.

"Brian likes me," I said.

"Not nearly as much as you think," Jesse said.

"Is such a thing even possible?" I said.

I bubble-wrapped the containers with the prints in them, filled out the FedEx air bill, and called in the pickup, then headed over to the statue of George Washington to meet Richie.

If the chief of police in Paradise couldn't help me identify Skinny Suit, at least not yet, maybe a son of the Irish Mob could. No one had a more wide-ranging support system than I did.

With or without benefits.

79

FOURTEEN

We still got together occasionally, and when we did it was always as the family Richie had hoped we would be: him; his son, Richard; me. He hadn't moved off that. When Richie Burke made up his mind about something, you had a better chance of moving the Hynes auditorium.

It wasn't as if either of us had lost our feelings for each other. It wasn't that I hadn't come to love the little boy, because I had. I loved him, he loved Rosie, I really did still love Richie. But I knew enough about myself to know that if we had ever tried to make the situation permanent, if Richie and I had remarried, as I knew he wanted us to, and really tried to become one big happy family, I would have lost myself inside it. Or lost myself, period. Everyone had talked about the new abnormal during the virus. Now this was ours, mine and Richie's, and the son his second wife had given him, before Richie realized that there was no happy family for him without me as a part of it.

The equestrian statue of George Washington was in the Public Garden at the Arlington Street end, as if the father of our country was guarding Commonwealth all the way down to Kenmore Square. It was a slightly longer walk for Richie than it was for me, since he'd moved again, to a new condominium within walking distance of Fenway Park, high up over Beacon with a view of the Charles. Even though his boy had spent a lot of his growing-up years in London, his father had now turned him into a baseball fan, something at which he'd failed, rather spectacularly, with me.

I beat him to the statue and saw him before he saw me, collar of his tan windbreaker pulled up, pressed jeans even though hardly anybody wore pressed jeans anymore. I smiled at the sight of him, the grace he brought to something as simple as crossing Arlington Street. Much had changed for us over the years since our divorce, and then changed back, and then changed again. But one of the things that had not was this:

Every time I saw him it was still like the first time.

The last time we'd been together had been a couple weeks ago, when he and Richard and I had walked Rosie up here from River Street Place and then down to the Ben & Jerry's on Newbury.

We hugged each other tentatively, kissed each other chastely on the lips. When he stepped back he said, "You lose weight?"

I grinned. "I think my heart just skipped a beat," I said.

We sat down on the bench next to George.

"Unless you want advice on opening a bar," he said, "I assume you need help with criming."

He still owned his bar on Portland Street, the only thing in the world he loved as much as his son. Or me. His father, Desmond, now in his eighties, was still the head of what was left of the Irish Mob in New England. Whitey Bulger was gone, killed in prison. It really meant all the old Irish were gone except Desmond Burke. Not only had he survived the virus, so had his operation, the foundation of which was still loan-sharking. It was another reason why I had called Richie, beginning to wonder how my former father-in-law felt about someone such as Alex Drysdale — and his associates — operating off his playbook.

I showed Richie the picture I'd taken in

my office, told him about the picture of my dad left at the front door, told him about Drysdale and Spike and how Spike wasn't the only one Drysdale had squeezed.

"You've been busy," he said.

"Idle hands."

"But you don't know who this guy is," Richie said.

"Not who," I said. "But got a strong feeling what."

He nodded.

"All I've got is that picture," I said.

"Gonna send it to my phone," he said, and did.

"You think he left the one of Phil?" Richie said.

"Who else?" I said, choosing not to quote Jesse to him on the subject of coincidence.

"It would mean he has now threatened you at your office and at your home," Richie said. "We can't have that."

"I was hoping you could show the picture to your father, and have him show it around in his crew," I said. "I can't even get into the game with this guy until I know who he is."

"You could have called Desmond yourself," he said.

I smiled.

"There have always been certain protocols

in place," I said, "even when we were still married. Too late for either your father or me to change now."

He knew all of the protocols with his father, and his father's business, one Richie had somehow managed to avoid, even as Desmond's only son. Or perhaps because he was his only son.

"We could always just have my father have a talk with this Drysdale guy," he said. "Just to move things along."

"Not there yet," I said. "Not even close. Just looking for information Desmond might be able to provide."

"Not like you two haven't teamed up effectively in the past."

"Albeit reluctantly," I said.

"You've always had an interesting code," Richie said. "You have always been willing to cross over to my father's side of the street, or Tony Marcus's, when it suits your purposes."

"My therapist calls it a form of duality," I said.

He grinned. "I'll bet she does."

"She has a lot of interesting observations about me."

"You ever try to compute how much you've spent on her?" Richie said.

"I don't like to play this game," I said.

He told me he and Richard were having dinner with Desmond Burke later, and he would show him the photograph. Then gave me a long look with eyes that had always reminded me of black ink.

"You need protection, just in the short run?" he said. "I could mention that to my father as well."

I told him what I'd just told my father, that I could take care of myself.

"Until you occasionally can't," he said.

"Somebody has to know who this guy is," I said.

"If he and this maroon Drysdale have found what my father would call a lace-curtain way to shake people down, Desmond might already know who he is," Richie said.

"I'm not saying Spike's is small-time," I said, "but why would somebody like Alex Drysdale punch down like that?"

He smiled now, fully.

"I'm sure you'll find out whatever needs finding out," he said.

We stared over to the ornate old bridge over the Swan Boat lagoon. Silence had never seemed awkward for us in the past, but had grown increasingly so.

"How's Spike doing with all this?" Richie said finally.

"Badly," I said. "He seems broken."

"But you're going to make him whole."

"Or die trying," I said.

"Hoping that's a figure of speech."

Now I smiled.

"I don't like people threatening you," he said. "Never have, never will."

"I didn't imagine you would."

"Desmond *would* have you watched if I asked," he said.

"I know he would," I said. "For now, just ask him if there might be some new kids on the block."

"I've got regulars at the bar who are hedge-funders who aren't total dirtbags," Richie said.

"Drysdale is."

"And you're going to take him down a peg or two."

"Or just take him down, period."

"That's my girl," he said.

"That's what my father always says."

He sighed. "I never did like playing *that* game," he said. "Haven't you and your therapist sorted that out yet?"

We both stood and hugged again. When he pulled back he said, "How's Jesse?"

"You don't care," I said.

"You're right," he said. "I don't."

He said he'd call later after seeing Desmond; right now he had to go pick up Richard at The Advent School, a few blocks over from the park on Brimmer. We didn't kiss each other goodbye. I watched him until he crossed Beacon and then disappeared down Charles, then I turned and headed in the other direction.

I didn't need a therapist to tell me that duality could be a bitch sometimes.

Lee Farrell called a few minutes after I was back in my office. I asked if he'd been in contact with Emily and he said not in the way I might think.

"I just got a call from my sister," he said. "Emily is on her debit card, and forged her signature and took a ten thousand cash advance off her account."

"As in dollars," I said.

"As in."

"It's a lot of money for a college kid, Lee," I said. "Is she into drugs?"

"There has never been any indication," he said. "She's been at Taft three years and there wasn't a whiff of trouble until the other night."

I thought of what my father had said at lunch the day before.

"Everybody's got secrets," I said. "And she won't return your calls or texts, I gather?"

"Nope," he said. "Her mother has tried, too."

"She never asked you for money?"

"Never," he said.

"So she has ten grand in her pocket and she's out there somewhere," I said.

"I got a friend in the department to ping her phone," he said. "The last place she used it was at my place, before she took off with her boyfriend."

"If he even is her boyfriend," I said.

"Your guess is as good as mine," he said. "Prying information out of her about her romantic life practically requires the Jaws of Life."

I told him I'd been the same way when I was in college, for what that was worth. I used to tell my parents that I didn't talk about my love life, or what passed for a love life in those days, if caught behind enemy lines.

"I've got a bad feeling about this," he said. "What happened the other night has to have something to do with her needing money. Nothing else makes sense."

"Are you saying that as an uncle, or cop?"

"You know the answer to that," Lee Farrell said. "And does it even matter?"

"In the great grand scheme of things, no," I said.

"I'm asking you as her uncle," he said. "But the cop in me tells me something's wrong here."

There was a pause.

"You have to find her," he said.

Then: "Please."

"I will," I said, hoping I sounded more confident about that than I felt, and then told him I was on my way back to college.

This continued to show all signs of being a spectacularly shitty week.

FIFTEEN

Over time Taft University had grown from red bricks and ivy on what looked like the planet preppie into a futuristic McMansion of a school.

A couple decades earlier, the fourth-richest man in America — or maybe it was the fifth, I didn't actually check the rankings — had poured enough money into the school after his daughter had gone there to buy Vermont. I was aware, or as aware as I could be about sports, that they'd always had a pretty fancy basketball program, one good enough to occasionally make the front page of the *Globe.* Spike had recently told me that they'd also started playing big-time college football. I told him if he was happy about that then so was I.

Part of the Taft-improvement program was that senior men and women got to live in modern frame houses that had been built on the campus at the same they'd built the new football stadium. Emily lived in one of them, 323 College Road, across the street from the ancient stone library that looked older than the earth. By the time I'd parked in one of the public lots near the stadium and walked across the quadrangle, having passed kids who'd just finished their last class of the day or were on their way to one, it was four o'clock.

Emily's row house, white with green shutters, green being one of the Taft colors, looked exactly like the ones on either side of it. But they all still looked quite new, including picket fences in front that looked freshly painted. It was, all things considered, a long way from Myles Standish Hall at Boston University.

I rang the doorbell and got no answer, not having expected one. Then I knocked on the door, hard. Nothing.

"Ma'am?" I heard from behind me.

Ma'am. It was starting to happen less infrequently. To me it always sounded like "Grandma?"

I turned around. She wore a green Taft cap, jeans so tight I imagined her having to put them on in tiny increments, like it was part of a bar method stretch, old-school Converse sneakers, and a backpack.

"You looking for Em?" she said.

"I am," I said. "You live on the block?"

"Two doors down."

"You haven't by any chance run into her today?"

"Not for a couple, actually," she said. "You're not her mom, are you? The one from Hawaii?"

Ma'am-ed and mom-ed. I resisted a sudden urge to tell her that it was a pity she obviously hadn't had the grades to get into Harvard.

"More like an unofficial aunt," I said. "I was in the area and thought I might take her out for an early dinner."

"Sorry you wasted the trip," she said, and gave me a wave and walked across the street in the general direction of the library. Emily's side of College Road was empty for the time being. I sat on the front stoop and waited to see how long it would remain that way. My lock-picking set was in the cool new Isabel Marant shoulder bag I'd gotten on sale when Jesse and I had made a weekend trip to New York City. I imagined it was the first time a Marant bag had contained a hook, tension wrench, twist-free wrench, offset pick, half-diamond, short and medium hooks, and a Bogata rake.

If you were fast, and I was very fast when it came to the type of deadbolt lock on Emily's door, a passerby would think you were just using a key, even though I needed both hands to do the job right.

I had learned how to pick locks, and disarm alarms when necessary, from my friend Ghost Garrity. Another fine art not taught at BU.

The sidewalk in front of the house remained empty. I went back to the door and took out the small tension wrench and pick. Looked up and down the street again. Still no hard-bodied products of higher education. Turned and worked the pin along the shearline, felt the cylinder turn almost immediately.

And I was in.

The house was somehow smaller on the inside than it looked from the outside: living room to your left as you came through the door, tiny kitchen behind it. Both bedrooms were upstairs, connected by a shared bathroom. I remembered Lee telling me that her roommate was abroad. The roommate's bedroom was to the right, so clean and organized it looked as if she hadn't moved in yet. The one with the huge brass *E* on the outside of the door was Emily's.

I had locked the front door behind me, as to give myself some time if Emily suddenly showed up.

I checked the bathroom first. Her makeup stuff was lined up haphazardly on the counter. If she had taken some of it with her on a short road trip, or on the run, she had left a lot of hair and face product behind. There were still gel creams and face cleansers and face polishes here. Brushes in a Taft coffee cup. Blush. Foundation. The essentials. Mostly name brands. Some better than mine, damn her.

What was I looking for? The answer was simple enough: something. Or anything that might tell me if she'd left for a couple days, or longer. Or even for good. Maybe the beating hadn't been an attempted rape at all, maybe just a warning. But a warning about what? All I knew was that she had needed to put her hands on ten thousand dollars, and fast, and had been afraid to ask her mother for it, or her uncle. Her uncle the cop. Ten thousand *was* a lot. I knew it was for me, and for a homicide cop like Lee Farrell, no matter how much money he'd recently inherited.

I went into the bedroom, saw clothes on the floor and on the bed and on the chair facing her desk. At least, I thought, I wouldn't have to worry about her thinking the place had been tossed when she did come home. No laptop on the desk. A corkboard hanging on one wall. A ticket stub for a Maroon 5 concert at the Garden tacked to it. A picture of her and Lee at a Patriots game, Lee wearing his Brady jersey, one I knew he wore even when watching the games at home on television.

I'd asked him once why grown men did dress-up things like that.

"This jersey won us our last two Super Bowls," he explained, as if that should have been the most obvious thing in the world.

I went through the desk. I went through the drawers of her antique dresser. Underwear in the top two drawers. A couple bad-girl black things in the middle of the pile. Weed and rolling paper in a plastic Baggie underneath the underwear. I frankly wasn't even sure why you'd hide it any longer, kids were more likely to have marijuana on them than Tic Tacs.

I went into the closet then. A couple nice outfits, but mostly jeans, shirts, boots, and sneakers on the floor. A pair of Crocs, now that they'd caught the fashion wave again. The basics. A wire hamper for dirty clothes, overflowing. One long shelf over the bar from which the clothes were hanging, some caps to one side, sweaters stacked neatly next to them.

I reached up there, feeling around underneath the sweaters, and touched a small metal box, about the size of a shoebox. Brought it down, saw that it actually had a small lock on it. No challenge for Sunny Randall, master lock-picker. I brought the box over to the bed and used the pick I'd used downstairs for about five seconds, and opened it.

And whistled.

There were three sets of playing cards inside the box, the seal broken on each one of them. A folded pair of glasses.

And a plastic pint bottle of invisible ink.

"Better to mark the cards with, my dear," I said.

I put on the glasses, took a card out of one of the boxes. Ace of diamonds. Looked at both sides of it through the glasses.

I didn't see it right away, but the marking on the outside was clearly visible, dark blue against the red.

"You have got to be shitting me," I said.

I put everything back inside, placed the box back on the shelf where I'd found it, walked downstairs and out the door. There were a couple girls about fifty yards away, walking toward me. I quickly used the pick to set the deadbolt, went across College Road and the quadrangle and past the stadium to where I'd parked my car.

I wasn't any closer to knowing where Lee's darling niece was. But I knew *what* she was.

A card cheat.

SIXTEEN

I met Spike at Spike's. He was still going there at night. He said it was like the old Robert Frost line. "Home is the place where, when you go there, they don't tell you to get the fuck out," he said.

I told him that was my general sense of things, yes. Then I asked him about what I'd found in Emily's room, knowing he was a serious poker player. But also knowing that in the games he played, the most he had ever lost or won in a night was five hundred dollars.

"People actually wear those glasses to cheat?" I said.

"Rarely," Spike said, "and usually only with suckers." He grinned. "Put it this way. If you show up one night to play with pros and have started to wear glasses between one game and the next, you better have a note from your eye doctor."

"But you can cheat and get away with

it?" I said.

"Sure," Spike said. "A marked deck is like having a GPS in your car. You can't get lost."

"Explain."

"Having a deck like that doesn't mean you win every hand," he said. "You still have to have the cards. But when you *do* have the cards, you know you can bet them. Say you're playing a game like Hold 'Em and you have a low straight. You know what that is, right?"

"I have a general sense."

"Now, it might not be a great hand," Spike said. "But if you know the guy raising has three of a kind, you can take him to the cleaners. If you're playing a pot limit, it only has to happen three hands a night. It just lets you know you're on the right road and you don't make a wrong turn."

He had been at the end of the bar nursing a beer when I got there, staring into the back room as if worried a fire was about to break out. Then I saw it was Alex Drysdale he was looking at, Drysdale somehow acting as if he were seated at the head of the table though it was round, surrounded by young guys who looked as if they might have grown up with his poster on their bedroom wall.

As I sat down next to Spike there was a

burst of laughter from them. From experience, I knew Drysdale wasn't that funny. Maybe the boys were afraid not to laugh, for fear of being banished into the night.

Spike turned away and looked at me, and my outfit.

"I forget," he said, "are you a Shark or a Jet?"

He had me there. I was wearing badass clothes: black leather AllSaints biker jacket, black jeans, tee, boots. I thought I looked pretty damn good for someone who'd been ma'am-ed and mom-ed in the same day.

"He likes this," Spike said, nodding at Drysdale. "I swear, he likes being here even more when I'm here. Like he's rubbing my face in it."

"Down, boy," I said.

Beer was a good sign. Spike could drink beer from here to Samuel Adams's birthplace on Purchase Street and back and never show any signs of being overserved.

"Does he make you pay?" I said.

"No," Spike said. "All part of big-timing me. When he saw me sitting here he slapped me on the back and pointed to my glass and said, 'On me.' "

"Isn't it rich," I said.

It got a smile out of him.

"Are we a pair," he said.

100

Another burst of laughter.

"Send in the clowns," I said.

Jack, his favorite bartender, brought me a glass of my favorite pinot grigio without being asked. I drank some. Spike asked if I was making any progress looking into Drysdale's background. I told him about my meeting with Rita, and her having sent me a list of other people in town to whom Drysdale had loaned money before relieving them of their businesses. And then strongarming them into keeping their mouths shut.

"Technically you were the one who got threatened," Spike said.

"Happens to one of us, happens to both of us," I said.

"But we're not the only ones."

"No, sir," I said.

"You going to talk to some of the others?" Spike said.

"If they're not afraid to talk to me," I said, "I'd at least like to talk to one."

"If you start tomorrow," Spike said, "I could go with you."

I told him I would bring him with me when the time came, but had another plan for tomorrow. When I told him what it was, it got another smile out of him.

"When all else fails, annoy somebody," he said.

"Words to live by."

"Even when they don't know they're being annoyed."

"Boots on the ground beats a search engine any day," I said.

I sipped some wine.

There was now a burst of sudden applause from Drysdale's table.

"Maybe," I said to Spike, "there's some kind of escort service for ass-kissers."

"Unless they just come by it naturally," Spike said.

He waved at Jack for another beer.

"I'm glad you're here," Spike said, and we clinked glasses.

"I needed to talk to somebody who knows even more about poker than you do," I said.

"Want to learn about flops and turns and rivers?" he said.

"Please, no," I said. "I just want to know if a college kid could get in deep enough to steal money from her mother."

"Maybe she just thought of it as a temporary loan," Spike said. "But to your point, it could happen to anybody, especially if they fancy themselves players. Poker has gotten huge over the last ten years, especially since they started putting it on ESPN. One of the guys I used to play with, before he went looking for bigger games, called me up about six months ago and asked if I was ready to run with the big dogs. I asked how big the pots could get. He said half a million. I said I was going back to bingo."

"So you can lose that much," I said.

"Sure," he said. "Sometimes the trick in poker, once you've got a seat at the table, isn't knowing how to win. It's knowing how to lose. Sounds like she didn't."

"What if Emily got caught cheating?"

Spike laughed. "You better not get caught cheating."

"Would they beat up a woman?"

"Even if it was their mother," Spike said.

I had taken an Uber home from the house. Spike said he'd drive me home, in case someone had left another envelope.

Spike took one last look into the back room.

"I know they call asshole women Karens now," Spike said. "Can we just call fuckwits like this guy Alexes?"

"Works for me," I said.

I insisted on leaving a hefty tip for Jack. Spike and I were walking to the door when I heard Drysdale's voice behind me.

"Leaving so soon?" he said. "The night is young."

Spike was ahead of me. He turned around. There was nothing in his eyes that I liked. I casually got between him and Alex Drysdale.

"Go back to your table, Alex," I said. "The puppies look as if they might die of heartbreak if you don't."

There was the smirk again. I wondered if he practiced it in a mirror.

I looked at him and then turned and looked around at Spike's, which was Drysdale's now, and was overwhelmed in the moment at how wrong that was.

And then I turned and slapped Alex Drysdale as hard as I could, the sound like a crack of lightning. Not the punch I wanted to throw. Close enough.

After I did, I said, "Don't you touch me like that ever again," loudly enough to be heard on the Freedom Trail.

He seemed as stunned by the force of the blow as by the blow itself. I could see his cheek reddening. He started to put a hand up there, then stopped and turned to the room and said, "She's kidding."

"Am I?" I said.

I could see the two bruisers standing behind him now. But what were they going to do, toss me out onto Marshall Street?

"You need to leave," Drysdale said, keeping his voice low.

"Why in the world would I want to stay?" I said, and then followed Spike out to the sidewalk.

"What the hell was *that*?" he said.

"Better me than you," I said.

"How'd it feel?" Spike said.

I smiled.

"I'm much too refined to say."

"Since when?" Spike said.

SEVENTEEN

I spoke to Lee when I got home about what I had discovered at Emily's house.

"Could she have been hiding that stuff for a friend?" he said.

"The kind of friend who just basically stole ten thousand dollars off her mom's card," I said.

"Maybe I didn't know her as well as I thought I did."

"You're her uncle, not her roommate," I said.

"I'm also a detective."

"When you were with her," I said, "you were an uncle."

"Maybe trying too hard to be the funny one."

"She ever mention poker to you?"

"Never," he said.

"Nevertheless," I said.

"Losing the money at cards would explain a lot," Lee said.

"And she didn't want to come to you for it."

"Or she owes more than ten grand," he said. "And is in a lot more trouble than we think."

He said he was going to take a ride out to Taft himself, maybe tomorrow afternoon, and did I want to join him? I told him Spike's situation was going to have me jammed up all day and likely into the night, but that we'd touch base at some point. He said he'd call me if he found out anything more.

"A *card* cheat?" he said.

"What are the odds?" I said.

I couldn't make another trip to Taft because I had decided to spend all day tomorrow, and into the night, following Alex Drysdale. When all else failed with sophisticated modern detecting, trail somebody.

Something else that was in all the manuals.

EIGHTEEN

I knew, just because Drysdale had told us often enough at Spike's, that he lived at the Archer Residences on Temple Street in Beacon Hill. It was close enough that I could have walked there from River Street Place, but I needed my car, which I had parked halfway up from the block by seven-thirty the next morning.

The Archer was once two buildings owned by Suffolk University, but now had become one of the tonier condominium complexes in the Back Bay. Drysdale, who talked about the place as if it were a miniature version of Versailles, owned a two-story penthouse suite that he had once described as being maybe the greatest bachelor pad in Boston history.

"Pad?" I'd said at the time.

He'd winked and said, "Least I was polite enough not to say 'fuck pad.' "

There was a fountain out front, and a

circular cobblestone courtyard in case you had gotten disoriented and forgotten you actually were in Beacon Hill. I saw a black Mercedes pull into the driveway at a few minutes before eight o'clock and Drysdale came walking through the double doors about ten minutes later. One of the bruisers from last night, one of the two who had bounced Spike around, got out from behind the wheel and opened the back door. He then pulled the car out onto Temple. No reason for them to notice my car, or care about it. I followed them all the way to One Financial Center.

I wasn't entirely sure of what I hoped to accomplish. But as pleasurable as slapping Drysdale had been, I needed to be in motion, needed to feel as if I had some control of the action. It meant doing something more than talking to his former partner, or letting Rita Fiore do some legwork for me, or having some prints run. Skinny Suit had come to my office to warn me off. Somebody had left that picture of my father at the front door of my home. The French, as my father liked to say, had an expression for what I was feeling today.

Fuck 'em.

When the Mercedes pulled away, I miraculously found a metered parking space on the other side of the street from One Financial, one that afforded me a full view of the building's front entrance.

I prepared to wait, as long as it took. I had brought KIND bars, bottled water, an apple. I had brought my still-home-delivered *Globe* with me. I had brought along a book of Georgia O'Keeffe's watercolors. I had a new Joe Ide audiobook on my phone. I tried to remember the last time I had been on a stakeout and could not.

At eleven-thirty, the Mercedes was back. Drysdale came out. The bruisers drove him to the Equinox gym on Franklin Street. Drysdale must have had a locker there, because he had carried a gym bag with him out of One Financial, but had not had one with him when he'd come out of The Archer. Or maybe he kept one in the car. Wherever he kept his workout clothes, he stayed at the gym for an hour. From there he went to the Central Wharf Co., a restaurant on Milk Street. There was a drop-dead gorgeous woman waiting for him out front, light-skinned but African American, wearing jeans, a stand-up-collar blazer I knew came from Rag & Bone, a bag with DG in silver letters on the outside. Dolce & Gabbana, that bitch. I bet no one had ever mom-ed her. She pointed at her watch when

Drysdale was out of the car. He made a don't-shoot gesture with his hands, hugged and kissed her, then grabbed her ass for good measure. I wondered how he even got a good grip. She laughed and slapped his hand.

They came back out at two o'clock. I used to have the tuna tacos there when Richie would occasionally bring me for lunch. Today lunch for me was a second KIND bar. They finally came outside. He grabbed her ass again. She grabbed his back. He laughed. She laughed. The Mercedes took them back to the Archer Residences for what was most certainly a matinee. When Drysdale came outside an hour later, the Mercedes took him back to his office, where he stayed until six o'clock.

Then I was back on Temple Street in front of The Archer. I thought about Richie while I waited. Then Jesse. I thought about my marriage to Richie and how happy I had been until I wasn't. And why I wasn't. Not for the first time, I tried to imagine myself married to Jesse. He was easier than Richie, I knew that. Not less complicated. Probably more so when I really thought about it, with more sadness to him, and even darkness, so much of it tied to his drinking, whether or not he was sober, as he was now. I didn't love him more than I loved Richie. But for now, being with Jesse *was* easier, perhaps because he seemed quite content for us to continue on with things the way they were indefinitely.

But was I?

Or did I want more, and wasn't admitting that to myself?

Or less?

Fuckety fuck.

I could ask Dr. Silverman tomorrow, if today ever actually ended. I drank some water and finally ate my apple. I thought about Emily now, weighing what I thought I'd known about her against what I'd learned. I tried to imagine someone losing enough money playing cards that she had to steal from her mother to pay it. Or maybe the loss had led her to cheat to break even, even knowing the inherent risks, whether you were playing for a thousand dollars or ten thousand or a million.

I wondered if it was a form of sexism, or reverse sexism, or something else, not to be able to picture a beautiful young woman, which Emily certainly was, being a poker player at all.

Something else I could ask Susan Silverman, who pretty much knew everything.

The Mercedes hadn't come back. It gave

me time to run over to the parking garage two doors down and shamelessly flirt with the attendant so he'd let me use the bathroom. I'd done the same with a garage on Milk Street while Drysdale was at lunch. Spike was watching Rosie today. She'd probably never had a full bladder the whole day. My life was often less glamorous than the Duchess of Cambridge's.

I got back in the car and looked at Georgia O'Keeffe's watercolors and finally snapped myself out of my reverie as the black Mercedes pulled past me and back into the courtyard. Then Drysdale came through the doors and got back inside the Mercedes, and I was once again following them down Temple Street at a safe distance, determined to go the distance, even if they were on their way to the Berkshires.

This time the Mercedes dropped him at an impressive old brownstone on the river side of the Comm Ave walking mall, a four-story town house that looked even more expensive than the ones on either side of it. I was vaguely aware that the writer David McCullough had once had an apartment around here somewhere or perhaps still did, but couldn't remember exactly where it was.

The Mercedes pulled away. Fuckety fuck. He was going to be here awhile, which meant so was I.

I was starting to nod off when I saw that the Mercedes was back. It was five minutes after eleven o'clock when Drysdale came walking down the front steps, smiling, chatting with the guy in the skinny suit who'd come to my office. He had been inside since eight.

It wasn't nearly as noteworthy as the fact that when the door opened again, Emily Barnes came walking down the steps behind them.

NINETEEN

I sat in my car, on the opposite side of Commonwealth, as I watched Drysdale get back into the Mercedes, which headed west for a block before making a left turn and passing right by me.

I knew where he lived and worked and where he'd eaten lunch today and that I could find him most nights at Spike's. But Emily was right across the street, checking her phone, looking around as if waiting for her own ride. She wore a cropped blazer and jeans and Golden Goose sneakers, ones that went for at least five hundred a pair. I could see the huge star on the side even from where I sat.

Wait for her to be picked up, by an Uber or by the boyfriend, or go talk to her right now?

I got out of my car and called out to her as I started across Commonwealth.

When she saw it was me, she took off.

"Emily!" I said, running after her. "I just want to talk!"

I was wearing a pair of cute slip-ons. Very comfortable. Not made for the finishing kick of the Marathon. I had actually been doing a lot of running lately, distance and intervals. Not in my Toms. I was fast. She was a lot faster.

Another thing to hate about college girls.

She crossed Clarendon, heading for the park, had already put more distance between us as she caught a green light at Berkeley. I was still at Dartmouth, and had to stop when I heard the blare of a car horn, heard myself being cursed at through open windows as the car went past me before I was in motion again.

I saw her look back over her shoulder to see if I was gaining on her when she had to wait now for a light at Arlington. Then she was on her way across the street and into the Public Garden, raising her hand to her ear and leaving it there, obviously talking on her phone. Probably to arrange a new pickup location. Uber or Lyft or perhaps the red Mazda that had been her ride away from Lee's apartment that day. It didn't matter. I was going to lose her if I couldn't catch up with her. I remembered chasing a woman named Lisa Morneau up River

116

Street Place one night when she was headed for the park. Never caught up with her, either. She later ended up dead.

Emily Barnes was flying across the bridge over the Swan Boat lagoon, then angling toward Boylston, when I gave up, turned, and walked back to where I'd left my car, already feeling the pain in my feet, thinking:

Nice running, Grandma.

TWENTY

"That building on Comm Ave is owned by an LLC," Lee Farrell said.

Spike grinned as he turned to me.

"That's a limited liability corporation," he said.

I told him I knew stuff like that from watching *Billions.*

The three of us were at my kitchen table at nine the next morning. By now I had filled them in about my adventures the night before, all the way until I chased Emily and finally lost her in the park.

"She ran cross-country in high school," Lee said, "if that's any consolation to you."

"And, let's face it," Spike said, "everybody loses a step eventually."

"They had to be there for the same poker game," Lee said. "Nothing else makes sense."

"Very little makes sense at the moment," I said.

"Except that my world just collided with yours," Spike said to Lee.

I'd made a pot of coffee this morning, abandoning Mr. Keurig. I poured more for everybody. When I sat back down I said to Lee, "So there's no name on the lease?"

He shook his head.

"I ran the address through Records Management," he said. "Commonwealth Mall LLC owns the building. I could have gone deeper with the Regional Intelligence Center. But that would have started a paper trail that would have made me explain why I was doing a deep dive on something not attached to an active investigation. Which this isn't."

"Missing person?" I said.

"Not if you saw her on the street," Lee said.

"Maybe whoever was hosting the game, if there was a game, just rents the place," Spike said.

"From an owner who wants his identity kept private," I said.

"I'm guessing foreign owner," Lee said.

Spike said, "Makes sense. I read this piece in the *Times* about how these rich foreign guys love LLCs because it's one of the ways they can launder money." He grinned. "One of many."

"You told me you thought the guy who came to your office might be from some-where else," Lee said to me.

"I told you, it was something about the way he spoke," I said. "I just felt as if English might be his second language.

"There were just a couple little things that hit my ear wrong when I thought about it afterward," I said. "It wasn't just that I thought there was some kind of accent buried there, like with all those Aussies and Brits on TV shows. It was that his English sounded a tiny bit off."

"Maybe Drysdale is fronting for somebody who doesn't want his identity known," Spike said.

"Maybe even the guy who came to your office," Lee said.

Spike put his mug down hard.

"What's Drysdale into?" he said. "Other than me, of course."

"It could be nothing more sinister than a poker game," I said.

"But if these guys *are* high rollers," Lee said, "how did my niece get into the game?"

"Maybe she's a play-ah," Spike said.

"And maybe she didn't get beat up be-cause of a debt," Lee said. "Maybe it was because she got caught cheating."

"Or maybe the ten thousand was the vig,"

Spike said. He grinned again as he turned to me. "You know what the vig is, correct?"

"My ex-father-in-law is a legendary loan shark," I said.

"And then they just turn around and let her back into the game?" Lee said.

I saw him check his watch.

"I know some heavy players," Spike said. "I'll ask around. Maybe they've been in games with Drysdale. Or Emily. Or both of them."

"Be nice to know whose game that was last night," I said. "And what the stakes were."

"And who Drysdale's friend is," Lee said. "Send me the picture you took of him. If I get a chance later I'll run it through facial recognition."

My phone was on the table. I sent Lee the picture.

"Well," Spike said, "we've put the band back together, haven't we?"

Lee gave him a blank stare.

"I was never in the band," he said.

I patted him on the arm. "Well, you are now, sweetie," I said.

He said he was going to keep trying Emily's phone, and asked if I would do the same. I told him she had her chance to talk to me last night, so I wasn't hopeful that she'd take my call.

At the front door Lee said, "Who the hell *is* this kid?"

"We're going to find out eventually."

"We have to find her first," Lee said.

I went back into the kitchen and sat with Spike. He looked tired, and had clearly lost weight. Or maybe just looked lost. It made me want to smack Alex Drysdale all over again.

"I was thinking about something," he said. "Maybe I should have just borrowed the money I needed from Richie's old man."

"Even with the vig?" I said.

"Maybe he would have given me a family discount because of you," he said.

Then he said he was off to start investigating Boston poker, saying that it would feel like old times, him doing some legwork for me this way.

"See," I said, "I still need you."

He said, "Not as much as I need you," and then asked what my next move was.

"I'm doing what any self-respecting gumshoe would do," I said. "Going to see my shrink."

TWENTY-ONE

Even when I was meeting with Dr. Susan Silverman only by Zoom during COVID, having learned to live with Zoom the way I once had braces, her office on Linnaean Street still felt like a safe place for me from the chaos of the virus, fifty minutes at a time, in a world that had otherwise gone batshit crazy.

I mentioned that to her now. She smiled. Or nearly smiled. Sometimes her changes of expression were as imperceptible as light beginning to fade in the late day.

" 'Batshit crazy,' " she said. "I believe one of my professors in cognitive psychology occasionally referenced that."

She had somehow become even more beautiful in the years I had known her, without any visible signs that she was getting any older. I knew that eventually it would make me come to hate her the way I was hating on college girls these days, even the ones who weren't card cheats. Her dark hair gleamed, as always. Her makeup was both discreet and flawless. She wore a charcoal-gray cutaway blazer, black jeans, a white shirt with a gathered-neck collar. She folded her hands on the desk in front of her. Even her hands showed no signs of aging. What the hell?

"So," she said. "What's new and exciting in the world of Sunny Randall?"

I told her most of it then, about Spike and Drysdale and Emily, about seeing Emily with Drysdale the night before, and how what had seemed like a two-front war had suddenly become one somehow.

"Spike's still my number-one priority," I said. "I like Lee a lot. But I love Spike."

"And are motivated to avenge the loss of his restaurant," she said.

"Highly," I said.

"Slay the dragon," she said.

"If not slay him, then at least kick the shit out of him," I said.

"The knight errant," she said, "just as a woman."

"What," I said, "girls can't be knights, too?"

"I believe they're called dames," Susan Silverman said. "And you do happen to be a great dame."

"Not feeling like one at the moment," I said.

"It sounds to me," she said, "as if you are experiencing the same emotions you did after Richie was shot that time."

"I honestly believe that Spike is more damaged right now than Richie was," I said, "and Richie took a bullet."

"Which will motivate you even further."

"Fuckin' ay," I said.

I was sure only her steely will prevented her from smiling. Instead she leaned forward, tenting her fingers underneath her chin. Why *hadn't* the backs of her hands started to get veiny?

"How is Richie, by the way?" she said. "And Jesse?"

Somehow, I told her, I'd managed to ask both of them for help on the same day.

"That must have been interesting," she said.

"I guess *interesting* would be one way of describing it," I said.

"It actually makes perfect sense," she said. "Asking two men you love for assistance because another man you love is in trouble."

"You know how it is with us dames," I said. "Whatever it takes."

"You could have it printed on your new business cards," she said.

125

She forgot no details of my life, no matter how minor they might have seemed to me when I shared them with her.

"But," she continued, "being willing to do whatever it takes has enabled you to do what you do as well as you do it."

"Except when I get spun around the way I did when I saw Lee's niece and Drysdale together," I said.

"As a friend of mine likes to say, it just means the game's afoot," she said. "Which is something that has always brought out the best in you."

"You're saying I like this?"

"You certainly don't like Spike being in pain," she said. "And don't like watching what Lee is going through with his niece, being spun around this way himself. But you are back in the arena. I know what you sound like, what you *are* like when you feel the work doesn't matter. But this work clearly does."

Now she smiled. It was a truly luminous smile.

I thought, *Was that so hard?*

"You'll figure this out, Sunny," she said. "You always do."

"Is that my Ph.D. pep talk for the day?"

"Just an observation based on past experience."

"Are you as confident I'll eventually figure things out with the men in my life?" I said.

"Oh," she said, "them."

"Always in the room somewhere," I said, "hiding in plain sight."

"We'll save them for next time," she said.

She nodded at the new clock on the wall to my left.

"One last question?" I said.

"Of course."

"Who do you think is more likely to get me to where I want to go, Alex Drysdale or the girl?"

"Drysdale," she said. "He sounds like the factor affecting all other developments."

"Is that you thinking like a cognitive psychologist?" I said.

"More like a detective," she said.

"You're very good at it."

"You have no idea," she said.

TWENTY-TWO

When I was back from Cambridge I went for a run along the Charles, a long one, more interval work today after getting dusted the way I had by Emily Barnes the night before.

I finally came back across the river on the Mass Ave Bridge, made my way back up Commonwealth to the brownstone I'd seen Drysdale and his friend and Emily exiting the night before, walked up the steps and rang the doorbell. Waited a few minutes. No one came to the door. There was an old-fashioned brass knocker. I knocked it.

Nothing.

No one home. That was one possibility in the middle of the day. The other was that there was a security camera attached to the peephole and whoever might be inside just wanted me to think no one was home.

I went to the bottom step and sat down. Perfectly normal for a runner at rest, especially in Boston, the runners' capital of the world, whether you lived here or not. I had bought myself one of those water bottles you could attach to a wristband. I drank some water and decided to wait, hoping someone would come walking out or pass me on the way in. But no one did. My phone was in a zippered pouch on my running belt. There was a voice message from Lee saying he was on his way to Taft. There was a missed call from Spike. No message.

I was about to jog home when Jesse called.

"What's good?" I said.

"Keeping the streets of Paradise, Massachusetts, safe from marauders," he said.

"Are there marauders in Paradise?"

"Not at this particular moment," he said. "But I'll be ready when there are, don't worry about me."

He asked where I was.

"A stakeout," I said.

"What are you wearing?"

"Seriously?"

"I'm an officer of the law," he said. "We take all lines of questioning seriously."

"Sweaty sweatshirt and running pants."

"The tight spandex kind?"

"How old are you?" I said. "We talk about Lycra these days."

I told him where I was, and why, but that

I was about to give up, head home, take a shower. He told me how quickly he could get to downtown Boston if he used the flashing lights and siren. I reminded him how often he said that.

"Do you have dinner plans?" he said.

"I do not."

"I can be down there by seven," he said. "You pick the place."

"How about King & I for takeout," I said.

"Sold," he said. "I want the Paradise Beef-cake."

"It's called Paradise Beef on the menu," I said.

"You call it what you want," he said, "I call it what I want."

We had spread out the food on the coffee table in the living room. I had put pillows on the floor for us to sit on. It was understood that he would stay the night. Over the last couple months he had taken to leaving a change of clothes in a spare bedroom that had never been used, at least not since Rosie and I had moved here, and leaving a dopp kit in the bathroom attached to it. It made us, I felt, a lot more official than an Instagram post.

I was drinking Riesling, which I'd decided went perfectly with Thai food. He was drinking Coke out of the small bottles that he liked. It had long since become a non-issue that I drank in front of him.

"You drinking doesn't make me miss it any more," he finally said one night, before grinning and saying, "or any less."

As we ate I took him through everything that had happened, Spike and Lee, from the day Drysdale had come to Spike's until last night. He interrupted only one time.

"You slapped him?"

"I did."

"Badass," he said.

I told him it had just felt quite natural in my badass biker jacket.

"How quickly could you model that for me?" he said.

"Please try to stay on point."

"I thought that's what I was doing," he said.

I told him what Dr. Silverman had said about keeping my focus on Drysdale.

"There's a lot of ways to go at this," he said. "But I think she's right. There's a baseball expression that covers him."

"I was afraid of that."

"He sounds like the straw that stirs the drink," Jesse said, and reached over and effortlessly picked up some of my duck with his chopsticks. I used a fork.

"I watched the two of them walk out last

night," I said, "and felt like the girl had walked in from another movie."

"It will all make sense," he said, "when you find out why."

"You sound as confident as my shrink."

"I tell you all the time," he said. "If this shit were easy, everybody would do it."

He put down his chopsticks, leaned back against the couch, and closed his eyes. I knew he was reviewing everything I had just told him. There was almost a kinetic energy when he was like this, his cop's mind at work the way it was now. Like a river flowing. Mass plus velocity. The first thing he'd told me when he arrived was that he'd just gotten off the phone with Brian Lundquist, who had come up empty on the fingerprints we'd sent him.

Now he said, "Until we get a name, or some background on the fuckwit who came to your office, I would definitely keep digging on Drysdale."

Most of the food on his plate was gone. He reached over and handed one last small piece of beef to Rosie.

Somehow he had gotten closer to me.

"So it's a hard pass on the biker jacket?" he said.

I tried to wink at him in a saucy way, worried as always that it simply looked as if I had something in my eye.

"Who said it was?" I said.

He leaned over and kissed me then. I kissed him back. It went like that for a few minutes, and very well, I thought, even though I knew I was hardly an impartial judge.

It had been decided that we could clear the coffee table later when my doorbell rang. Rosie beat me across the foyer, barking and wagging her tail.

Dogs knew things.

When I opened the front door, Richie Burke was standing there.

"Surprise," he said.

I told him he didn't know the half of it.

TWENTY-THREE

By now Jesse and Richie probably felt as if they knew all about each other, especially Jesse, who had heard all about my relationship with my ex-husband when we first became intimate with each other. It was mostly because he was having even more issues about letting go with his ex-wife, Jenn. Lots more. But as deep as my feelings for Richie were, and still were, and always would be, I was never obsessed about him the way Jesse obsessed about Jenn, really until she finally remarried. She had always been enough, sometimes literally, to drive Jesse Stone to drink.

It was different with Richie. Most of the time his position was that he didn't want to know what he didn't want to know about Jesse Stone, even if he knew *me* well enough to understand that what I felt for Jesse was serious.

You could see all the way from the front

door into the living room, where Jesse was now standing. As Richie knelt down to greet Rosie he said, "Well, well, the gang's all here."

Then he looked at me and said, "I can come back."

"Don't be silly," I said, even though the whole thing felt as far from silly in the moment as if we all were from the Great Barrier Reef.

"It's just that I just got off the phone with my father," he said. "Call lasted all the way from the North End to here. One of his troopers knows the name of the guy who came to your office. And a lot more than that."

"I want to hear all of it," I said, and walked back into the living room, Richie and Rosie following me.

I felt like an idiot formally introducing them. But I did, anyway. They shook hands. It was Jesse who attempted to break the ice, grinning and saying, "Should we just go ahead and skip the parts about how I've heard a lot about you?"

"The Irish have an expression that covers situations like this," Richie said, grinning. "No use gurnin' about it."

Then he nodded at the food on the table and said to me, "King & I?"

"None better," and then I said I'd clean up later, and said we could go sit at the kitchen table. I absently ran a hand across my lips, hoping Richie wouldn't notice, glad I'd worn my favorite pale lip gloss tonight and not something more colorful.

First Spike and Lee had been here in the morning. Now Jesse and Richie. My kitchen was starting to feel like a conference room. Jesse was to my right, Richie to my left, as if they'd gone to neutral corners.

"The guy's name is Eddie Ross," Richie said. "But turns out that's short for Rostov. He's Russian."

"Oh, ho," I said.

"You still say that?" Richie said.

"Only when I feel as if a clue has presented itself," I said.

"There are times when it happens less than she'd prefer," Jesse said.

Richie nodded. I knew him, sometimes better than I knew myself. He was not here to banter with Jesse, or bond. Or like him.

"One of Desmond's top lieutenants, a rather brilliant young hotshot from Roxbury named Jalen, recognized him," Richie said. "He told my father that he became aware of Eddie Ross several months ago, when a friend of his ended up at one of Eddie's tables."

"So who is he, really?" I said, "other than the former Eddie Rostov?"

"Jalen did his homework," Richie said. "Or *does* his homework. It turns out Eddie's father once operated the biggest sports books in Europe, one that primarily catered to your basic oligarchs in Russia and Ukraine."

"I've always just thought 'oligarch' meant they steal bigger than everybody else," I said.

"In Russia and Ukraine they do," Richie said.

"They're fucking gangsters is what they are," Jesse said, then looked at Richie and added, "No offense."

"None taken," Richie said.

Richie told us more of what Jalen had learned, about Rostov's father having been the king of gambling, not just in Eastern Europe but all across the continent, and money laundering across the globe. At one time, he had also organized, almost on the side, the biggest and richest poker games in about a dozen countries.

"Jalen found all this out?" I said.

"When my father wants information," Richie said, "he doesn't fuck around."

"Young Jalen sounds like an up-and-comer," I said.

"He has quietly started to fill the role at Desmond's right hand that Uncle Felix once filled," Richie said.

He told us the rest of it about Eddie Ross, occasionally checking his phone to look at the long email Jalen had sent him. Vasily Rostov, Eddie's father, had disappeared a couple years ago, Richie said, under circumstances that would have been considered unusual, except for the fact that it was Russia. By then his son was long gone, the father having kept him away from their family business and sent him to America to college twenty years earlier.

"As thorough as your father's man Jalen clearly is," I said, "I'm sure he knows what college."

"Stanford," Richie said.

"Oh, ho," I said again.

TWENTY-FOUR

I told them that Alex Drysdale and his former partner had also gone to Stanford, and I was willing to bet that if I checked with the alumni office, they were all there at the same time.

I saw Richie scroll down the email.

"Before long our Russian prince was living the life in Los Angeles," he said, "and organizing poker games for the rich and famous. Actors. Professional athletes, even from the fucking Lakers. Movie moguls. Now Jalen believes he's doing the same thing in Boston."

"I take it he's not just doing it for the love of the game," Jesse said.

"Not so much, according to Jalen," Richie said. "He thinks money laundering might still be the family business, especially for rich foreigners."

"You said it was a little murky how Drysdale got back up on his feet," I said. "Maybe

139

less murky now."

"You're saying it could be something other than a passion for Texas Hold 'Em that brought them together here?" Jesse said.

"Texas Hold 'Em?" I said.

"I still watch ESPN sometimes when there's no baseball," he said.

I looked at Richie.

"What does Desmond think about Eddie Ross, now that he knows what you know?" I said.

"He thinks that perhaps one of the rich foreigners might be running Eddie the way Eddie runs games," Richie said.

"Desmond find any of this troubling," I said, "just in the area of criming?"

"Not yet," Richie said.

I got up from the table, went into the living room, came back with my wine, and drank some.

"Jesse doesn't believe in coincidence," I said to Richie.

"Who the hell does?" Richie said.

"Ross went to Stanford," I said. "Drysdale went to Stanford. Drysdale's former partner went to Stanford. Drysdale stole Spike's restaurant out from underneath him. Eddie Ross came to see me. I saw him with Drysdale coming out of the brownstone, along with young Emily Barnes."

"Maybe it's just the gambling that's the connection," Richie said.

"Gonna find out," I said.

"I'll bet," Richie said, without a hint of irony.

He pushed back his chair, then he was the one disappearing into the living room. When he came back, he said, "I did *not* feed Rosie off your plates."

"Thank you," I said.

"For lying about not feeding the dog?"

"For the intel on Eddie Ross," I said.

He shrugged.

"You asked," he said.

He turned to Jesse and said, "Nice to finally meet you."

"Same," Jesse said.

Richie nodded.

"Now we're both lying," he said.

"Speak for yourself," Jesse said.

Richie said that he'd call when Jalen came up with more on Eddie Ross, which Richie said he most certainly would. Then he gave me a long look and said he knew his way out.

When I heard the front door shut I said to Jesse, "Well, that was kind of a mood killer."

"Speak for yourself," Jesse said again.

He walked across the kitchen and told me to drink up, then took me by my hand and

141

walked me through the living room and up the stairs to my bedroom and the bed that Melanie Joan Hall had left behind, one as big as a helicopter pad.

"You know," I said, as I slowly began to undress, "I'm still worried about the mood thing."

"Makes one of you."

"I read somewhere once that a good mood is like a balloon," I said, "and that all it takes is a good prick to ruin it."

Jesse Stone smiled and then came over to the other side of the big bed to speed up the undressing process.

"I'll risk it if you will," he said.

And we did.

It was after midnight when my cell phone buzzed from the table on my side of the bed, and Frank Belson was telling me that somebody just shot a guy who had one of my cards on him, two to the chest, close range, center mass, dead.

I took a very deep breath, in through the nose, out through the mouth.

"The guy named Alex Drysdale by any chance?" I said.

"However did you know?"

"Women's intuition," I said.

"Are you even allowed to say shit like that anymore?" Belson said.

142

"When you got it, flaunt it," I said, and then asked him where he was before calling Spike to tell him that ding-dong, the bitch was dead.

TWENTY-FIVE

Jesse said that the last thing Frank Belson wanted or needed was some small-town cop mucking up his crime scene. I told him he was about as far from being just another small-town cop as I was from being the next Ruth Bader Ginsburg. He said I knew what he meant and he was just going to head back to Paradise.

"Never dull hanging with you," he said when we were outside next to our cars.

"I am truly blessed," I said, "in so many ways."

He grinned.

"And look at me," he said, "making a new friend tonight."

"It was all a cruel deception," I said. "Like when Rosie actually acts as if she likes other dogs."

I got into my new Prius and drove the few blocks to where Alex Drysdale used to live, saw that the cops had already blocked off

Ashburton at the corner of Somerset. I parked and walked the rest of the way, explaining to the first uniform stopping me who I was and that Belson had called me. He let me pass. There was another Ford Expedition parked next to another Crown Vic at the other end of Somerset. The bus with Drysdale's body inside was already gone. There was a perimeter of yellow tape at the entrance to The Archer. Chalk outlines were strictly for old movies now. I saw Belson standing where Drysdale must have been shot, out on the sidewalk.

Another uniform tried to stop me, but when Belson saw me he called out.

"Tragically," he said, "she's with me."

He took one more look around the immediate vicinity, but not the last he would take tonight, and nodded for me to follow him into the courtyard. I could have sworn he was wearing a new raincoat, to replace the one he'd been wearing the first time I met him. No tie tonight. Belson looked as if he'd last shaved a couple days ago, but he always looked like that, and was still carrying an unlit cigar. Even as we'd moved away from the street, his eyes were taking in everything around us at once. If I called him in the morning after he'd gotten a few hours' sleep, he would be able to provide an astonishingly detailed description of the scene, down to what kind of sneakers I was wearing.

As always, it was as if he had started the conversation between us a few minutes before I had arrived.

"He gets dropped off at the front entrance," Belson said. "His car pulls away. Doorman is behind his desk. But as soon as Drysdale is inside, doorman says he gets a call. Turns out the service isn't great in the lobby. Drysdale says to whomever he's talking to, 'Wait, let me go outside.' Doorman sees him walking toward the sidewalk, waving his free arm, looking agitated. Next thing the doorman hears is boom boom, sees a car heading toward Somerset, runs out. There's our vic, flat on his back, bleeding out. Doorman calls nine-one-one. By the time the paramedics show up, guy's dead as a doorstop."

"You have his phone?" I said.

Belson shook his head. "Gone."

"Security camera?"

"In here," Belson said. "Not out where he got it. A woman at the other end of the block was walking her dog. Heard the shots, saw the car pull away. Says she thinks it was a Lexus. Could have been an Audi. Said the noise was very upsetting to Mrs. Miniver."

146

"Mrs. Miniver?"

"Her Yorkie," Belson said. "Lady said the car was pulling away a few seconds after she heard the shots."

"There goes the neighborhood," I said.

"You care to tell me what your card was doing in the front pocket of the guy's sport jacket?" Belson said. "I didn't even know you had cards."

"I even have my own office now like a big girl," I said, and then told him about what Drysdale had done to Spike, and what Spike had done to him, and how I'd gone to Drysdale's office and left a card on his desk, and how he must have stuck it in his jacket and forgotten about it.

"Kind of a bad guy, Frank," I said.

"Ran into a worse guy," he said.

He jerked his head back toward the street.

"That's Russian-style, getting it like that," he said. "Not even a drive-by. They like to pull up, walk right up to you, look you in the eye, spit on you when it's done."

Belson told me he'd talk to Spike tomorrow, it was too fucking late tonight to act like he was a person of interest, then turned and walked back toward the street, pulling out a notebook and a pen as if he were about to write me up. I watched him go, thinking, *Russian-style*.

I knew a Russian.
Boom.

148

TWENTY-SIX

Spike and I were having coffee at my office the next morning. He stopped at the downtown location of Kane's on Oliver Street to get the donuts fresh out of their oven. He'd called to ask if I wanted gluten-free. I told him I'd lost some weight, not my mind. He'd gone to Kane's after visiting with Frank Belson at One Schroeder Plaza.

"You know I don't scare easily," Spike said. "But the idea of getting on the wrong side of Frank Belson scares the balls off me."

I smiled. "Same," I said.

"I didn't tell him about the former Eddie Rostov," Spike said.

"Only because I told you not to."

"Only because you held that back," Spike said.

"Not ready to show all of my cards," I said.

"I see what you did there," Spike said.

He took a bite of his honey jelly, washed it down with some coffee, licked his fingers.

149

"I can't believe he's dead," Spike said.

He'd spoken to Rita Fiore before she'd even gotten to Cone, Oakes, asking what Drysdale's death might mean about the ownership of Spike's, now and going forward. Rita said that she knew as much about contract law as she did celibacy, but did ask if Spike had signed the transfer papers. He said he had not, that he'd been putting it off until the last possible moment. Rita said it was a good thing, that it might take a while for accountants to go through Drysdale's books, and that the ownership of Spike's restaurant, no offense, might not be their principal focus in the short run. Spike asked what he should do. Rita told him to go over to the place in the late morning and open it the hell up for lunch.

"Then what?" Spike asked her.

"For the time being you go back to playing the part you were born to play," Rita said. "Yourself."

Before she'd hung up, Spike told me, she'd asked once again if he was absolutely certain he was gay.

"I'm not sad he's dead," Spike said.

"I know."

"I tried to be after you called last night," he said. "But I couldn't."

"You don't have to explain yourself to

me," I said. "I'm not *your* shrink."

"Bullshit you're not."

"So now we ask ourselves who killed him, and why," I said, "unless somebody just took it upon themselves to rid the world of one more hedge-funder."

"Russian-style," Spike said.

"But the Russian I met came to my office and told me to back off his friend Alex," I said, "and with vigor."

"And you saw them leaving what you believe was a poker game with *their* friend Emily the night before somebody shot him," Spike said.

"Get out of here now," I said. "You've got a restaurant to run."

"For the time being."

"Better than the alternative," I said.

"Ain't that the truth," Spike said.

He nodded at my own half-eaten donut, a plain, and raised his eyebrows. I gladly slid it across the desk to him. Those five pounds weren't coming back without a fight.

Spike said, "Will Lee tell Belson about seeing Emily and Drysdale and Eddie Ross together?"

"Only if asked," I said. "He's more worried about Emily than ever and would very much like me to locate her. I told him the best way for me to do that was to find Eddie Ross first. Find him, find Emily, maybe even find out who shot Alex Drysdale."

"And find out who beat the girl up," Spike said.

"Yup," I said.

"And I'm just guessing that you haven't forgotten that picture somebody left of your dad," Spike said.

"I'll forget when I'm the one who's dead," I said.

He came around the desk, kissed the top of my head, and said, "And Russians think they're badass."

I told him to stop before he embarrassed me.

TWENTY-SEVEN

I met Christopher Lawton for an early lunch at The Bell in Hand Tavern on Union Street, a short walk from where Alex Drysdale's office had been at One Financial.

The Bell in Hand advertised itself as the oldest tavern in America, and as the most famous alehouse in Boston. I had liked the place from the first time Richie had taken me there to meet his father, which is why I'd always taken it on faith that they were offering a legitimate version of their history.

Lawton said he didn't have a lot of time, he had to get back to The Carmody. I told him the Lobster BLT was great. We ordered two of those, and iced teas.

"When did you hear about Alex?" I said when the waiter had walked off with the menus.

"Saw," he said. "Early this morning on Twitter."

"Ah," I said, "the paper of record."

153

"Isn't that *The New York Times*?" he asked.

"Not anymore."

We had scored a table by one of the front windows. Lawton stared outside.

"It sounded like an assassination," he said.

"Not sounds like," I said. "*Was* an assassination."

"It's not as if Alex was one of the most popular boys in class," he said. "And I know better than anyone else the bullshit things he's done to people, your friend being the most recent evidence of that. But what did he do to make somebody get out of a car and shoot him on the street?"

The question hung in the air between us. I had no answer for him and so let it go.

"I'm actually only here to talk about Alex tangentially," I said.

" 'Tangentially?' " he said. "Are you sure you're a private detective?"

"Me talk pretty," I said.

I sipped some strong iced tea, freshly brewed Bewley's, over ice.

"Eddie Ross," I said when I put my glass down.

"Eddie Ross," Lawton said.

"Or Rostov, as they called him back in the mother country."

We briefly hit the pause button as our food was delivered, Lawton looking down at his plate and saying, "Looks delicious."

"Eddie Ross," I repeated.

"What about him?"

"He was at Stanford when you and Alex Drysdale were at Stanford," I said. "I called to make sure. He graduated a year ahead of the two of you, and then, lo and behold and all this time later, he shows up at my office, slick as spit, and tells me to lay off Alex. Called himself a business associate and told me that when Alex was unhappy, so was he. Not terribly long after that, a photograph of my father with a red dot on his forehead is delivered to my doorstep."

I took the top piece of bread off my sandwich and picked off a chunk of lobster meat and ate it.

"*That* Eddie Ross," I said.

"Don't know what I can tell you," Christopher Lawton said. "I haven't thought about Eddie much lately."

"Think about him now," I said. "I'm buying lunch."

"Alex was always closer to him than I was," Lawton said, "all the way back to college. I always just thought he was a shifty little mutt on the make."

Now we're talking.

"In addition to him coming to my office," I said, "I saw Alex and your old classmate

155

Eddie walking out of a brownstone on Comm Ave the other night, and intuited that they had just played poker together inside."

" 'Intuited,' " he said.

I sighed.

"Christopher," I said, "we have now established that you think I am a silver-tongued devil."

Now he sighed.

"I know his father ran a sports book back in Russia," he said, "and was regarded as a very bad man."

"One who eventually got disappeared, as they say over there."

He pushed his plate to the side and leaned forward. The BLT was listed at "market price." Shame, I thought, for it to go to waste. Maybe I could bring it back to the miniature fridge in my office.

"He really was Alex's friend, not mine," Lawton said. "Alex started hanging with him in college because he thought Eddie was dangerous, because of his father. For the drama of it. Alex loved drama."

"When you and Alex were still together," I said, "did some of Eddie's daddy money find its way into your business?"

"No," he said, perhaps a bit too firmly. "Eddie was living in Los Angeles by then,

156

trying to be the thing he'd always most wanted to be in the world: a celebrity. He was in the process of figuring out that you could achieve a level of celebrity in the modern world just by hanging around with some."

"And playing cards with them?"

"Apparently so."

"So when might he have become an 'associate' of Alex's?" I said, putting air quotes around *associate*.

"Well, it had to be some time after Alex and I had dissolved our partnership," Lawton said.

"Could he be one of those who provided the mysterious infusion of capital to save Alex's ass at that time?"

He sipped some iced tea now, and winced. "This will put hair on your chest," he said.

"Hoping not," I said.

"Could Eddie have used some of his old man's money and given Alex a boost?" Lawton said. "Perhaps. But I honestly don't know. What I do know is that Alex was so desperate to stay out of bankruptcy he would have taken money from the Taliban at that point."

"There's no shame in bankruptcy," I said. "My friend Spike would have done it in a heartbeat if it meant saving his business."

"Alex didn't look at it that way," Lawton said. "Death before dishonor. Like that. At least in his mind." He shook his head. "He literally would have done anything to not look like a loser. And to still be Ace Drysdale. You know the type? His personal code of morality was actually amorality, but he just never saw it. Steal your money, steal your restaurant, steal your wife or your girlfriend. Didn't matter to him. It was why I had to finally get away, as I tried to explain to you. But with all that? I knew him for half my life."

He picked up a fork, put it back down, stared at me.

"Eddie's a lot of things," he said. "But he's not a murderer."

"Who said he was?"

"Something *I* intuited," he said, smiling thinly.

He looked at his watch.

"I really need to get going if I'm going to get to my meeting on time," he said.

"When was the last time you saw Eddie Ross?"

"When he first moved back to Boston," Lawton said. "Maybe a year or so ago? Said he wanted to have a drink. But what he wanted was information, mostly about the dynamics of Alex's and my partnership.

158

Who was the real brains of the operation, me or him?"

"What did you tell him?"

Lawton smiled so thinly I wondered if I could have slipped a piece of paper between his lips.

"I told him Alex's specialty was BS," he said. "Mine was making the money."

"Is there any chance you could get an address for me," I said, "or at least a way to contact him?"

"I can try," he said. "But if I do find him for you? I'd appreciate you not telling him that I did."

"You never signed an NDA with him, right?" I said.

"There was no reason, Eddie and I never did business together," Lawton said. "But all the way back to Stanford, there was something about him that made me reluctant to turn my back on him."

"Could he be running the kind of poker games here he did in L.A.?" I said.

"He was running them all the way back to college," Lawton said. "Maybe nothing *since* college has changed with him."

"Alex play in those games?"

Lawton laughed.

"Only when Eddie would let him cheat his ass off," he said.

TWENTY-EIGHT

"I need some information," I said to Tony Marcus.

He smiled. I would have called it a Cheshire Cat smile if referencing *Alice's Adventures in Wonderland* didn't make me feel older than Alice. So I just thought of it as a Tony smile, smug and condescending and arrogant as hell, all at once.

"What am I," he said, "fucking Google?"

We were in his office at Buddy's Fox. I had not been in contact with him since we had formed another of our temporary alliances to solve the murder of Lisa Morneau by a dirty cop. It changed none of the realities of our relationship. Mine and Tony's. I still trusted him about as far as I could throw a vending machine.

"I thought you still owed me a favor," I said.

"Ain't no more owed between us no more," he said. "You add it all up, the one who ought to be coming up with a little sugar is you, Sunny Randall."

"You ever notice how you occasionally talk to me like I'm one of your girls?" I said.

"You still holdin' on to your looks," he said. "But truth be told, you a little past your sell-by date."

He'd grown a beard during COVID and still had it, even though there was a lot more gray to it than to the hair on top of his head. I loved it when guys did that. Who did they think they were fooling?

He wore a dark suit today, white shirt, purple tie with a knot as big as a fist. As usual, his nails looked better manicured than my own. Junior, his body man, was on one side of the door, as wide as ever, making you wonder if he had to get himself at an angle to enter the room, like he was moving a desk in. Ty-Bop, Tony's shooter, was on the other, a dreamy look on his face, staring at either nothing or eternity. But I knew how quickly he could produce whatever handgun he was carrying if necessary, and then shoot the numbers off a bank card.

I jerked my head in their direction. "At this stage of our relationship," I said to Tony, "do you really feel threatened in my presence?"

"They get they feelings hurt they get left

161

out," he said.

He asked me if I wanted some of the latte his bartender had made up special for him. I told him I'd pass, I didn't want to take up too much of his time.

"Bulllllllllshit," he said. "You just worried that I'm takin' up too much of your time."

"I was hopeful that we could move things along," I said.

"You a piece of work," he said.

"Long since established," I said.

"So how can I help you, be I so inclined?"

"You know a guy named Eddie Ross?" I said. "I think he might be into a lot of things, but I'm almost certain poker is one of them."

"Why do you want to know about him?" Tony said.

"So you do know him?"

"Didn't say that."

"He's involved in something I'm working on," I said. "Couple things, actually."

"Does one of them have something to do with that rich white boy got his ass shot up in your neighborhood?" Tony said. "One you slapped upside his head at your buddy's gay bar?"

I didn't acknowledge that he knew. He just did. He was Tony.

"Spike's gay," I said. "The clientele at the

restaurant is quite ecumenical."

"Ec-u-men-i-cal," he said.

"Eddie Ross," I said.

"Little Russian dude," he said, "even though he trying to pass."

"So you do know him."

"Know *of* him," Tony said. "Like I know of a lot of people I think I might need to keep eyes on, see if they might have something I want or need. He let it be known when he got to town, through somebody who knows somebody knows me, that there was some big-time money games about to be played, and did I want a seat at the table."

He smiled again. "I had to let it be known that if I was to get involved in a game like that, it would be my fucking table. That in games of chance, I ain't likely to be the one taking the chances."

"His father ran a sports book in Russia," I said, "which I believe is something in which you dabbled at one time."

"*Hell,* yeah," he said. "Least back in the day, until the online shit and all the other legal sports betting took the entrepreneurialness of it out of play. I mean, all's you got to do is turn on your television. They's more commercials for sports gambling these days than they is about ways to save fifteen percent or whatever the fuck it is on your

163

car insurance."

He looked over at Junior and pointed to his mug. Junior walked over and wordlessly picked it up, wordless generally being Junior's normal state, and walked out the door toward the bar area.

"One thing don't change, though," Tony continued. "Boys do love they poker games. So I'm keeping an eye on Mr. Eddie Ross, seeing if I might need to take some of those tables away from him one of these days, I feel one of my urges coming on."

"How big is the state of play?" I said.

"Like he's got a league of his own going," Tony said. "Some big games, some smaller. These are the type of arrogant assholes think that if they had the time and inclination, they could be raking in the big pots at the World Series of Poker."

"Who gets in?"

"Anybody willing to pay the buy-in," Tony said.

"How big is that?"

"Depends on the game."

"Money laundering involved?"

"Lots of ways to rinse money and repeat," he said, "poker being one of them."

Junior came back with a steaming mug. Tony sipped some of the latte, then almost daintily placed the mug back on the coaster

164

in front of him. I knew enough by now of what he used to do with those manicured hands when he was making his way up on the street, before his troopers did that sort of work for him.

"Give me a general idea of the floor for the buy-in," I said.

"What I hear?" he said. "Ten grand, or thereabouts."

I wondered, and not idly, if Emily Barnes would have been willing to steal that kind of money from her mother to buy into one of Eddie Ross's games.

"But the price goes up from there," Tony said. "Twenty, twenty-five, up to a hundred for them that want to feel like a play-*ah.*"

"At a poker game."

"They'd be the type that look at that like damn tipping money," Tony said. "They got they private planes. They just bought the lot next to them in the Vineyard, so they don't have to worry about a neighbor having a better goddamn view than they do. And some of them? They just happy to be out the house again after the virus, trying to take some money off some mo-fuck who's got more than they do."

"Thrill of victory," I said.

"Like Viagra, just with poker chips," he said. "Guys like we talking about would rather pay for poker than pussy. Thrill lasts longer."

"You know where I might find Eddie Ross?" I said.

"Sure you want to?" Tony said. "I hear he thinks he's bad, but you don't set up an operation like this if you don't have bad behind you."

"I've just got some questions for him," I said. "And he did threaten me recently."

"I did mention that he's Russian, did I not?" Tony said. "What I know and what I hear, Russians aren't as understanding as somebody like me. Or as, uh, flexible when it comes to being transactional."

"Our friend Frank Belson referred to the shooting as being Russian-style," I said.

Tony closed his eyes and slowly nodded, as if appreciating the image.

"Out the car, then you dead, then back in the car, goodbye," he said.

"I don't believe those particular details were in the news account," I said.

He gave me a big smile now.

"See right there?" he said. "That's why you here, girl. I know how you slapped the boy and I know how he got it. Sometimes I do know more than Google and Safari and Firefly put together."

"Firefox."

"Who gives a shit."

"There you go," I said.

"Say I can get you an address for Eddie Ross," he said. "You know that means we back to you owing me a favor."

"I just assumed I was running a tab."

Junior was already opening the door.

"Couple more questions before I go?" I said.

"Might mean we talking about two favors, then," Tony said.

"You ever hear about anybody cheating at poker games like the ones we're talking about?" I said.

Tony snorted out a laugh. "*Hell,* yeah," he said. "All you need is a dealer willing to risk that shit."

"What about a player cheating and getting away with it?" I said.

"Only if they in on it with a dealer," he said.

I stood and turned to leave. Tony said he'd let me know when he had something on Eddie Ross. Junior was still holding the door. Ty-Bop was still leaning against the wall.

"How we goin' there, Ty?" I said. "All your carry permits up to date?"

He didn't change expression, even though I knew he secretly wanted to. As I was walking out the door the sound of Tony's voice stopped me.

"Hey?" he said.

I turned back around.

"I might've heard one other thing about Eddie Ross," he said. "Boy like *his* pussy."

"Good to know," I said.

"College pussy," Tony said.

TWENTY-NINE

I dropped my car at home after leaving Tony at Buddy's Fox and walked to my office from there.

I hadn't heard from Spike, or Lee. I'd been checking Emily's Instagram account every day, but she hadn't posted anything since she'd been roughed up. Frank Belson had not called about the murder of Alex Drysdale to pick my brain about investigative technique, or crime-solving in general. His loss.

I opened my laptop and put a search on "Eddie Ross and poker" even though I was not expecting him to be advertising his games on social media. The only significant mention of Eddie I found was a *Los Angeles Times* story from a few years ago about celebrity poker. Eddie wasn't described as the organizer of the games. Just one of the players. He was described as a "talent agent," but only in passing, well into the body of the piece.

There were two movie stars mentioned, one Oscar-winning director, a former Laker, former Dodger, the guy who'd made a small fortune with his chicken-burger franchise, a screenwriter, a former diving gold medalist in the Olympics. The basics of the piece were that playing poker for serious money had become as cool in Bel-Air and Beverly Hills and Brentwood as buying kids into college had been until the Feds started perp-walking the rich and famous into courthouses.

It was three o'clock by now. Noon on the West Coast, where it was a little early for power lunches. I called a number that I had briefly known by heart, but now had to look up in my contacts.

Tony Gault, an actual talent agent, picked up on the first ring. He did that, as if afraid his phone would explode in his hand if he didn't.

"I believe you might have told me when we last spoke that you were losing my number," he said.

"I reconsidered," I said.

"So since you *haven't* lost my number, I can only conclude that you want me, or a favor," he said. "Even though many see them as one in the same."

170

"Latter," I said.

"But you did want me once," he said.

"Not sure *want* is the word you're looking for, Tony," I said. "You were an occasional urge, like mint chocolate-chip ice cream."

"Is this how you want to begin our deal-making?"

It had been fun with the other Tony in my life while it lasted, even if it hadn't lasted very long. He was handsome, almost as charming as he thought he was, almost as good in bed. But he had become an even bigger Hollywood player since I'd last seen him, merging his agency with one of the other alphabet agencies Out There.

"I'm looking for someone who once traveled in your circles," I said.

"Which one?" he said. "I have so many."

"Of course you do."

"Name, please?"

"Eddie Ross."

I heard Tony Gault chuckle.

"Now, there is an authentic blast from the past," he said. "Fast Eddie. I wondered what happened to him after he skipped town."

"Skipped?" I said. "Why?"

"He got some people even more prominent than I . . ."

"If such a thing could ever be possible."

". . . into a couple investment-type things

171

that ended up losing them a boatload of money."

"Did you play poker with him?"

"Couple times," Tony said, "with a couple of my brilliant actor clients."

He named them, and I stopped myself from pointing out the distinction between "brilliant" and "famous," though he'd probably stopped making the distinction himself long ago. One was the second lead in a sitcom. The other was an action star who generally killed more people than the Allies had in World War II.

"What were the 'investment-type things'?" I asked.

"I'm still not sure what he was talking about," he said. "Microblogging, or some goddamn thing."

"What was he doing for a living?" I said.

"He said he was a venture capitalist," Tony said. "But his poker buddies were supposed to provide the capital. Eddie managed to convince them that if they didn't get out ahead on it, they'd be kicking themselves like they'd missed buying Apple at the beginning. That was right up until the thing blew up the way the dot-com bubble did back in the day."

"How'd his poker buddies who'd coughed up dough take that?"

"Couldn't find him."

"Hard to take a flier in the modern world," I said.

"He did," Tony said. "Hadn't thought about him until you brought him up just now. So he's in Boston?"

"Still living the poker life," I said. "Still hanging around with rich guys."

"If they shake hands with him," Tony said, "tell them to count their fingers."

I heard a buzzing noise at his end of the call, then heard him say, "Tell her I'll call her back."

To me he said, "Sorry."

"You gonna call whoever-she-is back?"

He chuckled again. "Eventually."

"You may be the biggest bullshitter I've ever known," I said.

"No business," he said, "like show business."

He asked me why I wanted to know about Eddie Ross. I told him. When I finished, Tony Gault said, "You think Eddie might lead you to the girl?"

"*Will* lead me to the girl," I said. "But I have to find him first."

"Wish I could help you," he said. "I'm not sure anybody knew where he lived when he lived out here."

There was another pause.

173

"Was I your first call on this?"

"Actually, Tony Marcus was."

"The gangster you used to talk about?"

"He considers himself kind of a talent agent," I said. "With an even bigger commission than yours."

"Don't be so sure."

"Anything else you can remember that might help me?" I said.

"Maybe not something that will help you," he said. "But something you need to be aware of. There had been this game one time, up in the Hollywood Hills. The usual crowd, just with a couple randos added to the mix. Kind of young guys who said they were friends of somebody. As I recall, one of them had been in a Leo movie. Long story short?"

"They rarely are," I said.

"Ouch," he said. "Anyway, Eddie apparently caught the other young guy cheating. He was in on it with the dealer. The young guy walked away with about twenty grand. Two days later he's in the hospital. Face so messed up he didn't work for six months. I heard it from the kid's agent. Everybody assumed that it was Eddie got it done."

"I'll be careful," I said.

"You with anybody these days?" Tony said.

"Kind of," I said.

"Kind of?" he said. "That kind of sounds like my second marriage."

"I thought you told me you'd only been married once."

"Did I?" he said.

I heard another buzz.

"Listen," he said, "if you're ever out this way . . ."

"I'll have my people call your people," I said, and ended the call.

THIRTY

His name was Matt Dunn. He was the young guy who'd driven away with Emily Barnes in the red Mazda. Now sitting across my desk from me, having told me she was missing, and not just from her uncle and me.

"How did you find me?" I said.

"Emily gave me your card," he said.

I should have had the cards made up sooner. Clearly just about everybody had one of them by now.

He said he'd graduated from Taft two years ago, but had started dating Emily when she was a freshman and he was a junior.

"You guys still dating?"

"Better than saying 'fucking'?" he said.

"Beautifully put."

"We didn't last long," he said. "But we stayed friends. Poker friends. She still crashes at my place sometimes."

"She going around with somebody else now?"

" 'Going around with'?" he said.

"A generational thing," I said.

"There's a guy," he said. "She won't tell me who it is."

I asked if he wanted something to drink. He asked if I had beer. I told him I did, actually, an IPA called Hazy Little Thing. Richie had put me onto it. Matt Dunn told me I had good taste. I told him I was a closet beer nerd, but not to let it get around.

"But you're . . . ."

"A girl?" I said. "Let's have that be our little secret."

He popped the tab and drank down a fair amount of beer.

"When was the last time you saw her?" I said.

Two nights ago, he said, at a poker game on Comm Ave.

"I saw her come out of the building," I said. "Not you."

"What were you doing there?"

"Following Alex Drysdale," I said. "Not that it did either one of us much good. He came out that night with Eddie Ross and Emily. Where were you?"

"Still dealing," he said. "There were a few guys left at the table still trying to get even."

"Is dealer your current occupation?" I said. "Other than card cheat, I mean?"

He finished his beer. Second gulp. Wiped the back of his hand across his mouth. Put the bottle on my desk. Didn't act insulted. But also didn't respond right away.

So I told him then what I'd found in Emily's closet that day.

"You broke into her apartment?"

"I did," I said. "But just so you know? I come by my lock-picking skills honestly."

He asked if he could have another beer. I asked if he had driven to my office. He said he had. I told him he was shut off. He said that beer didn't affect him. I told him I used to get a lot of that from guys when I was Emily's age.

"What are you, my mom?" he said.

"Don't start with me, Sparky," I said.

He had that scruffy, young-guy look. Long hair, shortish beard, Taft hoodie, skinny jeans, motorcycle boots. He'd pulled up the sleeves of the hoodie to his elbows. I could see the tattoo of a playing card, pretty good-sized, inside his right forearm. As always, I wondered how he'd feel about the tat when he was sixty. Or sooner.

"How much poker does she play?" I said.

"A lot," he said.

"She addicted?"

"What does that even mean?" he said. "If she's addicted to anything, it's action."

"That's what's known as a distinction without a difference," I said.

"Whatever."

"How did she play herself into Eddie's games?" I said. "Seems like they'd be kind of rich for a college girl's blood."

"I got her in," he said. "And Eddie didn't think it hurt to have somebody who looked like her at the table."

"Did she lose enough money at one of Eddie's games to get herself beat up when she didn't pay up?"

"Yeah," he said. "We got sloppy. A game in the South End. Not one of Eddie's. We didn't even know we'd gotten caught until the guy went after Emily at school."

"Why her and not you?"

"Maybe to send a stronger message by beating up a woman? Who the hell knows? I didn't have the money to pay him back. Em said she had a way to get it."

"A guy I know told me that back in college, Eddie used to let Alex cheat his ass off," I said. "That still going on?"

"Occasionally," Matt Dunn said. "Him and Eddie were boys, and Eddie liked to keep him happy. I think they had some deals going, apart from poker, but I never knew what kind, and didn't ask. With Eddie, you get the idea pretty quick that he only wants you to know what he wants you to know. He's always using that line from *Rounders,* about how if you don't know who the sucker at the table is, it's you."

"So you got the idea that Eddie and Drysdale were partners?" I said.

"That was the weird part," he said. "Drysdale was the rich guy, but sometimes he acted as if he worked for Eddie."

Dunn reached into the side pocket of the hoodie, came out with his phone, checked it for the first time since he'd knocked on the door, put it back in his pocket.

"No messages from her?"

"Not since I woke up the morning after you saw her and she was gone."

"Do you have the ability to track her phone?"

He made a snorting noise. "She's got more than one phone."

"Why?"

"So people *can't* track her, that's why," he said. "Starting with her uncle the cop."

"Are you here because you want me to find her for you?" I said. "I'm already trying to find her for her uncle the cop."

"I'm worried that something has happened to her," he said. "That maybe she

180

ended up at the wrong table, or screwing with the wrong guy."

"You think she might have gotten beat up again?" I said.

"Or worse," he said. "Let's just say that Emily will play poker with just about any-fuckingbody."

"You know I'm going to tell her uncle that you came here," I said.

"Do what you gotta do," Matt Dunn said. "Just find her. I know she dumped me a while ago, but I still care about her."

He stood, checked his phone again, disgustedly shook his head.

"Gonna need your number," I said, "and your address."

He told me and I wrote them both down.

"Is that *your* only phone?"

I said. He assured me that it was.

"Where are you going now?" I said.

"Check out a couple places where she might be."

I walked across the office and opened the door for him.

"Before you go?" I said. "Where does Eddie live?"

"What the hell do you mean where does he live?" Matt Dunn said. "You were there the other night."

181

THIRTY-ONE

Richie called as I was cutting across the Public Garden and asked where I was. I told him. He asked if I was on my way home. I told him I was, and he asked if he could stop by.

"Somebody I want you to meet," he said, "who might be useful to your sleuthing."

"Sleuthing?" I said.

"You'd prefer private-dicking?" Richie said.

"You're right," I said. "Sleuthing it is."

I made it home quickly enough to change clothes and fuss with my hair and makeup and generally make myself look made for my ex-husband, while telling myself I wasn't trying too hard to look good for my ex-husband.

When I was checking myself out in front of the full-length mirror in the upstairs bathroom, I noticed Rosie staring at me.

"What?" I said to her. "A girl can't want

to look her best?"

She continued to stare.

"Okay, okay," I said. "You got me."

When I opened the door Richie was standing next to a young African American guy about his size, cute as hell, hair cropped close, no beard, a white tee showing underneath a zippered sweater, white Stan Smith sneakers that looked as if they'd just come out of the box.

"Hi," Richie said.

"Hi," the young guy said.

"This is Jalen," Richie said.

"Jalen," I said.

"I told you about him," Richie said. "He works for Desmond. *That* Jalen. The up-and-comer."

"I wish," Jalen said.

Everybody smiled at everybody else.

"Oh," I said. *"Jalen."*

"I believe that's been firmly established," he said.

"I don't want this to come out wrong," I said.

"Y'all didn't expect me to be black," he said.

I put my hands out in a helpless gesture.

"Think of me as black Irish, that work for you?" he said as I showed him in.

It wasn't yet six o'clock. Close enough to

the cocktail hour for me. I asked if anyone would be opposed to me opening a bottle of wine. Richie and Jalen said that would be fine for them. I asked if they preferred red or white. Richie said I could decide. I went into the kitchen and opened a bottle of Malbec and came back with three glasses.

"Sorry about my reaction," I said. "But I just assumed that everybody who worked for Desmond looked like they'd just walked off the set of *Peaky Blinders.*"

"That's about the English, that show," Jalen said, "not Irish. But I get your meaning."

He and Richie sat on the couch. I pulled up a chair and sat across from them. We all leaned forward and clinked glasses.

"It's Jalen Washington, by the way," he said.

"Nice to meet you, Jalen Washington," I said. "How'd you end up working for Desmond Burke?"

"I won't wear your ass out, all the details," he said. "But the bumper-sticker version is I was working as a lookout for Gino Fish when I was in high school. Running some numbers for him when Gino turned that into a side business. Even helping him out, his books, not that he ever told anybody that. This was right before Gino took himself out. You know about all that, right?"

"I do."

"Well, if you did what I did, you got to know all the players," he said. "Like lookin' out was a full-time situation. One day I saw a couple of Mr. Burke's men, who *did* look like *Peaky Blinders,* walking into a trap on collection day over at Blue Hill, in Roxbury, near where I live."

"At which point Jalen promptly saved their asses," Richie said.

"Anyway," Jalen said, "Mr. Burke found out what I got done in that situation. He tried to give me money. I told him I'd rather have a job. He gave me one. An upgrade from Gino, you ask me, even if I didn't say that to Mr. Burke."

I watched him and listened to him talk and thought of what Tony Marcus might have looked like and sounded like at his age. More than anything, it was Jalen Washington's attitude, the cool way he presented himself, the way he streeted his language down, just enough, to let you know where he came from.

"I became Mr. Burke's eyes and ears in that part of town," he said. He grinned. "What you call your black community. Paying attention to which criminal en-ti-ties were doing what."

He stretched out the word as if it were a rubber band.

"And the more things I saw on the street, the more I thought that there were several growth opportunities for Mr. Burke's operation, and likewise opportunities for someone with my, ah, skill set, I guess you could call it, if so inclined."

He smiled. He was probably older than he looked, the way Chris Rock was.

"I figured out something young," he said. "You don't have to be the smartest guy in the world. Just the smartest guy in the game."

"What game?"

He smiled again. "Whatever game you in," he said.

"How would *you* describe your skill set?" I said. "You don't mind me asking."

He tapped the side of his head with a forefinger.

"I got a head for numbers," he said. "And for those, ah, opportunities I just referred to."

"Richie made you sound more like your field was research."

The smile held, bright as his kicks.

"Think of it as research and development," he said.

"Jalen finally convinced my father to do

186

something that Uncle Felix could never quite convince him to do," Richie said. "Diversify."

"Think of me as his one-man diversifying program," Jalen said.

"All legitimate, I'm sure," I said, looking at Richie.

"Little of this, little of that," Jalen Washington said.

"And so how is this going to help me in my sleuthifying?" I said, addressing both of them.

"I think Jalen could do a deeper dive into Eddie Ross's business relationship with Alex Drysdale," Richie said. "I told him what you had going on and asked him if he might be able to help you out." Richie grinned. "Knowing that you most certainly do not have a head for numbers."

"You acting as his agent?" I said to Richie.

"Yours," he said. "Same old, same old."

"I told Richie," I said to Jalen Washington, "that there was much more I needed to know about the old Stanford buds."

"Which I explained to Jalen," Richie said.

"Did you really volunteer to help me," I said, "or did Richie and Desmond draft you?"

He shrugged. "Little of this, little of that," he said again.

"You really want to help?" I said.

"What Mr. Burke wants, I want," Jalen said. "He also believes that there might be a way for him to come away with a piece of whatever Eddie might have going on, apart from poker."

Then he stood up, thanked me for the wine, and said he'd be in touch. "When I have a better sense of the lay of the street," he said. Then he was gone.

"Interesting young man," I said.

"He's really only afraid of one thing," Richie said.

"What's that?"

He smiled. "My father," he said.

"Who isn't?" I said.

I walked him outside.

"I don't like the idea of you going after Russians," he said.

"I really haven't."

"Yet," he said.

We were facing each other on the front walk in the gathering twilight. I thought he might try to kiss me. Hoped he would not. And he did not.

"Think of Jalen as a forensic accountant," he said.

"I'm still not sure that Eddie is fronting for the Russians," I said.

"But he *is* a Russian," Richie said. "His

father, by all accounts, was a bad one."

"Sins of the father don't always get passed on," I said, smiling at him.

"Be careful," Richie said.

"Always."

"You know you're not as tough as you think you are, right?" he said.

"If you really think about it," I said, "who the hell is?"

THIRTY-TWO

I thought about taking a walk over to what I now knew was Eddie Ross's brownstone. Maybe poker was already being played there. Maybe if he answered the door I could ask him if Emily was the one who could come out and play. But I decided to wait. When I next got face-to-face time with him, the real thing, I planned on knowing a lot more about what kind of games Eddie might be playing *apart* from poker than I did now.

I decided to go over to Spike's instead. Private-dicking, as my ex-husband called it, could resume in full in the morning. For now I just wanted to have a drink with Spike, and hope for at least one night that things felt the way they used to at his place.

I took an Uber over there, in case I wanted to have more than one drink. When I walked in, Jack the bartender waved me in the direction of the back room. Spike was at his usual table near the door, good view of the big crowds in both rooms, sitting with a man I did not recognize.

They looked like a doubles team, just from the gym, both of them wearing black T-shirts that were at least a size too small, showing off as much of a ripped upper body as you could with your clothes on. The other guy also showed off two sleeves of tats. Spike had never been a tattoo guy. The other man seemed to be in Spike's general age range. I thought he might be a date he hadn't told me about, even though Spike generally told me about all romantic possibilities — or realities — as if I'd injected him with truth serum.

Spike pulled out a chair. The other man stood and extended a hand that looked as big as an oven mitt.

"Victor Morozov," he said.

"Sunny Randall," I said.

He smiled. "I am already hearing much about you," he said. "Spike tells me that your real first name is Sonya. Russian, you know."

"My dad just always liked it," I said, "and he's more Irish than Guinness. He says my name means 'wisdom' in your country."

"In your case it should mean 'beauty,' " he said as we sat down.

Spike winked at me and said, "I know what you were thinking."

"Do not."

"Not gay," he said. Grinned and said, "Not that there's anything wrong with that, of course."

I decided to stay with wine. When the waiter was gone Spike said, "Drysdale took Victor's gym the way the fuck-monkey tried to take this place. And still might, dead."

He looked over and said to Victor Morozov, "You tell it."

He had been a boxer in Russia, and on his way to the Sochi Olympics before he lost a fight that just turned out to be against the son of a government official.

"Would have been what you call a controversial decision," he said, "but that is only if I had complained about it."

He tried again four years later. But he was, he said, past his best boxing by then. It turned out he had a cousin who lived in Allston. He came here and thought about opening a boxing gym, and heard about Henry Cimoli's. But Henry told him there was no money in boxing, that all he had left of his original gym for fighters was one room. The rest of it, Victor saw, was Peloton machines and a Pilates room and what Morozov described as a sea of blue yoga mats, and the biggest room of all, filled with weights and machines and more exercise bikes.

"I have some money," he says. "My sister and her husband have more. I opened my own gym on Front Street."

"It's not far from where my ex-husband owns a bar," I said.

I told him the name. Morozov smiled. "My home away from home," he said.

He drank what looked like straight vodka.

"Then the COVID comes," Victor Morozov said, "and suddenly in my new life I am starting to die a little, day at a time."

"Guess who worked out there before Victor had to close the doors?" Spike said.

I nodded. "I didn't know your name, Victor," I said. "But I heard about what happened to you from a lawyer trying to help out Spike."

"They beat up Victor, too," Spike said. "But I think he got in more good shots than I did."

Victor held up his left hand, which was still swollen to twice the size of his right. Which was saying plenty.

"I followed Drysdale to the gym at lunch the other day," I said, and Victor Morozov said, "Сукин сын."

"Translation?" I said.

193

"Son of a bitch," he said, and drank. "The last thing they said to me after they had me on the ground and stomped on my hand was that if I went near Drysdale again they would beat up Ilsa next. My cousin."

"Did you shoot him, Victor?"

"Did you ask that of Spike?" he said.

"I know what Spike is capable of," I said. "And not."

Morozov leaned across the table and gave me a long look, close enough for me to see the scarring around his eyes.

"If I am killing Alex Drysdale," he said, "I am doing it with my bare hands."

"I had to ask," I said.

"And now you have been answered."

I looked around Spike's. It was crowded and noisy and there were half a dozen people standing near the hostess stand, waiting for a table. I heard a burst of laughter from a large table of young women in the front room, who appeared to be celebrating something, maybe being young. *I'll drink to that,* I thought.

"Has anybody yet come to claim ownership of the gym?" I said to Morozov.

He nodded at Spike.

"Am in the same boat as him," he said. "I am waiting for somebody to walk in and tell me it is time for me to leave."

"But not yet," I said.

Morozov said, "Now I die a little when a stranger comes walking in."

"What neither of us can figure out is why a hedge-fund guy would want to pick off his place or mine," Spike said.

"Been asking myself the same thing from the start," I said. "Maybe guys like Drysdale can't stop themselves from being complete pigs."

"Or maybe it is something different, I have been maybe thinking to myself," Morozov said. "What if he was not really as rich as we think he was?"

"Or maybe," Spike said, "the people propping him up are the ones with the real money."

"I've got a guy might be able to help find that out," I said, and told him about Jalen Washington.

"Desmond hired a brother?" Spike said. "Seriously?"

"Might have been the last frontier for inclusion," I said.

Victor Morozov said he had to get back to his gym, and left. Spike and me now. He asked if I had any leads on Emily. I told him about the visit from Matt Dunn, dealer and card cheat, and how he'd told me the brownstone belonged to Eddie Ross.

"It seems like a lot of this runs through those poker games," Spike said.

"I just have to figure out how, and why," I said.

I sighed. "Fuckety fuck," I said.

"When are you going back to the brownstone?" Spike said.

"Tomorrow," I said.

"Please take me with you," he said.

I told him I would. He went to work the front room. I went outside to wait for my Uber. The car was eight minutes away. When I got home, I told myself, it was time to get out one of my yellow legal pads and make one of my famous lists and see if writing down everything I knew would make more sense when I saw it on the page. Then I was going to call Jesse and run it all past him. I'd told him once that he was a far more linear thinker than I was.

He'd grinned and said, "In certain areas more than others."

I was scrolling through emails when the car showed up early, switching screens to make sure I had the right make of car and license plate. I was still looking at my phone when car doors opened in front and back and two guys got out and had me by the arms before I could scream or stop them and then I was in the backseat with the bigger of the two and the car doors were shut and the car was pulling up Marshall Street.

The guy in the passenger seat, turning to face me, was the one who had his gun pointed at me.

Now he was the one smiling and saying something in Russian to me.

"Means now we are being up in your shit," he said.

THIRTY-THREE

The car made a series of quick turns. I wasn't paying much attention to where it was going because my attention was focused on the gun. Mine was in my bag, on the seat between me and the man next to me. He reached in there now and quickly rummaged around through my stuff, easily found my .38, the new one Jesse had given me, with my initials engraved on the handle, stuck it into his pocket.

"If you want lip gloss," I said, "all you have to do is ask."

"Funny girl," he said to the men in the front seat right before he backhanded me across the face, snapping my head to the side and nearly putting me on the floor, my bell fully rung.

I leaned back against the seat, angling my body so I could see him and the gun at the same time.

"Eddie send you guys?" I said to the man

198

next to me.

He was big enough to remind me of Tony's man Junior. Full black beard. Wearing a crimson cap with an *H* on the front. Harvard. I resisted the impulse to ask what his major was. The side of my face still felt raw and hot and hurt like hell.

"We are told not to kill you," he said. "But make sure you are not tempting me, ha?"

I took a closer look at his gun. A Glock. I had not yet heard the slide racked. A good thing. It didn't mean he wasn't going to shoot me, Russian-style or otherwise. Ever hopeful.

"You guys leave the envelope at my house?" I said.

No answer.

"One of you shoot Drysdale?"

No answer.

"What do you want from me?" I said.

"Not what we want," Harvard said. "We are told to tell you that this is maybe your last warning. You walk away now and nothing, no more bad shit happens."

"To me?"

He reached into the side pocket of his windbreaker and came out with his phone.

"Not right away," he said, touching the screen with his index finger.

Then he held up the screen so I could see.

It was another picture of my father. But he wasn't with me this time. He was walking out his front door, my mom standing on the porch behind him.

"Did whoever it is who sent you mention that he's a cop?" I said.

"Old cop," Harvard said.

He pulled the phone back and swiped the screen. Showed it to me again.

The next shot was of Richie standing at the end of his bar.

"You know his father is a gangster, right?" I said.

Harvard chuckled now.

"Old gangster," he said.

"Is that the end of the slide show?" I said.

He shook his head and swiped the screen again.

"Best for last," he said.

This one showed Richard Burke with what I knew was a Boston Bruins backpack standing in front of The Advent School.

Son of a bitch, Victor Morozov had said in a language I knew the sons of whores in the car with me would understand.

"So here is thing," Harvard said. "Is up to you whether something happens to them, or no. I am to tell you that includes the college girl. Your queer friend even keeps his restaurant. Just walk away from it."

200

"From what?"

"Our business, you stupid cow," he said.

"Ask you something else?" I said. "How come none of you are wearing masks? You use them all up during the pandemic?"

Harvard chuckled again.

"Because next time you won't seeing us," he said.

"Maybe we shoot your dog first," the guy with the gun said. He winked at Harvard. "Unless maybe we are doing that already."

The driver slammed on the brakes then. I heard him yell something in Russian. The guy with the gun turned his head around to see what had happened. Either another car or a pedestrian.

Made no difference to me.

I leaned back harder into the seat and pushed forward, giving all praise to Pilates as I flipped my legs up and kicked the gun out of his hand.

Now he growled something in Russian as he scrambled to bend down and get it.

Harvard raised his hand and was about to hit me again. This time I was ready for him, grabbing his wrist and biting down as hard as I could on his hand as I reached for the door handle, hearing him scream and hoping at the exact same moment that the door was unlocked. It was. Why not? Three of them, one with a gun. What could go wrong?

A lot was happening now, at once. The guy in front probably had to have his gun back by now. I didn't think he'd shoot now that the whole thing had turned into a shit show, but wasn't going to hang around to find out. Even if the guy wanted to take a shot at me, Harvard was between me and the gun, Harvard clumsily trying to get himself out of the car behind me, head and shoulders first. It gave me just enough time to turn and slam the door as hard as I could into his face. Ringing his bell. Me. The funny girl.

I stumbled over the curb now, pitching forward onto my hands and knees, scraping my right hand as it hit the sidewalk first, rolling to my feet as quickly as I'd landed, starting to run in the opposite direction from the direction the car was facing.

Thinking as I did how dumb it had been for the guy in back with me not to have locked the doors.

And him a Harvard man.

THIRTY-FOUR

The car had stopped near City Hall Square, on Congress Street. I kept going up Devonshire, glad I hadn't changed out of my running shoes before heading over to Spike's. I didn't think the sluggers had any chance of catching me on foot, but still wasn't taking any chances, keeping up a good pace as I went past the old Granary Burying Ground, and finally passed the King's Chapel before I was finally on Beacon.

I had never taken my bag off my shoulder, even when Harvard was taking the gun out of it. It hadn't fallen off as I'd gotten myself out of the car. Maybe he thought, maybe they all thought, I'd faint with terror at the sight of their guns. Or being outnumbered.

As I made the turn past the Meeting House, I knew I was hardly in the clear. If they were the ones who had left me the picture of my father, it meant they knew where I lived. If they thought I was going home, they knew where home was.

They could be there waiting for me. One possibility. Another was that even though I showed their asses up by getting away from them, right after showing them I was a biter, they had delivered the message they'd been instructed to deliver, by Eddie or somebody else who was pulling Eddie's strings.

I stopped halfway down River Street Place. I didn't see their car. Didn't mean they hadn't parked it somewhere else. Didn't mean they weren't inside the house. There was an app on my phone that would theoretically alert me if the alarm system that Ghost Garrity himself had installed after the place had been broken into last year had been breached.

There was no such alert.

They could still be inside. Or waiting outside to grab me again. Still three of them. Jesse had always said that being overly cautious had never gotten anybody killed. But a lack of caution could. So I circled around to Mugar Way and came at 4 River Street Place from the back. Their car wasn't in sight. Neither were they.

Still didn't mean they weren't waiting for me.

I reached into my bag for my .38, then realized it wasn't there. I had backups, but they were all inside the house, the first available in a drawer in the foyer.

Front door or back?

I decided on back.

I made my way along the side of my building, got my keys out of my bag, opened the back door, hearing the beep of the alarm as I did, punching out my code on the pad next to the door.

I heard Rosie the dog then, barking happily as she came running and skidding through the kitchen. Alive and well. I couldn't remember who had first written or said that their vision of heaven was all the dogs you'd ever loved running for you when you got there. But whomever it was sure was right.

I went into the back bathroom and checked my face. Still some redness. No swelling. No bruising. Maybe the guy who hit me wasn't as tough as he thought *he* was.

I fixed myself a big pour of Jameson and sat down in the living room and called my father first. Then Jesse, who said he was on his way. I told him that wasn't necessary.

"For you, maybe," he said. "Feels very necessary for the chief."

He was at the front door half an hour later. I told him he clearly hadn't been lying about the kind of time he could make with the lights and sirens about which he frequently bragged.

When he had his arms around me I said, "Thinking it might be time to go to the mattresses."

He pulled back, grinning, and said that first we needed to talk about the case.

THIRTY-FIVE

Jesse wanted to know what my father had said.

"You mean after *I* told *him* that he and my mother might want to head down to the small house on the Cape they'd bought about ten years ago?"

"After that," he said.

"He wanted to know if I was going to leave town," I said. "I told him I was not. He said that neither was he, good night."

"What about Richie?"

"Richie said that he was going to have Desmond's men watch him and Richard," I said. "And that they could do the same for me."

"How did you respond to such a generous offer from the Irish Mob?"

"I told him I could take care of myself," I said.

"Wow," Jesse said, "didn't see *that* coming."

207

We had pushed back the coffee table and were sitting on the floor, legs stretched out underneath the table, Rosie between us, me holding my whiskey, Jesse with a mug of high-test black tea that he liked to sip on late at night. He was still wearing his old Dodgers cap. I told him he could take it off now, nobody else was going to be calling him out of the bullpen tonight.

"You don't call shortstops out of the bullpen," he said. "You call pitchers."

I drank some of my whiskey and then smiled at him.

"So much about baseball I don't care about," I said. "So little time."

It was past midnight by now. Rosie was snoring. Jameson usually leveled things off for me, especially at this time of night. Just not this night. I was still running hot.

"Don't you think you *do* need somebody watching your back?" Jesse said.

"Wasn't that what I was doing not so terribly long ago with Deputy Chief Crane?" I said.

Molly. Not just his deputy, but Jesse Stone's best friend. I'd always wondered what would have happened between them if they had both been single when they met, instead of Molly being the happily married mother of four.

"Didn't answer my question," he said.

"Is this an official police interview?"

"Ish," he said. "What about Vinnie Morris?"

"I called him on another thing a few weeks ago," I said. "He was in Miami, on a thing of his own."

"I assume there weren't many specifics on the thing," he said.

"Vinnie deals less in specifics and more in absolutes," I said, "as you well know."

He put his arm around me and pulled me closer to him. I put my glass on the table and told him I was glad he was here. He said that he knew that already. I said I wanted to talk more about the case. He said he knew that, too.

"I don't just need to know who killed Drysdale," he said. "I need to know why. Working back from that and not him taking Spike's place and you getting involved."

"Yeah," I said, "even though that might have gotten him killed."

"You don't know that," Jesse said.

"Well," I said, "it's not as if I did much to keep him alive."

"Love or money," he said. "Comes back to one or the other most of the time."

"How about love *of* money?" I said.

"You said that this guy Drysdale had a lot

of money, lost a lot, made it back," he said. "And that the guy who might have helped him get it back is Eddie Ross."

"Who's Russian," I said, "and who sent Russians after me tonight."

Jesse said, "You think that Russians might have been running Drysdale?"

"Yes, sir," I said, "I do."

"And you said you talked to Drysdale's old partner," Jesse said.

"Lawton, his name is. Not a big fan of our Alex."

"You believe him?" Jesse said.

"I believe he liked what he'd become as much as he liked Alex Drysdale," he said. "He sounded like a drunk who's gotten sober, no offense."

"None taken."

"Drysdale, Lawton, Eddie Ross," I said. "They went to college together, and all this time, some form or fashion, end up together in Boston."

"You know what I think about co-incidence."

I smiled. "People in outer space know by now."

"So who was really in charge?"

"Be nice to know," I said.

Rosie stirred, stretched, poked her nose up over the coffee table in her endless quest for treats. Jesse got up and went into the kitchen and came back with a Ritz cracker that he fed her after breaking it in two.

"If you have to pay her to get her to love you," I said, "doesn't that cheapen your relationship?"

"Damn right," he said.

He sat back down and pushed my glass and his mug aside, picked up the small pile of magazines and placed it on the floor. I knew what he was doing, I'd seen him do it before. It was as if the top of the coffee table had become a blank canvas.

"Trying to see all the pieces," he said.

I told him *I* knew *that* already.

"Spike and Drysdale and Ross and the goon squad he sent tonight," he said. "And the Russian dude who owns the gym, at least for the time being. And Lee's niece." He was still staring at the table.

"I know I'm leaving people out."

"Lawton," I said. "Old partner. And the kid Matt Dunn, the dealer."

"Right," he said. "Tea must have gone to my head."

He leaned back now.

"Time to go talk to Eddie Ross," Jesse said.

"Maybe," I said, "Drysdale did something

to get sideways with him. Or with his master."

"Maybe get him talking about these poker games," Jesse said. "The only thing that connects Drysdale and Ross to the girl."

"You're reading my mind," I said.

Now he smiled, fully. "Hope so," he said.

Then he said, "Listen, I'd take a few days off and watch you myself, but I have to go to L.A. tomorrow afternoon. An old teammate of mine, in Albuquerque, died. If Vinnie can't cover you, I know some people who can."

"I've got Spike," I said.

"How come you called me tonight and not him?"

I stood and, with just a bit of a hip swing, headed for the stairs.

"Can't go to the mattresses with him," I said.

"No, you certainly cannot."

Over my shoulder I said, "Two birds, one Jesse Stone."

THIRTY-SIX

Jesse left a little after seven. His flight to Los Angeles was departing at noon and he needed to get back to Paradise and pack. He told me again that if I needed anything while he was away that I was to call Molly Crane.

"She owes you one," he said.

"No," I told him, "she does not."

After he left I went for a run along the Charles, free and easy, no longer being chased by men with guns. Or maybe they hadn't chased me once I was out of the car. But I hadn't been willing to take any chances, and had been prepared to run all the way to Wellesley if necessary. Jesse liked to quote some old ballplayer who'd said one time not to look back, because somebody might be gaining on you.

He quoted a lot of old ballplayers. I'd just grown more accepting of it over time.

I showered and dressed and sat at the

kitchen table and read the *Globe* and decided that before I went looking for Eddie Ross again I wanted to have another conversation with Matt Dunn. It bothered me, and more than somewhat, that he couldn't locate Emily Barnes.

He'd told me that he'd call if he learned anything. Didn't mean that he would. Didn't mean he'd been telling me the whole truth, and nothing but, about her and Eddie and poker and cheating and the whole damn thing. Nobody ever told the whole truth, or all that they knew. Before he'd left, I hadn't even gotten to ask him about Alex Drysdale, to whom Dunn had been dealing cards, honestly or dishonestly, before somebody had walked up and shot Drysdale dead on the street where he lived.

It wasn't so terribly long before I had continued to be enough of a nuisance that I had been threatened again, this time in spades.

Good one, Sunny, I thought. *In spades. Look at you.*

A friend of mine from Boston College had lived in an apartment on Foster Street in Brighton her sophomore year. The street, feeding off Commonwealth, was more gentrified than I remembered it, mostly old two-story houses, some of them brick, some with big lawns in front, stretching all the way down past St. Elizabeth's Medical Center. Matt Dunn's was smaller and more run-down than the ones on either side of his. For a full-time dealer and at least part-time cheat, it wasn't as if the kid was living on the margins.

There was no sign of the red Mazda parked on the street in either direction. There was no bell for me to ring. The mailbox next to the front door was empty.

I knocked, and waited, and heard no voice or stirring from inside. I knocked again, much more emphatically this time. If Dunn was inside, and unless he was in the shower, he had to have heard. If not, I had wasted a trip down here. Maybe the early cheat caught the worm. I was considering another round of lock-picking, despite the foot traffic on the sidewalk heading in both directions, when I decided to try the knob first.

The door was unlocked.

I knocked one last time before opening it and stepping inside, taking my gun out of my bag as I did. No idea that it was needed. Perhaps force of habit. Perhaps the Russians had made me do it. Or just a feeling. I'd had them plenty of times before and been wrong.

Just not always.

Dunn could have just forgotten to lock the door on his way out. One way looking at things. The other was that he'd been at the table with Alex Drysdale and Emily the other night and now Drysdale was dead and Emily was missing.

And I had been taken for a ride the previous night by men with less-than-honorable intentions.

Only a fool, I told myself, *would be less than vigilant.*

"Matt, it's Sunny Randall," I called out. "You here?"

My voice sounded as loud as a bullhorn.

The only thing I heard in response was the hiss of an old-fashioned radiator in the front room, speaking to the age of the house. I couldn't remember the last time I'd seen one like it.

The small living room, furniture looking older than the radiator, was to my left. The same Taft hoodie he'd been wearing in my office was draped over one of the chairs. An acoustic guitar was on the couch. There was an ashtray on the coffee table, a half-smoked joint in it. Those were the days, my friend.

The kitchen was beyond the living room. There was a Mr. Coffee machine, half-full. I touched the pot. It was still warm, the brewing light still lit. There was a piece of toast, uneaten, on a plate next to it. An empty mug next to the plate.

If he'd left, he'd left recently, and in a hurry.

No sound of a shower running from upstairs.

I could hear my own breathing now.

Something wrong here, I told myself. Something wicked this way comes. Who'd written that? Wait. I knew that one. Ray Bradbury. Jesse was right. The things you remembered when you least expected to.

I started up the narrow stairway almost directly across from the front door, startled by the loud creak of the first step, and then the second.

I could see the open door to the bathroom at the top. What looked like bedroom doors to my left and to my right. I gently pushed open the one to my right. There was an open canvas overnight bag on a twin bed, made. I looked inside. A couple women's T-shirts, a pair of jeans, a few bras and panties. I held up the jeans. Long enough to fit Emily. Didn't mean they were hers. This wasn't sleepaway camp. She hadn't written her name into her undies. Or, now that she was gone, maybe Dunn had already found a replacement.

The other door had to be the master

bedroom, if there were such a thing in the small house. The door was ajar. I pushed it open and there was Matt Dunn, on his back on the floor next to the queen-sized bed, eyes wide open, the front of his gray T-shirt covered in blood, another gunshot wound in the center of his forehead, the blood spreading in both directions from behind his head.

There was a queen of clubs stuck in his mouth.

I put away my gun and took out my phone and called 911 right before I called Frank Belson.

THIRTY-SEVEN

The crime scene people, who always looked to me like a small invading army, were gone. So was the body of Matt Dunn.

It had taken the first car right around eight minutes to get to the address I gave them on Foster Street. Belson had been there in twenty. By now his people were canvassing the neighborhood. The elderly couple who lived next door were still standing on their porch. They looked to be in their eighties. Frank Belson had walked over and talked to them when they'd first come outside. When Belson was done chatting with them, he told me they hadn't heard anything resembling gunshots.

"How would you rate their hearing?" I said.

"Not sure they would have heard a small plane hit the guy's house," he said.

He took out one of his cigars and actually lit it this time.

"Well," he said, "you are on some fucking roll, aren't you?"

I looked behind me, and did my bad De Niro.

"You talkin' to me?" I said.

He blew some smoke in my general direction.

"A noted wit," he said, "day and night."

By now I had taken him through it, step by step, from the moment I'd found the door unlocked until I found the body. I told him about first seeing Matt Dunn with Emily outside Lee's place. I told him about their relationship and how they appeared to have occasionally been working as a team to cheat people at poker and how Dunn had come to my office when he was concerned that Emily had disappeared.

I didn't tell him Emily and Alex Drysdale had been in the same game at Eddie Ross's place, at least for now.

"Maybe he cheated the wrong guy," Belson said.

"Or they did," I said. "It had happened before."

"Tell me," he said, and I did.

Belson walked over and sat on the bottom of the three steps leading up to Matt Dunn's front door. He held up the cigar.

"Don't tell Lisa," he said.

His wife.

"Not unless I absolutely have to," I said, and sat next to him, despite the smoke.

"Tell me again why you were here," he said.

"I thought he might know more about Emily and her possible whereabouts than he'd let on," I said.

"That's it?"

"That's it," I said.

He took the cigar out of his mouth and stared impassively at me. I knew the look. I had seen it before and felt it before. It made me feel as if he could see secrets stretching all the way to the backseat of Brian Foley's Firebird when we were in high school.

"I told Lee I'd find out who beat up his niece," I said. "I can't do that if I can't find her."

"People generally disappear, or try to, when they're afraid of something," Belson said.

"Or somebody."

I knew I should be telling Belson that there was a connection between Dunn and Alex Drysdale, if a tenuous one. I was certain of how he'd react when he found out. But to give that up meant giving him Eddie Ross, and Eddie was mine, at least when I finally caught up with him.

I felt Belson staring at me again.

"No phone on the dead guy here," he said. "No phone on the other dead guy."

"The shooters appear to be very thorough," I said.

"Interesting, though," Belson said, "that the only person who'd been in contact with both of my vics is you."

"What are the odds?" I said.

I told myself that I would tell *him* about Eddie Ross eventually. Just not yet. And not until I had to. It made this just one more time when I did so many contortions involving right and wrong that I was surprised I didn't pull a muscle.

Belson got up and nimbly stepped between the yellow crime scene tape across the door and went back inside. When he came back outside, I told him that I had an appointment downtown.

"Try your best not to get whoever it is killed," Belson said.

He told me he'd be in touch. I smiled my most winning smile and told him I'd be counting the minutes. Then I pointed at him and said that cigars could kill you, too.

THIRTY-EIGHT

Jalen Washington called right after I'd walked into my office.

He said, "Checking in."

I asked if he had anything to report. He said that he was starting to think any financial link between Eddie Ross and Alex Drysdale might turn out to be a dead end.

"But I'm still gonna do a deeper dive," he said.

I giggled.

"Something funny?"

"I always get a kick out of somebody talking about deep dives," I said. "Not quite sure why."

"Good for a brother to know," he said.

"Could there be a money trail from Eddie to Drysdale that's just well hidden?" I said.

"All right to that," he said. "Hedge-fund returns supposed to be private, way it's supposed to work. Now, there's some services *try* to report performance numbers. But if

223

Drysdale was lying his ass off about his returns and how he was getting them, it's like I say, a dead end. But I'm trying to ask around with people who know investors who might know who his were, you follow. But most of those investors are about as likely to tell the damn truth as whores."

"You mind staying on it?" I said.

Now he laughed out loud.

"I'll get off this shit when the Burkes tell me to get off it," he said. "But it might end up like trying to find a damn buried treasure, with your LLCs over there and your offshore accounts over here, and that's before you maybe bring your Swiss banks into it. Then, if they *is* money laundering, that's a whole 'nother rabbit hole. I hear some of these people doing the laundering got money stashed in lockers at airports all over the world."

"Maybe if I want to start putting money away for a rainy day," I said, "I should think about Logan Airport."

"We done?" he said.

"One more question," I said. "Could there be big enough poker games that Eddie could have funneled money to Drysdale that way?"

"Hell, yeah," he said. "That's where I'd

be looking, I was you. You ever watch *The Wire*?"

"Picked it up late," I said. "Never went all the way back to the beginning."

"Well," he said, "I like to have that shit memorized."

Jalen was more street today. I wondered if it was conscious with him or not.

"Season four," he continued, "they was this one guy running for mayor, and he was inviting some of his big-ticket donors to play poker with him. Talking about dudes maxed themselves out on legal donations. Then they'd pretend to lose to the guy running for mayor, and then he'd be the one, guy running, putting the money back into his campaign. So if you're asking me if Eddie could do something like that, I'm telling you he could. But I just don't see if there'd be *enough* money in those games to make it worth his while."

"Maybe I need to find out just who the players are in these games," I said.

"Could look into that for you," Jalen said. There was a pause and he said, "You talk to Eddie yet?"

"On my way over to the brownstone right now, as a matter of fact," I said before we ended the call.

Spike was at the brownstone already,

watching it from across the street in his car. If it turned out Harvard and his friends were inside when I went calling, I wanted Spike with me this time.

I called Spike and told him I was about to walk over.

"Nobody in or out?" I said.

"No, ma'am."

"Don't 'ma'am' me," I said.

"Sorry," he said. "I forget how sensitive women of a certain age get *about* their age."

"Blow it out your ear," I said.

"See there," he said.

I was making the turn onto Commonwealth from Arlington when Spike called me back.

"Somebody just came out," he said.

"Eddie?"

"Woman," he said. "Young. Tall. A knockout."

I described Emily Barnes.

"Could be," Spike said.

"Follow her," I said.

"Already am," Spike said.

"Where is she right now?" I said.

"Newbury Street," he said.

"Don't lose her before I get there," I said.

"Gonna be hard to do unless there's a back way out of Cartier," he said.

THIRTY-NINE

"Where is she now?" I said to Spike as I was passing the Arlington Street Church.

"Max Mara," he said. "You know where it is?"

"Like I know my alarm code," I said.

He was waiting for me at the corner of Newbury and Berkeley, near the side entrance to Brooks Brothers. Max Mara was on the other side of the street, half a block down. It was one of my favorite stores. I sometimes thought that if I even tried to walk past without going inside, a saleswoman would come running *out* side and tackle me.

"She hasn't spotted you?" I said to Spike.

He was wearing an old leather bomber-type jacket and a black cap that I'd given him, with BU written in red on the front. Jeans. High-top red Converse sneakers. It was about as incognito as Spike could manage.

"Did she spot me?" he said. "I'm going to have to ask you to take that back."

"I apologize."

"Doesn't make the hurt go away," he said.

I nodded across the street, both of us watching the entrance to the store.

"She either doesn't know her old boyfriend got shot up this morning," Spike said, "or doesn't care."

"Maybe we're about to find out," I said, and pointed.

Emily Barnes had just come back outside carrying a shopping bag. But before the light changed and we could get across to her, she had walked into Vince. I had no idea what her real story was, or what she was doing at Eddie Ross's residence, or what her current relationship had been with Matt Dunn before somebody shot him. But I liked the girl's taste in stores.

"We just go grab her," Spike said.

"Or we could wait patiently, Mr. Impatient."

"Look who's talking," he said. "By the way? You did tell me that Eddie Ross liked them young, right?"

"Tony Marcus told me he liked college girls," I said. "And she's a poker player and Eddie's been a poker impresario on both coasts. Maybe it was destiny that brought them together. That and marking cards."

Emily took her time in Vince. I would have done the same. She came out a half-hour later, carrying another shopping bag, and took a right and then another right on Dartmouth, heading back toward Commonwealth. Spike and I jogged after her now. When she got to the corner of Dartmouth and Commonwealth she waited on a red light and checked her phone. It was a two-way street, separated up here in the middle by a walking mall. After the light changed she was nearly to the other side when Spike was suddenly on her right and I was on her left.

"What did you get at Max?" I said. "I'll bet it was a sweater. I got a cotton turtleneck on sale there a couple weeks ago that is to *die* for."

"Well, not literally," Spike said.

She looked at him and then at me and started to pick up her pace. Spike put a hand on her forearm.

"I'll scream," she said.

"And I'll call my friend Frank Belson at Homicide and tell him about your relationship with Matt Dunn," I said.

"*Homicide?*" she said. "What are you talking about?"

"You don't know?" I said.

229

"Know *what?*" she said.

"I found Matt Dunn shot to death at his house earlier this morning," I said.

She opened her mouth and closed it.

"Matt's dead?" she said.

"Comprehensively."

I don't know what reaction I was expecting, shock or surprise or actual grief. None of the above.

"Well, I didn't do it," she said.

"No one said you did," I said.

We were only a block now from Eddie's brownstone. But we weren't going there. Emily didn't know that yet. But I did.

"You hadn't heard?" I said.

"Where would I have heard?" she said. "On my uncle's police scanner?"

I let that one go.

"I want you to leave me alone," she said.

She looked down. Spike's hand was still casually on her arm.

"Not until we talk a bit," I said. "Matt told me you two had been together once."

"Told you when?"

Then she said to Spike, "You can let me go now."

He did.

"But if you do a runner," he said, "I will catch you and we will take you directly to the cops." He nodded at me and said, "I'm

230

faster than Sunny."

"Are not," I said.

To Emily I said, "So were you and Matt an item at one time?"

"Item?" she said. "Jesus, how old are you?"

Here we go again.

She said, "We were hooking up when we first met. *Briefly.* When a game would run late and I didn't want to go all the way back to school, he'd let me stay in his guest room."

"That's what he told me."

"Gee," she said, "there's a relief."

I asked Spike where his car was parked, and then for his keys, telling him to stay with Emily until I pulled around. It would be easier than each of us taking an arm and walking her down there.

"I'm not going anywhere with you two," she said.

Spike smiled his customer smile.

"Oh, sweetie," he said, "of course you are."

"Eddie's not going to like this when he finds out," she said.

"May I handle that one?" Spike said to me, still smiling.

"Have at it," I said.

"Emily," Spike said, "Ms. Randall and I are well past the point where we give a flying funt what Eddie Ross does or doesn't like."

FORTY

We sat in my living room. Emily Barnes, hair pulled back into a ponytail and looking even younger than she was, acted like a kid who'd been forced to sit in the principal's office.

"This is like kidnapping," she said.

"It would require a broad definition," I said, "since we will shortly let you go."

"You're saying that if I tell you the stuff you want to know, you'll let me leave?"

"Yes," I said.

She took the couch. Spike and I sat across from her.

"You had no idea Matt was dead," I said.

"I already told you I didn't."

"He said the last time he saw you was the night I chased you into the park," I said.

"I was late for another game," she said. "You made me later by being a pain in the ass."

"Kind of her thing," Spike said. "One of

233

them, anyway."

"A game was starting up at that time of night?" I said.

"You really don't know shit about poker, do you?" she said.

"Apparently not."

"There's always a game somewhere," she said.

"I'm wondering when you still have time to be a college student," I said.

"I'm not going to be one for much longer," Emily said.

Rosie was at my feet. I reached down and scratched the back of her neck. Every once in a while she would look over at Emily and emit a low growl. My girl.

Rosie, not Emily.

"You're quitting school?" I said.

"In my mind I quit a long time ago," she said.

"And what are your post-higher-education plans, if you don't mind me asking?" I said.

"Become a professional poker player," she said. "Or marry a rich guy. Whatever comes first."

"Wow," Spike said brightly, "I didn't know you could cheat your way into the World Series of Poker."

"Fuck you," she said.

"As you wish," Spike said.

" 'As you wish'?"

"It's from *The Princess Bride,* Buttercup," he said.

She gave him a blank look, as if he'd just spoken to her in Cantonese.

"Spike is referring to the fact that I found marked cards and your special decoder glasses in your room at Taft," I said.

"You broke into my *house*?" she said.

"It was nothing, really."

She stood up. "I'm leaving," she said. "You searched my room? Fuck you, too."

Spike was out of his chair and over at the door in a blink, arms folded in front of him.

Emily sat back down.

"You said I could leave," she said.

"After I get a little more information."

"Fine," she said. "But I'm not dishing on Eddie. You want to get sideways with him, go right ahead. Not me."

"Who beat you up?" I said.

"You don't give up, do you?" she said.

"Hardly ever," Spike said from across the room.

"Somebody Matt and I had cheated," she said.

He had been telling the truth about that, too.

She smiled, almost smugly. "Let's just say that he won't be doing anything like that to

235

me ever again," she said. "Or anybody else."

"Why'd you lie to your uncle and me?" I said.

She smiled again. "Kind of *my* thing," she said. "One of many."

College girl, I thought. Lee's niece, one he treated like a daughter.

"Why did you need to steal ten thousand dollars from your mother?" I said.

"A previous debt that needed to get paid off," she said.

"If Eddie's your boyfriend," I said, "why couldn't he pay it off for you?"

She looked at me quizzically. "Is that what this is about?" she said. "You think Eddie's my boyfriend?" Her eyes widened. "It's not just poker you don't know shit about."

Her phone buzzed. She checked it.

"I need to go," she said.

"Soon," I said. "How well did you know Alex Drysdale?"

"I was just at the table with him a few times," she said, "when Eddie wanted him to win."

"Why did Eddie want him to win?"

"Ask Eddie," she said.

"He told me he was in business with Drysdale."

"Eddie's business is Eddie's business," she said. "He just wanted Alex to feel like the big player he wanted to be, even when he wasn't."

"Emily," I said, "listen to me. Two people you played poker with a few nights ago are both dead. You need to get away from Eddie Ross."

"Are you insane?" she said. "He's helping me get to where I want to go."

"Homecoming weekend?" Spike said.

"I told you," she said. "Vegas."

I nodded.

"How did you go from Taft to this?" I said. I knew she was there on a math scholarship.

"This?" she said.

"Poker, Eddie, Matt Dunn," I said. "The whole damn thing."

"You want to know the truth?" she said. "Well, check it out: You get to college and you think you're some kind of math whiz. Only then you look around the classroom and *everybody* is a math whiz, and most of them are smarter than you. One day somebody asked me if I wanted to play some poker. And I did. And I found out I wasn't just good at it, I was *awesome.* And just like that, I was the smartest girl in class."

"Where's Eddie right now?"

"Somewhere," she said.

She stood up again. "Now can I leave?"

"Sure," I said. "But first, one last question."

"Fine," she said.

"Why did you tell me as much as you did?"

"Because this is the last time I am ever going to tell you anything," she said. "About anything."

"I can help you," I said.

"Go help somebody who thinks they need it," Emily said.

She walked over to where Spike was standing and he just hesitated briefly before stepping aside and opening the door for her. As she went past him he said, "Good luck with midterms," but I knew that was more for my benefit than hers.

It happened a lot.

FORTY-ONE

Before Spike left he said, "I know you're a bear for saving wayward girls. But pretty sure you could throw this one back with no regrets."

"You mean just walk away?" I said.

"Yup," he said.

"That's the same advice I got from that Russian ape Eddie Ross sent after me," I said.

I went upstairs to paint then, thinking it might be good for the soul after what I'd just heard from Emily Barnes. I got out my paint set and brushes and put on an old gray DODGERS sweatshirt Jesse had given me. Rosie was on the floor, snoring, in what I constantly assured her was a very cute way. The light in the late afternoon was nearly perfect, as if this were a different world, a different space, from the one Emily Barnes inhabited. Different, better, cleaner air. Had she been telling the truth about who had beaten her up, and why? I had no way of knowing.

Was Eddie, who liked college girls, her boyfriend even though she said he wasn't?

You came up here to paint, I told myself.

So paint, girl.

I did. The lighthouse began to take real shape now, and the sky around it became the color it had been that day, more gray than blue, almost like the color of the ocean in what had been a late afternoon like this, time frozen between day and night. I painted and at least felt some sense of form, and order, on the board in front of me.

It was past seven o'clock when I finally finished. I had taken a picture on my phone of where I had been before I started today. I pulled it up now and saw much how good work I had done. I put the tops back on the paint cups and my brushes in water. Even the simplest tasks in this studio made me happy. I was happy here, Rosie seemed happy here, at least when awake. Sunny Randall, in an uncomplicated state. Not my natural state, not by a long shot. But close enough. Painting made me happy. Jesse made me happy, even when we were apart. Forever? Who knew. Just for now. Of course, that made Richie *un*happy. But then it had been an ongoing problem, keeping all the men in my life happy.

I picked up Rosie and we walked down to the bedroom.

Spike was right.

I *could* walk away.

If Emily had been telling the truth, I had done what Lee had asked me to do. He wanted to know who'd bounced her around. Now she herself had told me. Someone she'd cheated at cards, if she had been telling the truth. The Russian who'd grabbed me had told me Spike could keep Spike's, free and clear, if I'd walk away from him, them, Eddie.

So why not walk away from all of it?

I knew the answer, and so did Spike, just because of how well he knew *me.*

They had threatened me, and people I loved, because they saw me as some sort of threat to them. But why? And a threat to what?

I wanted to take a shower. It could wait. I walked back up to my studio and picked up one of my oversized drawing pads and brought it downstairs and put it on the kitchen table and fixed myself a glass of Jameson, even though I hadn't eaten yet, and told my dear friend Alexa to play Carol Sloane singing the songs of Ella and Louis with Clark Terry playing trumpet behind her. It was one of my favorites, recommended by Susan Silverman, who said a friend had recommended it to her.

I then began writing down everything that had happened since Alex Drysdale had showed up at Spike's that day and ripped up his check. Everything that involved Drysdale and Christopher Lawton and Drysdale's hedge funds, past and present, was on one side of the page. And Drysdale trying to screw over Victor Morozov the way he had Spike.

And Eddie.

Emily and Matt Dunn and poker were on the other side, starting with the night Lee drove Emily back to his place from Taft. And then Emily and Drysdale together on the sidewalk that night, not long before Drysdale got shot. Russian-style. Eddie was Russian. I'd talked to him only one time, in my office. I still felt as if I couldn't turn around without bumping into him.

He said he was working with Drysdale. Now dead. Matt Dunn had worked with Eddie, and was also dead.

Was Eddie the big boss here?

Or was there a bigger one?

Or an equal partner?

I drank my whiskey. Carol was singing "Don't Be That Way." I stared at everything

I'd written down. I felt as if I was looking down at one of those five-hundred-piece puzzles. There was something nagging at me. Something Emily had said.

Then there it was.

About Alex Drysdale.

He just wanted Alex to feel like the big player he wanted to be, even when he wasn't.

What had she meant by that?

I wrote down what she'd said and circled it, finished my drink, closed the pad, took it back upstairs in case I wanted to add anything to my lists before I went to sleep, put Rosie's leash on her, had her secure the perimeter one last time, came back in, locked the door, set the alarm in case any bogeymen with accents came back.

I put Rosie on the bed, cleaned up, took one last look at my notes.

Out loud I said to Rosie, "Who's the boss?"

As always, what she seemed to hear was "Should I run downstairs and bring back treats?"

So she was up on the bed, doing one spin, tail wagging, ever hopeful, my adorable treat ho.

"And if it's not Eddie, then who is it?" I said. "A Russian to be named later?"

I found an emergency bag of treats in my

bedside table and gave her one, and asked her one last question knowing I had her at a disadvantage now.

"And maybe here's the biggest question of all, Rosebud," I said. "Why are they so worried about a nice Boston University girl like me?"

In the middle of the night, a little after three a.m., somebody firebombed Spike's.

FORTY-TWO

They had the fire under control by the time I got to Marshall Street a half-hour later.

The fire truck, which had barely had enough room to squeeze onto Marshall and was now parked out front, had ENGINE 8, LADDER 1 written on the outside. The guys from the BFD had stopped hosing the interior of Spike's, but the place was still full of smoke. I saw firemen talking to cops and cops talking to firemen. There were a lot of flashing lights on Marshall, and two television trucks parked at the north end of the block, even in the middle of the night.

The front window, with *Spike's* in flowing, cursive script, had been shattered by whatever kind of goddamn incendiary device somebody had thrown into my best friend's goddamn restaurant.

I found Spike sitting on the opposite side of the cobblestone street, staring at his phone.

"Hey," I said, sitting down next to him.

He held up his phone.

"Bet you didn't know that Molotov cocktails were named after a Russian foreign minister during World War Two," he said.

"No," I said, "I did not know that."

He was Spike. He'd get to it when he got to it.

"Actually," he said, "it was the Finns who came up with the name. Apparently the Molotov guy was talking some shit about cluster bombs and acting as if the Russians were doing the Finns a favor by dropping them. But the Finns, being bad sports, decided to return the favor, and called their bombs Molotov cocktails."

"Ironic," I said.

"Right?" Spike said.

He put away his phone and made a sound that was like some sad note he'd blown on a trumpet.

"What the fuck," he said.

"My sentiments exactly," I said.

"I believe I might have to kill Eddie Ross," he said.

"Not," I said. I put an arm around him. "Because I might have to do it first," I said.

"And both of us normally such peaceful souls," Spike said.

"Not," I said again.

I had brought goggles with me, ones I'd kept from when I'd been with the cops, just in case I needed them. I didn't, because I had no plans to go inside. And for now, just the smell of burning plastic made me want to stay right where we were.

I looked across the street and saw fire marshals coming outside with evidence containers that looked like empty paint cans, and sample bags. Two arson inspectors were staring at what was left of the front window. They were wearing Tyvek suits and white Tyvek booties and breathing apparatuses. I knew a fair amount about arson investigators, having dated one right before I met Richie.

"We actually don't know this was Eddie's doing," I said, "as much as we both want to make him for it."

Spike said, "And we don't know for certain that he sent those Russian sluggers after you. Or that he had Drysdale and the poker kid taken out. Or that he threatened not just your family but your extended family. But you know it's him, and so do I. Know *why*? Because it can't be anybody else *but* him."

"They're after me, not you," I said. "Only now they've dialed it up like this to get *at* me. It's why I keep asking myself the following question: If I'm such a threat to whomever is doing this shit, why not just take me out?"

"Maybe they know it would be the same as killing a cop," Spike said. "Or they're worried about bringing the wrath of Desmond Burke down on them. Or both."

"So they continue to try to back me off," I said.

"And you," Spike said, "continue to show the inefficaciousness of that."

" 'Inefficaciousness'?"

"They blew up my restaurant," Spike said. "Not my vocab."

I kissed him on the cheek.

"No, they certainly did not," I said.

"What do we do about this?" Spike said. "Because we sure as shit have to do something."

"*You* are going to think about rebuilding, as soon as you get some sleep," I said.

"I'm not entirely sure whose insurance covers this," he said.

"Call Rita Fiore," I said. "If she doesn't know, she knows somebody who will."

I smiled at him. "That would be the efficacious thing to do, in my opinion."

Spike nearly smiled back.

"And after *I* have gotten some sleep," I said, "I am going to make it my mission to have a conversation today with Eddie Ross. Who can run, but not hide."

"You know that's a boxing expression, right?" he said.

"You mean Phil Randall isn't the one who came up with it?"

"Joe Louis," Spike said. "An old sportswriter once called him a credit to his race. The human race."

"As are you," I said.

"Not feeling it," he said. "At least not presently."

The arson guys kept going in and out. The odor from inside, coming from everything that had burned up, had become far more pungent in a predawn breeze. One police car left. Another remained. I did not recognize any of the cops. I stood up, goggles in hand. Spike said he'd walk me to my car.

"I could end this," I said, "with a full retreat."

He stopped. I stopped. He put his arms around me. He was as strong as anybody I had ever known. But he had been tested during COVID and now he was being tested again. First somebody took Spike's. Now somebody had bombed the holy hell out of it.

"You know you're not going to do that," he said.

"And why is that?"

"Because you're the one who's a credit to her race," he said.

"Me and Joe Louis."

"He did like blondes," Spike said.

FORTY-THREE

"You have to know that what happened to Spike, and *at* Spike's, isn't your fault," Dr. Silverman said.

I had called when I knew she'd be at her office and asked if she had an opening. She did. Now here we were. I was wearing a square-neck Ann Taylor dress, navy, that looked more expensive than it was. Slingback heels. Considering how little sleep I'd gotten, I thought my makeup, at least upon last check before I got out of the car, was providing me stellar coverage.

She never looked as if it took any effort whatsoever to look as spectacular as she did. Hair. Makeup. Oversized blazer with the sleeves pulled up to her elbows. She'd even looked like a million damn dollars when we'd Zoomed during COVID. When I'd look at my own face during those sessions, I thought I looked as if I were cutting a hostage tape.

251

"That's nice of you to say," I said. "But I was specifically told that if I stopped making a nuisance of myself, those near and dear to me would be left alone."

She offered one of those tiny smiles that made me speculate about how few muscles she actually used.

"You making a nuisance of yourself is practically a mission statement, wouldn't you say?" she said.

"Them's still the facts," I said.

"But ask yourself a question," she said. "The people who told you they'd back off if you backed off — why would you trust anything they said?"

"I *don't* trust them," I said. "But if they can go after Spike this way, what's to stop them from going after my father, or Richie and his son?"

"So many people to protect," she said, "for just one woman."

"Are you being ironic?" I said.

"Trying to quit," Susan Silverman said.

"Maybe a therapist could help with that?" I said.

Now she smiled, fully. The force of it, as always, was something. Like the force of her. "Didn't this all start with you trying to protect a young woman who really didn't want your protection?"

252

"End of the day?" I said. "She's near and dear to Lee, not me."

She reached for what appeared to be an expensive pen and took a note. Every time she did that during one of our sessions I wished that I had the ability to read upside down. Jesse did.

Sometimes I felt myself wanting to pull out a notebook and take notes of my own. That would show her.

She said, "I referenced a mission statement just now. What do *you* see as your own mission right now? To find out who committed these murders? To avenge what happened to Spike? To discover if this Eddie Ross fellow is the man behind the curtain?"

I sighed, so loudly that it surprised me.

"I want to know what Eddie Ross and Alex Drysdale were up to," I said. "Or into. I want to know why it got Drysdale killed. And how the death of Emily Barnes's old boyfriend factors into all of this, and why him talking to me might have hastened his demise. And why I pose such a threat to whoever is behind it all."

I looked down at my hands, folded in my lap. I needed a manicure, but felt as if Dr. Silverman wouldn't be much help in that area.

"Something Alex Drysdale was doing, or

about to do, or had just done, got him killed," I said. "That's my story and I'm sticking to it."

"So find out what?" she said.

With just a slight inflection, she turned it into a question.

"It would certainly make me feel better about everything."

Time up.

"But then you wouldn't need me, would you?" Susan Silverman said.

FORTY-FOUR

Jalen Washington was sitting on the floor next to my office door when I got back from Cambridge.

"Think I got something," he said. "But I wanted to tell you in person."

I made us both coffee. He sat in one of my client chairs. He still had impossibly white sneakers, skinny jeans so faded they were on their way to white. A dark green hoodie with HARMONY written on the front. He looked like a Gap ad.

"Drysdale's fund is officially a dead end," he said.

"Do tell."

"First off," he said, "I got it on solid that he wasn't working off nearly as big a number as he used to."

"Wouldn't something like that get around?" I said.

"Not necessarily," Jalen said. "They're all playing a shell game, some form or fashion,

255

even the big ones. Look over there, not over here. Like that."

"But wouldn't the people entrusting their money to him know the numbers?" I said.

He smiled. Lots of white teeth, too. Extremely white.

"All's they care about seeing are returns," he said. "Returns keep coming in, they don't wanna know what they don't wanna know. How you suppose old Bernie Madoff kept the line moving, leastways till he got caught?"

"You're telling me that Drysdale was running a Ponzi scheme?"

He shook his head.

"No," he said. "But even though the returns *was* still coming in, he was about to run dry. Boy had kept that shit up as long as he could. Guy I know who knows people like him told me he was pretty sure Drysdale was about to cash out. Get out while the getting was still good. Pay out and hold on to what was left."

"Who told you this?"

"A guy who doesn't want people to know he knows what he knows," Jalen said. "And knows he shouldn't even have been talking to me."

"Jalen," I said, "not sure if you're aware of this, but you're not the one bound by a cli-

256

ent confidentiality agreement."

"May work like that in your world, Sunny Randall," he said. "But not in mine, if your motivation is to stay aboveground."

He shrugged. "Anyway," he said, "Alex Drysdale was about to take what toys he had left and disappear. Maybe go collect whatever money he had stashed offshore and go live the life where nobody could find his ass."

He shrugged.

"Hard to keep all the plates spinning the way he did, long as he did," Jalen Washington said. "Especially after he reinvented himself."

"Were the people in the fund going to get paid in full?"

"Thinking no," Jalen Washington said.

"Could one of them have found that out beforehand and been a bad sport?"

"Still looking into that piece," he said. "But if I was a betting man, be the way I'd bet."

"But you're not a betting man."

"I prefer fixed income investing," he said. "I don't need the thrill of chasing money. I want it right where I can put my hands on it."

"You sure you didn't go to Harvard Business?" I said.

He smiled again. "What I learned," he said, "I learned at the Orchard Park Houses, Eustis Street, Roxbury, Massachusetts. Finally worked my way all the way up to working for Mr. Desmond Burke. Help him invest his money a little better than he was 'fore I came along."

"That a long-term play for you?" I asked him.

He paused and frowned, as if considering his options about what to say next.

"Speaking freely?" he said. "Like I *was* the client?"

"Desmond and I have a complicated relationship," I said. "But it doesn't mitigate in any way what people tell me in confidence when they sit in that chair."

"You got a nice way of conversating," he said. "Anybody ever tell you that?"

"I try to hang around with people smarter than me," I said.

"Here's the deal," he said, leaning forward, eyes bright. "I'm not just learning *his* business. You understand what I'm saying? I look at what I'm doing for him as my own management training program."

"That include helping me?"

"That's just more networking on my part," he said. "Maybe someday I might be the one needs a favor."

"The money Drysdale *did* plan to cash out on — where's it going now?"

"Efforting that," Jalen Washington said.

"I keep asking myself if Eddie could have been the one running Drysdale, and not the other way around," I said.

"*I* don't think so," he said. "Everything I hear is that Fast Eddie was always more of a fixer than a boss, whether it was his poker games or something else."

"Drysdale was in his games," I said.

"Probably recruiting players to be players in his fund until the end," Jalen said. "That's my opinion. Maybe hoping to screw them on his way out the door."

"Sounds like there was a lot of money in those rooms," I said, "and not just on the tables."

"You know them frisky one-percenters."

"Before you go back to your day job," I said, "maybe you could poke around a little more and find out who put Drysdale back up on his feet when he was about to go under. And how much money might have been in the fund when he was still Alex 'Ace' Drysdale."

"And you still want to know where it might have gone."

"Bingo," I said.

"Bingo?"

"I'm older than I look," I said.

He was gone about twenty minutes when my phone buzzed.

The screen said *Unknown Caller*.

But the voice wasn't unknown, at least not to me.

"We need to talk," Eddie Ross said.

"That's my line," I said.

Then he said, "You got this all wrong."

FORTY-FIVE

I waited. He waited. It felt like a stare down, just over the phone.

"You still there?" he said.

"Waiting to hear what I have wrong about you," I said. "Two people you know are dead. Some of your people took me for a ride. My friend's restaurant got firebombed last night."

"You knew the dead guys, too," he said.

"Really, Eddie? You called me for bullshit like that?" I said. "Not gonna lie. You're starting to give the mother country a bad name. And we both know how hard *that* is to do."

I was up and pacing the office as I talked to him.

"Listen," he said. "I admit I wanted to scare you off."

"Scare me off what?"

"My business," he said.

"What might that be, exactly?"

"Business that never should have had anything to do with you," he said.

"Does now."

"I had nothing to do with killing those guys," he said.

"I have a friend who has an expression he likes to use about coincidence," I said. "No way God would leave that much to chance."

"Let me write that down."

I said, "There's only one person in this bit whose business involved both Alex Drysdale and Matt Dunn. And that's you."

"I can explain," he said.

"Go ahead."

"In person," he said. "That's what you've been looking for, no? A face-to-face? No way you're turning that down."

"I'm at my office," I said. "Come here."

"You're the one wanted this meeting," he said. "I get to pick the place. Charlestown Shipyard. Seven o'clock. Just the two of us."

"No," I said.

"No, you're not coming?"

"Not coming alone."

"Trust me on something," he said. "We wanted you dead, you'd already be dead."

" 'We'?"

"Figure of speech."

"Be that as it may," I said, "I will be accompanied by my friend Spike. And by the

262

way, Eddie? Spike wants *you* dead."

"I didn't do his restaurant."

"You can tell him that yourself."

"There's a playground at the shipyard," he said. "Meet me there."

"Where's Emily Barnes," I said. "Just out of curiosity?"

"Working tonight."

"For you?"

"Who better?"

Then he said, "Seven o'clock."

"I'll count the minutes."

I heard him snort.

"Yaytsa," he said.

"Excuse me?"

"Russian for 'balls,' " he said.

There was no need to tell him that was a recurring theme of my life, so I simply ended the call. Then I called Spike and told him where we were going and who we were meeting and made him promise not to turn the former Eddie Rostov into a piñata when we got there.

I made one more call after that, since Vinnie Morris was still out of town.

Jesse Stone was the one who liked to brag that he'd been a Boy Scout.

Didn't mean a girl couldn't be prepared, too.

FORTY-SIX

We met near the sandbox, surrounded by a low concrete wall, at the children's playground. Even at seven you could see night coming fast.

Spike wore an L.L.Bean sweater with a Henley collar I had given him. It had been form-fitting once. Now it just reminded me of how much weight he'd lost since the start of COVID, and was baggy enough on him now to hide the Glock 26 in his belt holster.

"Promise me again that you're going to be nice," I said as he walked toward the playground from 1st Avenue.

"I promise."

"This is a fact-finding mission, if Eddie is capable of giving us actual facts," I said. "Maybe even an Emily-finding mission."

"Are you still worrying about that ungrateful bitch?" Spike said.

"Is that being nice?" I said.

Ross was sitting on the concrete wall,

alone. But just because I hadn't seen any backup as Spike and I closed in on him didn't mean there wasn't any.

"You didn't need to bring him," Ross said, and stood up. Looking as he had in my office. Skinny black suit, red pocket square this time. White shirt. He hadn't appeared to be much of a threat that day, as tough as he'd talked to me. By now, the threat level had increased exponentially.

"I come in peace," Ross said.

He put out his hand to Spike. Spike ignored it.

Spike said. "You and the KGB."

"There isn't a KGB any longer," Eddie Ross said.

"Yeah," Spike said. "Go with that."

"You need to know I didn't try to burn down your restaurant," Eddie said.

"And you need to know that if you annoy me I am going to stick your head in this sand," Spike said.

I smiled at Ross. "My friend's having a bad month," I said. "It's better that you don't annoy either one of us."

He sat back down. I sat, too, but as if social distancing were still in place.

"So talk," I said.

"Where would you prefer I start?" he said.

"Your partnership with Alex Drysdale," I

said. "Whatever brought us here started there."

"It *was* a partnership," he said. "Just not the way you might think. I had the poker, something he had a big jones for all the way back to college. He had the hedge fund. And they were connected. But, like I said, not the way you think."

"Eddie?" I said. "You are going to annoy me if you don't stop telling me what *you* think *I* think."

Spike was slowly circling the sandbox, and was behind Ross now.

Ross said to me, "He's not really going to try anything, right?"

"The night is young," I said. "And so you know? He'd be doing more than trying."

I made a motion with my hand, as if telling him to carry on.

"I was his recruiter," he said. "The kind that maybe you don't find at the Boston Preservation Alliance."

"Bad guys with money," I said.

"*So* much money," he said. "And a lot of them liked playing poker as much as Alex did."

"You're telling me that you were the roper?" I said.

"You know what a roper is." He smiled. "Look at you."

"And Matt Dunn and Emily Barnes helped you when you wanted to turn the games into a grift," I said.

"We had a system," Ross said. "We decided who needed to win on a given night. Usually, the way we worked it, Alex would win big the first night. Then he would lose even bigger the next time we brought one of the whales back. And you want to know something? Sometimes we had to sit on him when he needed to lose."

"Even knowing it would benefit him in the long run," I said.

"All the way back to college," Eddie Ross said, "he just fucking needed to win."

"And Emily let you use her that way?" I said.

"She didn't look at it that way," he said. "And she wasn't sleeping with the whales. Or Alex, as hard as he kept trying. She thought she was using us. In her mind, she was really only whoring herself out to poker. She really is a hell of a player, in a legit game. I'm not bullshitting her when I tell her she could make it in Vegas. I've been looking at players half my life."

"So who killed Drysdale?" I said.

He took out a pack of cigarettes from inside his jacket pocket and lit one, blew out some smoke, almost exasperated.

"Alex turned into a pig," he said. "The money wasn't disappearing in the fund. Wasn't like that. But it was going down, so he was grabbing for every buck. So he took that guy's gym. He took the restaurant. Just to feel like a winner. But the bottom line is when he tried to fuck over your friend, he brought you into his business. And mine."

"Little old me," I said.

"It didn't take much investigating by me to find out you were a professional pain in the ass," Ross said. "I had a deal with him, after all the recruiting I did. I got paid when he cashed out. Not enough to live off the rest of my life. But more of a pot than I'd ever had."

He put his head back, closed his eyes.

"But then you weren't just up into his shit, like you promised. You were into mine, too."

Almost like he was talking to himself.

"Who killed him, Eddie?" I said.

"He'd started to organize his own games, with Matt as his dealer," Ross said. "Strayed outside the parish, so to speak. And I believe he cleaned out the wrong guy one night."

"Who?"

"An old friend of my father's," Ross said. "Ivan Kuznetzov. Owned art galleries in Ukraine, but they were just a front for money laundering. He was in town talking to people about opening a 'gallery' here."

He put quote marks around *gallery.*

"He called when he got to Boston and asked if I could find him a game," Ross said. "I told him there was always a game. This one was legit. But one of the guys at the table knew Alex and hooked Ivan up with him. Matt was the dealer. Ivan ended up losing big. The number I heard was half a million. He was sure he'd gotten cheated, even if he couldn't prove it. But Ivan was never the kind who required much proof."

He shrugged.

"By the next week, Alex and Matt Dunn are dead," he said.

He blew some smoke into the air.

"Where's Kuznetzov now?" I said.

"He could be anywhere," Eddie Ross said.

"But you believe he had it done?"

"If he thought somebody cheated him?" he said. "He might have done them himself. But more likely, he'd use his own shooter, if the guy's still with him. My father used to talk about him. The shooter. Boyko. You don't forget a name like that, right? My father said he was seven feet tall if he was an inch."

I stared out at the water, wondering how much of this, or if any of it, might be true. It all sounded quite plausible. Hustlers like

Eddie Ross had a way of doing that when they were trying to sell you something. Or get you off their backs.

I knew this: I wouldn't automatically believe him if he told me the water at which I was staring was wet.

"You talked about getting paid," I said. "Where's Alex's money going now?"

"No one knows," he said.

"Why should I believe you?" I said.

"You made enough trouble for me already," he said. "I'm trying to do you a solid here so you don't make more."

"Where's the girl?" I said.

"You don't give up."

"Hardly ever."

"She's crashing at one of my places," he said.

"There are more than one?"

He tossed the cigarette butt to the ground and stepped on it.

"Moving target," he said.

"I need an address," I said.

"What's in it for me?" Ross said.

Spike stepped forward then, so quickly it startled me as much as it did Ross, and grabbed him by his skinny lapels and lifted him up into the air as if lifting a child. When he had him high enough, he put his face close to Eddie's and spoke quietly to him.

"Were you under the impression that I was joking when I talked about burying your head in the sand?" Spike said.

In that moment the guy with the Harvard cap was walking across the playground, gun pointed at Spike, saying, "Put him down."

Eddie smiled, but only briefly. "That's Vadim," he said.

"As you know," I said, "we've met."

"Put him down," Vadim said again. *"Now."*

"You put *that* down." Phil Randall said from behind him. "Or I will shoot you dead."

My backup plan, just in case I needed one.

Without looking at me, my father said, "Thanks for calling."

"Thanks for coming," I said to him.

The situation resolved itself in a rather straightforward fashion after that.

FORTY-SEVEN

The address Eddie had given me for Emily Barnes turned out to be at the Washington Square Apartments on Comm Ave in Brighton. Spike had driven us to the shipyard in his car. I asked if he minded swinging by her apartment before we called it a night.

"Why wouldn't we want to seek out a young woman who has no use for you and doesn't want you coming to her rescue and whose last known job wasn't college student, but rather allowing herself to be poker-pimped by a lowlife like Eddie Ross?" Spike said.

"Well," I said, "when you put it like that."

"She is Lee's problem, not yours," he said.

"I'm thinking that if we can get her to open up," I said, "maybe we can find out if this Kuznetzov dude really does figure into all this."

"Great!" Spike said. "And then maybe we can get ourselves into more trouble with the

272

Russian Mob than we already are! What could possibly go wrong with a plan like that, Nancy Drew?"

"I knew you'd come around," I said.

Spike found a parking spot in front of the building. He called it his parking karma. I told him there was no such thing. He asked me how many times I'd ever had to walk more than half a block when he was behind the wheel. I had no answer for that.

"You're welcome," he said.

She didn't answer the bell. There were no lights on inside. I banged on the door. Still no answer. It was nine o'clock by now. Maybe Ross had been telling the truth and Emily was at a game. Maybe he'd sent us here just to mess with us, knowing she wasn't home. Or maybe she didn't even live here at all.

"You could break in," Spike said. "Everybody knows what a passion of yours that is."

"Been there," I said, "done that. I break into her residence twice and I move up into the stalker category."

We were back in the car by now.

"Gotta ask you something," Spike said.

"I know what you're going to ask me," I said. "Why are we really here?"

"It's practically existential," Spike said.

"Bottom line?" I said. "I want to know who killed those people."

"Neither of whom you knew was on the planet before last week," he said.

"And if I can find out who killed them, *we* can find out who blew up your restaurant."

"My money's still on the little weasel we just left," Spike said. "I think he told us that tale just to deflect your attention."

"The thought did occur."

"He cops to some of it so you don't think he's responsible for all of it," he said.

"And the bad Russian boss turns out to be him."

"The thought did occur," Spike said and grinned. "And just because he says he didn't have his fingers in the hedge-fund pie doesn't mean he didn't."

I put my head back and closed my eyes as he started the car.

"Nancy Drew would probably have figured it all out by now," I said.

Normally we would have stopped first at Spike's for a drink. Or two. But Spike's was still being rebuilt, even as he was preparing to open back up for business before the job was finished. So we stopped at the bar at The Newbury. He had a martini. I had half of one. When he finally took me home I opened my laptop and tried to learn more about Ivan Kuznetzov, born in Kiev but raised in Moscow. The biggest stories about him were out of the past, the biggest being the one from fifteen years ago that Ross had referenced, when he was one of the people accused of providing backing for what was described as a "massive gambling operation" that stretched from the back of his gallery in Moscow to similar galleries in Spain and London and New York. There were a dozen men charged. Seven ended up doing time in this country. Ivan Kuznetzov wasn't one of them. For all intents and purposes, despite the flurry of news stories and headlines after that bust, Kuznetzov had gone off the grid.

Until he had shown up in Boston looking for a poker game, at least according to Eddie Ross. And had not only found one, but had apparently been cheated out of a shitload of money at one where Alex Drysdale was a player and Matt Dunn was dealer.

Both now deceased.

When I finished my research, such as it was, I was suddenly in need of an Upper Crust Pizzeria fix. And needed some air. Upper Crust stayed open until eleven. It was still only ten-thirty. I called in an order for a medium mushroom-and-green-pepper pie, small Caesar salad with extra anchovies.

"We could deliver if you want, Miss Randall," Brian, the kid who answered, told me.

"Walk'll do me good," I said.

For some reason, just the simple act of grabbing a pizza felt like a brief return to some sort of normalcy, something that would take me out of what was starting to feel like a bad Russian novel. I explained to Rosie that I was going it alone, but then told her my destination. She loved the crust from Upper Crust. I inferred that she wanted me to get back as quickly as possible.

I stuck my backup .38 into the back pocket of my jeans. The gun was like my security blanket, even though I knew it wouldn't do me a lot of good if my intended target was outside of spitting distance.

As I walked up toward Charles Street, I thought about how few times in my life I had discharged any of my weapons outside a shooting range. But I practiced a lot, with all of my guns. I knew what a good shot Phil Randall was, and how he'd saved my life by putting down the Spare Change Killer, Bob Johnson, before Johnson could shoot me. My father hadn't hesitated. He knew what kind of shot he was. And knew he wouldn't miss.

Now somebody had put down two men involved in my case.

But *was* it my case?

How much skin did I have in this game, really?

I knew I'd left too soon. My pizza wasn't ready when I got there. I went outside and checked my phone. No messages, which meant no new calamities involving dead bodies or fire-bombings or college girls on the make.

Maybe this really *was* a time to just turn the whole thing over to God and let Her figure it out.

The Beacon Hill Hotel, right across the street, had closed down during COVID. Now they were giving the old girl a make-over. I loved the food there. I loved the rooftop terrace. Another place in Melanie Joan's neighborhood that felt like one of mine.

I walked across Charles Street to maybe peek through a window and survey the progress. They had vaguely said something about opening in the fall. The main entrance was on Charles. Branch Street ran alongside, another narrow cobblestone street that wasn't much wider than a driveway. Beacon Hill, to the max.

I was leaning under some scaffolding and looking in a side window when the car pulled up at the end of Branch.

A man got out.

He either had a long revolver in his hand or was just glad to see me.

Even in the dim light, he looked very tall.

FORTY-EIGHT

Nothing good for me on a side street empty except for him and me. I turned and started to run back toward Charles, where there was light, and traffic, and people.

Another man was walking toward me from that direction.

The basketball player who'd gotten out of the car was closer.

As casually as I could, considering my current circumstances, I reached back and felt my hand on the .38 and pulled it out of my pocket.

The tall guy was getting closer. Unless I missed my guess, and I knew my guns because of my father, it was a Colt in his hand, likely single-action. And a lot bigger than mine.

I'd never shot at anybody with the .38, though I'd put it on people a few times.

They're no longer just trying to scare me.

It was quiet on Branch Street. When the

hotel was still open, when the place wasn't a construction site, there was plenty of foot traffic out here, even at night. Not this night. If these were Kuznetzov's men, it somehow meant he knew I had talked to Eddie. Or Eddie had told him.

Maybe there was some kind of convention for Russian baddies this week.

Both of them kept closing in on me, both about fifty yards away.

It was quiet enough on Branch that I could hear the hammer on the tall guy's gun.

I dropped to the ground as he fired over me and put both hands on the .38 and hoped I was close enough to him and fired back at him, hearing him yell and then grab his leg. He didn't go down, but I had enough time to roll and fire two more shots at the guy, smaller and much wider, coming from Charles.

Missed him.

But he stopped when he heard the shouts coming from behind him on Charles Street. I scrabbled underneath the scaffolding and saw the giant up on one knee and raising his gun and firing again, the bullet hitting one of the metal bars well above me.

I fired another shot back at him, hoping he wasn't counting my bullets. Missed.

Lights went on above me now, from the old apartment building across from the Beacon Hill. I heard shouts from the windows, and saw the other guy in retreat toward Charles as I heard the first sirens in the distance.

I looked in the other direction and saw the car pulling away. I ran toward Charles, realizing I still had my gun in my hand, when I saw a tall kid carrying a pizza drop it and put his hands up in the air.

"I'm the good guys," I said.

When I was on the corner I saw the first flashing lights of the first cop car coming from the park. I got my breathing under control and leaned against the brick wall next to what had been the entrance to the Beacon Hill Hotel in far better times than this.

"A freaking shootout?" the pizza kid said. "In freaking Beacon Hill?"

"Happens in the best of neighborhoods," I said.

I waited to talk to the cops. As I did, I thought: It was a lot easier for these guys to shoot somebody Russian-style when the other person wasn't shooting back.

FORTY-NINE

The next morning I sat with Frank and Lee Farrell at two small tables we'd pushed together along the wall at Thinking Cup on Newbury Street. Lee had asked if he could tag along because he at least partially blamed himself for putting me in this picture in the first place.

"Like she needs help getting herself into the shit," Belson said.

"At least nobody died this time," Lee said, as if trying to be helpful.

"I owe it all to dedicated gym work and lightning-fast reflexes," I said.

"Yeah," Belson said. "You're a real peach."

Belson sipped black coffee. His unlit cigar, well chewed, hung over the table next to his cup. His idea of being decorous.

"I'm here to help, Frank," I said.

"Somehow I doubt that," he said.

I had determined not to hold anything back, even though holding things back from cops seemed to be my natural state. So I painstakingly took him through all of it, as linearly as possible, starting with the day Spike had tried to pay off on Drysdale's loan. I told them everything from, and about, Matt Dunn, and the grift he had been running with Emily. I watched Lee's face as I told him about Emily and Eddie and poker.

I knew Belson would remember all of it later, and remember where he wanted to jump in and ask a question. For now he allowed me to continue uninterrupted, as I told him about Eddie Ross and what he'd told me about Ivan Kuznetzov and his seven-foot shooter.

I circled back when I remembered I hadn't included the photographs left at my house, the unspoken threats against my father, and Richie, and his son.

When I finished I was hungry enough for a Morning Glory muffin. I asked Belson and Lee if they wanted anything to eat.

"Could you run over to the Dunkin' on Boylston and get me a Boston Kreme?" Belson said.

"You know those have three hundred calories?" I asked him.

"And me always worrying about my girlish figure," Belson said.

When I came back from the counter with my muffin Lee said, "Why did it take them this long to shoot at you?"

"I can only make the assumption that it had something to do with my meet with Eddie in Charlestown," I said.

"But," Lee said, "you told us that it was Eddie who gave you the heads-up that Kuznetzov might be in play, correct?"

"Eddie's got a lot of moves," I said.

"I'm gonna need to talk to him," Belson said.

He gave me his cop face and said, "Something I would have done already, as he is connected to two stiffs that occurred on my watch, had I known about his potential involvement."

"My bad?" I said, and ate some muffin.

"The bigger, badder Russian could be the one who had them killed," Lee said.

"Or not," Belson said.

"Well," I said, "there is that."

"You gotta think about standing down now," Belson said. "Not because you're in my way. You always seem to be in my way. But as tough a cookie as you think you are, if this is some new branch of the Russian Mob, they're not going to stop because they missed."

"The thought has occurred."

"You could call Vinnie Morris," Lee said.

"I am told he's out of town on a thing," I said.

"What kind of thing, you don't mind me asking?" Belson said.

"It's Vinnie." I shrugged. "Use your imagination."

"Maybe Tony Marcus could loan you Junior or Ty-Bop," Lee said.

"I'd rather not start running another tab with Tony if I can help it," I said.

"Jesse?" Belson said.

"Kind of has a day job," I said.

We sat and stared at our coffee. I asked Belson if he was sure I couldn't interest him in a cherry ginger muffin. He casually gave me the finger.

"I could put a car in front of the house," Belson said.

"If I think I need one," I said, "I'll ask for one."

He pulled his phone out of his pocket. I was not at all shocked to see that he was still using a flip.

"I'm gonna have a chat with a guy from Major Case when I get back to the office," he said. "See what kind of chatter and all-around bullshit he might have going with Russians."

He drained the last of his coffee, grabbed

his cigar, and stood up.

"You know any Russians you could talk to?" Belson said.

I smiled.

"One," I said.

FIFTY

"You need me to kill somebody else for you?" Gled said.

"Not to make too fine a point of things," I said, "but you didn't kill anybody for me. You settled a score for Tony and I didn't stop either one of you."

"If you are saying so," Gled said.

The last time he had been in my house he had engaged in some techy voodoo and found a bug in my kitchen left by a dirty cop named Jake Rosen. And the last time I'd seen Rosen had been when Gled and some other guys had driven off with him, after which the guy who had murdered Tony's ex-girlfriend went on the list of the permanently disappeared.

Gled had still been working for Gabriel Jabari, whose brother Tony once had shanked in prison. Now Jabari and Tony had mutual business interests. The heart wants what the heart wants.

Gled was big and broad and bald, and certainly armed, and undoubtedly dangerous.

"Actually," I said, "I was just looking for information about one of your countrymen."

Gled grinned. He was sitting on my couch but made it look as small underneath him as a barstool. He still looked strong enough to stop a Green Line train with one punch.

"If I tell you everything I know about my country," Gled said, "maybe I am having to kill you, huh?"

Jabari had told me once that Gled had spent a fair amount of his adult life working for the Federal Protective Service, one of the supposedly legit government agencies that had replaced the KGB, which meant separate from Putin's secret police. But he finally decided he needed to get out, out of government service and out of Russia, and had ended up in Boston, working as a bodyguard for Jabari.

"You still with Gabriel?" I said.

He shook his head.

"Working for him meant working for Mr. Tony Marcus," Gled said. "One time working for him was enough."

"Tell me about it," I said.

Now he smiled.

"A man's got to know his limitations," he said.

"Dirty Harry?" I said.

"Magnum Force."

It was the middle of the afternoon, but I asked if he wanted a drink. He said vodka. I told him I could do that. He asked what kind I had.

"Beluga Gold Line," I said.

"The good stuff," he said. "You keep it in the freezer?"

"Where else?" I said.

I brought him back a healthy pour and asked him what he was doing for work.

"Some of this and the other," he said. "Some protection. Some private security. I am even doing some consulting for Major Case." He grinned again. "Maybe I'm a little like another movie. *Taken?* You know that one?"

I told him I would watch Liam Neeson if he were conducting the Boston Pops.

"People, they seem to appreciate I have a particular set of skills," Gled said.

I explained to him then that somehow I had gotten sideways with Mother Russia. When I mentioned Eddie Ross's name, Gled barked out a laugh that sounded like rolling thunder.

"The mouse," he said, "who grew up to

be a rat. Little, little boy desperate to be his father."

"How much of a threat is he, really?"

"Only to himself," Gled said.

He drank. I could almost see the vodka settling inside him. Then he sighed. He wore an electric-blue suit and black sneakers with white soles.

I told him about my ride in the car with Eddie's guys that night, and how I had to bite one of them to escape.

"You get a rabies shot?" Gled said.

Then I told him about the scene on Branch Street last night, and what Eddie Ross had told me about Kuznetzov before that.

Gled put down his glass.

"Kuznetzov is in Boston?"

"Sounds like."

"Nobody has been seeing or hearing from him for a long time," he said. "People I know who are still with the government thought he was dead. Who did he send after you, huh?"

I told him about the giant.

"Boyko," he said.

"I shot him," I said.

He smiled fully now and said something in Russian that sounded to me like "you bought some."

"Help me out," I said.

"I was talking about admiring you," he said.

"For shooting him before he shot me?"

"For not being dead," Gled said.

"Eddie said he might be opening a gallery here," I said. "Kuznetzov."

"If he is, it would not be because of his love for art," he said.

"Is he a poker player, by any chance?" I said.

"So much so," he said. "He is not just playing. He was always obsessed with playing. Almost as obsessed as he was with winning."

I told Gled about Drysdale and Matt Dunn.

"Would he go so far as to kill somebody he thought was cheating him?" I said.

"For sport," Gled said. "In either poker or business, if he thought someone had been — what you call it? — boning him. No offense."

"None taken," I said.

He held out his glass. I went and got him more Beluga and hoped he wasn't driving.

"Just because Eddie Ross says he is in Boston does not mean he is in Boston," Gled said.

"But if he is, do you think you could do

me a favor and find out why?"

"For you, yes," he said. "I owe you."

"No, you don't."

"Yes," he said. "One of the girls that the cop you don't want to talk about killed? One of the young whores? She was the sister of a woman I know."

"I don't suppose I want to know where you took Rosen that night," I said.

"You are supposing so much correctly," he said.

He leaned forward and looked at me intently. He had very bright blue eyes and was, in his own odd way, good-looking.

"If it is Kuznetzov, he will come for you again," he said.

"I'll be careful."

He shook his head. "You need protection," he said. "North End and South End and everywhere."

It came out "norse" and "souse."

"That's what they're saying," I said, "*all* over town."

"I am doing this for you," he said. "You will not even be seeing me."

He reached inside his jacket and came out with a .44 Magnum.

"You can't cover me by yourself," I said.

He smiled again. "You have friends," he said. "I have friends."

Then he placed the Magnum across his lap and said, "Do you feel lucky today?"

I told him I did now.

"See what I did there?" he said.

FIFTY-ONE

After I'd fixed myself a dinner of pasta and vegetables I sat in the living room and did some reading about the Russian Mob, which seemed to have never had much of a footprint in Boston.

The capital of the Mob in the United States was still Brighton Beach, in Brooklyn. There was occasionally a money-laundering case involving Russians in a place like Atlanta. But the biggest and best money laundering seemed to be going on abroad. There had been a lot of arrests a couple years ago when the front had been one of the country's largest insurance companies, that case stretching all the way to Spain. There had been a bigger bust of a lot of hard guys from both Russia and Ukraine in Atlantic City involved in a literal laundry list of bad behavior, from extortion all the way to slot machines.

I closed my laptop and said to Rosie,

parked next to me on the couch, "This is another fine mess I've gotten us into."

She gave me a look that I interpreted as her saying, *What do you mean 'us'?*

I had recently branched out from Jameson and Bushmills Black Bush to try bourbon as a sipping drink, and was working on a glass of Heaven's Door. I was still on my Eddie Harris kick. I sipped bourbon and listened to Eddie and wondered all over again if a Taft girl I didn't like and a restaurant that was now back in Spike's hands were worth getting killed over.

I took out my phone and called Jesse and asked him that same question, even feeling it was classically rhetorical.

"Were you under the impression that I might tell you it was a good idea to get into a shooting war with the Russian Mob?" he said. "I know you're not any better at letting shit go than I am, but this one you need to let go."

"It may be too late for that," I said.

"I have this rule," Jesse said. "Would you like to hear it?"

"You have a lot of rules."

He ignored that.

"When you've got no skin in the game, make sure to save your own," he said. "Skin, I mean."

"Did you just come up with that?"

"Yes."

"You're not the only person who thinks that way."

"I'll bet." He paused and said, "You need protection, either way."

"Got some."

"Who?"

I told him.

Jesse said, "The guy who helped you with Tony and the cop?"

"Turns out he had some skin in that game," I said.

"You trust this guy?"

"He's a Russian, but he's my Russian," I said.

"So you're not walking away."

"Would you?" I said.

"Guys like we're talking about, they kill people to stay in practice," he said. "Not that they generally need much practice."

"Stop me if you've heard this one before," I said, "but I need to figure this out."

"I'll take a few days off and come down there," he said.

"You just took a few days off," I said. "But if I really need you, I'll holler."

I heard him chuckle.

"You often holler when you need me," he said.

"Oink," I said.

I walked Rosie after ending the call. I didn't see Gled, or any of his sidemen. I hadn't expected that I would. But I was sure they were around. I wasn't sure why I trusted him this way, but I did.

I had left my phone inside. Not a gun. I generally moved the guns in the house around. You could do that when you lived alone. Tonight I was carrying a Smith & Wesson M&P9. A personal favorite. The newest one I had. Lighter trigger. No manual thumb safety. Extended finger grip.

The neighborhood around us was quiet and still as Rosie took longer than usual to perform her nightly duties. A neighborhood that would have been out of my price range, and more than somewhat, if not for the largesse of Melanie Joan Hall. Someone else who had come to the determination that she owed me something because I had done my job.

I had always felt the world ought to be far less transactional than that.

Rosie and I walked all the way up to the Public Garden and back. I had brought treats and gave her all of them because her nightly walk was far longer than usual.

Still no sign of Gled, or whomever he had shadowing me tonight. I thought back to

the night he had silently come up behind
Jake Rosen and stuck a gun into the small
of his back before shoving him into the
backseat of the car, Rosen never to be seen
or heard from again.

Gled was right:

I didn't know what I didn't want to know.

Rosie and I went back to the house. I set
the alarm when we were inside and was
about to head up to bed when Richie called.

Jesse and Richie. Richie and Jesse.

"Can you get over to Desmond's house as
soon as possible?" Richie said.

"Has something happened to him?" I said.

"Not him," Richie Burke said. "Jalen."

FIFTY-TWO

Two of Desmond's troopers, neither of whom I recognized, were stationed at his front door. I knew there was at least one other between the back of the house at Flagship Wharf in Charlestown and the water. The property was on the old Navy Yard. From the top floor of the place you could see both the Bunker Hill Monument and the USS *Constitution.*

Desmond was in the living room, wearing an old-fashioned wool cardigan. I could have sworn that he was wearing the same sweater the first time I ever met him. The sweater was gray. So were his pants. So, I often thought, was he.

Jalen Washington was sitting up on Desmond's couch, his left arm in a sling, a bandage wrapped around his upper arm. Richie had pulled up a chair next to him.

"What happened?" I said.

"Got myself shot, is what happened," he

said. "Done a lot of things in my life. Had a lot of things happen. Never took a bullet."

"Coming after one of my people is like them coming after me," Desmond Burke said, looking at me. "What is this *shite* you're into, for *fook's* sake."

The Irish in his conversation, I knew by now, came and went, as if the language he were speaking was Desmond Burke.

"It's complicated," I said to Desmond.

"What isn't with you?" he said.

I turned to Jalen.

"What happened?" I said.

He had, he said, been visiting his lady friend over in Blue Hill.

"There's more than one," he said. "But Kerry is my main situation."

He had decided not to stay the night, but said they'd had some wine and what he described as "whatnot," which he knew was going to happen before he got there, so he'd taken an Uber over to her house, a couple miles from his own.

"But I had myself a nice buzz going," he said, "and it was a nice night, so I decided to walk a little bit, see if I had it in me to make it all the way home. Maybe even have myself a nightcap at Reggie's. You know Reggie's?"

"I do," Richie said.

"Anyway," he said, "I headed up toward Franklin Park."

He shifted slightly on the couch and grimaced. There was what looked like whiskey on the coffee table in front of him. He started to reach down for it. Richie picked it up instead and handed it to him and Jalen drank and handed the glass back to him.

"Then this car, coming the other way, stops about fifty yards up," he said. "Maybe a little more. Big guy gets out the passenger side and I see his hand come up, but just as he does, I hear somebody yell, 'Gun!' " He shook his head, and smiled. "Probably some kid doing the same kind of lookout business I used to do over there. Probably saved my life, 'cause I make a move toward the park as he shoots, so he only gets me where he got me."

"But didn't put you down," I said.

He shook his head.

"Hurt like a mother, though," he said. "You ever been shot?"

"I have," Richie said quietly. "Guy back-shot me one time."

"Dude fires off another one," he said, "but I'm running now into the park, and then I hear people yelling from in there. I'm still running when I hear a siren. When I got to

301

the other side of the park, I got my sweater off and took off my T-shirt and wrapped it 'round my arm and called Richie and he came got me, and brought me here."

Richie said, "Desmond called a doctor he has on call."

"One who wouldn't report treating a gunshot victim," I said.

"Not bloody likely," Desmond Burke said.

"How big was the shooter?" I said.

"What bloody difference does that make?" Desmond said.

"Might be important," I said to him.

"Big enough to be a big man for my Celtics," Jalen said.

"Somebody like that tried to shoot me last night," I said. "Couple blocks from my house."

Richie's head whipped around.

I said, "Tell you about it later."

I pointed at Jalen's drink and said to Desmond, "Could I get a taste of that?"

Desmond walked over to the wet bar near the door to the kitchen. I saw him reach for the bottle of Midleton Very Rare. He poured some and came back and wordlessly handed me the glass.

I drank. It was, as always, quite fine.

"Who have you been talking to about Drysdale since we last spoke?" I said.

"Could there have been a precipitating event for things to escalate like this, for both of us?"

"Was getting to that," he said. "I'd been over to Drysdale's office this afternoon. Just see who was around. See if I could get somebody talking, just on account of how I'm good at getting people talking."

"Who was there?" I said.

"Practically nobody," he said. "Hot shit of a woman still sitting outside Drysdale's office. Some mouth on her."

"Gina," I said.

"Other than her, it was just a couple traders," he said. "Both of them looking like they were clearing out their desks, boxing up their stuff. I asked one of them what was shaking and he said, 'Circus is about to leave town.' Then I asked the guy, coming out of the men's, if I could ask him a few questions about the fund and he said he couldn't talk."

"NDA," I said.

"There you go," Jalen Washington said.

He gently rubbed his shoulder, wincing as he did. "Maybe somebody made a call after I left," he said.

"Apparently so," I said.

"So you've now dragged us into some *shite* with Russians, is that it?" Desmond

303

said to me.

"Apparently so," I said again.

I knew I could explain it all to him, and it might even make some sense to him. But I knew he didn't care whether I made sense of it or not. And I was tired of explaining how we'd all gotten here.

Wherever that was.

"I've always got wars being fought on various fronts," Desmond Burke said. "I don't need another one, Sunny, not with Russians."

"Trust me on this, Desmond. Neither do I."

"I was glad to help Sunny out, Mr. Burke," Jalen said.

"I asked him to help," Richie said.

"It was supposed to be about somebody's fooking *money!"* Desmond said now. "And now these men send pictures of my grandson and shoot at you and shoot at Jalen and I want it to *fooking* end."

"Jalen," I said, "I am so sorry."

"Cost a doin' business," he said, forcing a smile. "I just wish I knew what the damn business really was."

Now he reached over and picked up his own glass and finished his Midleton and slowly got to his feet.

"I need little more of Kerry's weed," he said.

Richie said he'd drive him home, and asked me if I wanted one of Desmond's men to follow me home.

"I got this," I said.

"Obviously," Richie said, "you don't. You need someone watching your ass."

"Like you always did," I said.

"This isn't funny," Desmond snapped. "None of it."

I walked with him and Jalen out to Richie's car. When Jalen was inside and had fastened his seat belt with his right hand, he said, "We're out now, right?"

"So out," I said. "This ends here, and now."

Richie looked over at me across the roof and said, "You mean that?"

"I do," I said. "I can't have the next person the big Russian doesn't miss be someone I care about."

"Good," he said.

He drove off. I saw the black Audi pull out behind him and watched until the taillights of both cars disappeared toward Bunker Hill. I took it as a matter of faith that Richie knew I had been lying when I'd said I was out.

Having known me as long as he had, it was frankly on him if he didn't know.

FIFTY-THREE

I sat with Spike and Gled at a Russian bar in Cambridge actually known as The People's Republik. It was hard to miss, with the mural of a nondistinct Communist man out front, the guy wearing onc of those classic green caps with a red star squarely in the middle. I'd always assumed that the GUINNESS sign over the front door was just their way of being more free-market capitalists.

I hadn't been inside for years, but once we were, I saw that the place hadn't lost its sense of irony about the Red Menace. There were red walls and a black-and-white portrait of Lenin and an army boot above the bar and a drink on the menu called the Bloody Trotsky. Spike was the one who had first brought me here. At the time he said the place was cheeky, in a Commie sort of a way. He loved the fact that the house specialty, at least food-wise, was a Philly cheesesteak.

I said to Gled, "I don't see anybody in here who looks like the guy Harrison Ford threw off the plane in *Air Force One.*"

Gled nodded. "Gary Oldman. Playing Ivan Korshunov." He grinned. "Get off my plane," he growled.

I turned to Spike. "Gled likes his movies."

"The truth about this place is that the crowd is mostly grad students who get the joke," Spike said.

"I haven't spotted you or any of your guys following me," I said to Gled.

"And you are sounding so much surprised about this, huh?" he said.

"I'm usually good at spotting tails," I said, "whether they're on my side or not."

"We are better at not being spotted," Gled said.

Our drinks had arrived. We were all having Beluga Noble. It was forty dollars a glass. I told him he was well worth it. He said it was difficult for him to disagree. He'd called and said he wanted to talk about Kuznetzov, and had picked this place for the fun of it.

"Is Kuznetzov still in town?" I said.

He gave a quick shake of his head.

"Not only are my sources telling me he is not in town," Gled said, "they are telling me that they do not know that he ever was."

"So Eddie was lying?" I said.

"Maybe yes, maybe no," Gled said. "I just cannot nail it down that he is telling the truth."

He threw down what was left in his glass and wiped the back of his hand across his mouth and motioned for the bartender to bring him another.

"You good?" he said to Spike and me, nodding at our glasses.

"I'm trying to get out of here without having to take out one of those reverse mortgages," I said.

"So you're saying that the guy we thought sent a shooter after Sunny and one of her friends isn't the guy we thought it was," Spike said.

"Or maybe it was like a poker bluff," I said.

I drank some of the Beluga. It wasn't as icy cold as when my glass had been set down in front of me. But it still went down quite smoothly and tasted as powerful as a speeding bullet. I imagined that if I had another one Spike would have to use a fireman's carry to get me to his car.

"If Kuznetzov isn't the one behind this, then who?" I said.

"Maybe is not a Russian at all," Gled said. "Maybe another bluff from Eddie."

"There were three guys at Stanford back in the day," Spike said. "Maybe you need to have another chat with Drysdale's old partner. Maybe it turns out he's the one who knows more than he's telling."

"Or is the best liar of all," I said.

Gled had already finished with his second vodka, then looked at his watch and said he had to meet somebody in the North End.

"Another source?" I said.

"Woman friend," he said. "A smoke, like you say."

"Before you go," Spike said to him, "I just want you to tell me straight up that you and your guys can keep Sunny safe."

"I told her we would," Gled said. "So we will. That is it and that is all." He paused. " 'A deal is a promise, and a promise is unbreakable.' "

"Another movie line?" I said.

Gled smiled now, fully.

Wonder Woman," he said.

FIFTY-FOUR

I had left several messages for Christopher Lawton throughout the day. He had not responded to any of them. So a little after five the next afternoon I was parked up Comm Ave across from what Eddie Ross had said was Emily Barnes's new crash pad, employing a variation of one of my investigative fundamentals: When you don't know what else to do and don't know which lies you've been told or who sent Russians to shoot at you and your friends, go back to following somebody.

I'd followed the late Alex Drysdale and learned a lot, until he had ended up dead. But I had been able to link him to Eddie and poker and Matt Dunn, at least until Dunn ended up dead with a playing card stuffed in his mouth. Now I knew Eddie was lying to me, I just didn't know about what. Maybe he'd even lied about where Emily Barnes, who had turned out to be something less than the Queen of the May, currently resided.

I could just ring the doorbell and see if Emily was home. Or break in. Or I could do what I was doing and wait for her to come out and take me somewhere I wanted to go.

And if I ended up somewhere that was a less-than-happy place, at least for me, I was banking on Gled or his guys to make everything a fair fight.

Theoretically.

I had come to think of Gled as "My Russian Vinnie."

As in Morris.

With all that, I needed to make something happen. Move the line. I had brought a couple apples with me this time, but no water, because hydrating properly also meant bathroom breaks. I didn't want to miss Emily. Talking to her again seemed less meaningful to me, at least for now, than seeing the places she might go.

No audiobook tonight. I was listening to the Stones. The *Let It Bleed* album. Singing along loudly with Mick, windows closed, on "You Can't Always Get What You Want."

I sat behind the wheel and continued to belt out the lyrics in my shower voice.

She finally came out at seven-thirty, looking as if she were on her way to a slutty prom. *Extremely* short black skirt, tight pink V-neck sweater cut low. Hair loose and hanging to her shoulders. Thigh boots, also black. Leather clutch that I was betting was Tory Burch.

What I assumed was her Uber arrived a minute later. She leaned forward to talk to the driver, then got into the backseat. The car pulled away. I waited and pulled out behind it. The car went west for a block, then made a left across what I still thought of as the trolley tracks to make a U-turn on Commonwealth, and then a right toward Cleveland Circle. We both stopped at a light there, the new Marriott in front of us, the Boston College reservoir off to our right.

The Uber took a left on Beacon. So did I. I stayed close, because there was no good reason for Emily Barnes to think she was being followed. It might turn out there was no good reason for me to be following her. At least nobody had shot at me tonight. It was what passed for progress.

As we approached Kent Street the driver put on his left blinker, waiting for the light, and made the turn, as did I. When I saw the car begin to slow, I pulled over and waited, with a full view of the block ahead of me.

Emily got out, checked her hair in one of

the car windows, gave it a fluff, straightened out her skirt.

Then she walked into The Carmody.

Owned now by none other than Christopher Lawton.

"Oh, ho," I said.

FIFTY-FIVE

She could be here, I decided, for only two reasons.

Either she was here to play poker or she was meeting the new boyfriend about whom she had spoken of, and whom Matt Dunn had referenced, for a night of unbridled passion. Maybe she was dressed for both.

Just because she was here didn't mean Lawton was here as well. Or that he knew she was here, or had anything to do with her being here.

But if there was a game here, Lawton would know. He struck me as the type who would want to know everything going on at his hotel. And if it were a game being run by Eddie Ross, his old Stanford pal, he'd know that, too. Maybe Eddie had called, one Stanford guy to another, and had Lawton book him a suite for one of his movable feast games.

And what were the odds that Emily

Barnes, who once played poker with Alex Drysdale, would just happen to end up at a game being played at a hotel owned by Drysdale's former hedge-fund partner?

I was tired of not knowing things I wanted to know, about her and all of it. My concealed carry of choice, the M&P9, was in my bag. I got out of my car and locked it and walked underneath the lemon-and-white awning and into the lobby of The Carmody.

The concierge was tall and silver-haired, wearing a tight blue suit that featured what I was pretty sure the fashionistas called a shadow plaid. Underneath was a dark blue shirt with polka dots, buttoned to the collar. He reminded me of Anderson Cooper. It was just him on one side of the lobby and the woman working the front desk on the other. Somehow the concierge managed to look busy. And officious as all get-out without saying a word.

I stood in front of him until he was forced to notice me.

"May I help you?" he said.

He was trying to sound vaguely British. I nearly told him that we both knew better.

"I'm sorry to bother you," I said. "But I forgot my phone and I'm late, so I was wondering if you could tell me what room the game is in?"

"*Game?*" he said.

"The poker game," I said. "The one that the girl with no clothes on who just walked through the lobby is on her way to."

I took notice of his nameplate for the first time. MR. GAYLORD.

"Young lady," he said. "I have absolutely no idea what you are talking about."

I sighed. Almost a mournful sound.

Then leaned forward.

"Here's how we can do this," I said. "You can either tell me the room number where tonight's poker game is being played, and I head on up there." I smiled. "Or," I continued, "I can call my father, the former police detective, and have him call some of his old friends in Vice and tell them that there is a high-stakes poker game going on at this establishment, perhaps one that includes some extremely sketchy characters. At which point they will head on over here and you will then be forced to tell *them* where the goddamn game is. Then they, and the Good Lord, can sort things out."

He picked up the fountain pen in front of him, put it down. He stared at me. I stared back, still smiling.

"Actually," I said, "there's a third option. We can call Mr. Lawton. I assume you have the same number for him I do."

I took my phone out of my bag.

"You said you didn't have your phone," he said.

"Well, Mr. Gaylord," I said, "I lied."

We stared at each other a little more. I had gotten close enough to his stand-up desk that I got a whiff of his cologne.

Finally he reached into his drawer and came out with one of his cards and picked up his pen and wrote something on the card before sliding it across to me.

I looked down and saw "842" under his name and title.

"Top floor," he said. "To your right after you come out of the lift."

"Lift?" I said. "Really?"

He shrugged.

"You didn't get this from me," he said.

"Do people ever tell you that you look like Anderson Cooper?" I said.

Now he sighed, an even sadder sound than I had made.

"More than you could possibly imagine," he said.

I took the elevator to the eighth floor, took the right as he'd told me to, walked down to the end of the hall to 842, knocked on the door.

Christopher Lawton was the one who answered.

"Room service," I said.

FIFTY-SIX

I walked past him before he could even attempt to stop me.

It was a large suite, tastefully decorated, more old Boston than new. Beyond the living room was a dining room, dominated by a round antique table. That's where the players were. Emily Barnes was one of them, looking at me as if a swamp creature had just entered the room.

"What up?" I said too brightly.

No one at the table answered. There were three men at the table with Emily, and a much younger guy with an unopened deck in front of him. All of the players had chips in front of them. One was much older, bald, overweight, his belly stretching against a cashmere sweater. The other two were both lean and hard-looking.

"Hey, girlfriend," I said to Emily.

Still no answer. Lawton still hadn't spoken, or moved far from the door. The air in the room felt suddenly brittle. So I reached into my bag, came out with my wallet, and took out all the cash I had in there, counting it out in front of them.

"I've got eighty-six dollars here," I said. "Is that enough to buy me a seat?"

The big guy was closest to me, seated to Emily's left. He jerked a head at Lawton now.

"What the fuck kind of shit is this?" he said.

If it wasn't a Russian accent, it was from the same neighborhood.

Lawton finally closed the door and walked over to where I was standing.

"What are you doing here, Sunny?" he said.

"Funny," I said, "but I was about to ask you the same thing."

"You know I own this hotel," he said.

I gestured toward the table.

"Which means you sort of have to own this, too, am I right?"

"Enough," the hard guy with the accent said, and stood up. *"Enough."*

"She goes now or maybe you find somebody's money whose is better than mine," he said to Lawton.

"You need to go," Lawton said to me. "I don't know what you think is going on here, so I'll tell you: just a game with some friends."

"These people friends of yours, Emily?" I said.

"I don't have to tell you shit," she said.

"Well put," I said.

She stared at the stacks of chips in front of her, just as a way of looking anywhere except at me.

I turned back to Lawton.

"This is one of Eddie's games, isn't it?" I said.

"No," he said.

"Yes," I said. "But you gave me the impression, rather earnestly, as I recall, that you and Eddie weren't all that close anymore. So you were being less than honest with me, weren't you?"

The hard guy with the accent was standing now. His focus was where everybody else's was, on Christopher Lawton and me.

"Which," I continued, "makes me wonder if you've been lying to me about, oh, I don't know, everything."

"Eddie and I have an understanding," Lawton said. "I'd be happy to explain it to you, I'd just rather it wasn't here."

"I'll bet," I said.

"Enough," the guy with the accent said again.

He covered the distance with surprising quickness for somebody his size, and before I could do anything grabbed me roughly by my left arm, his grip hard enough that it hurt as he pulled me toward the door.

I didn't let him, even with his size advantage. Instead I planted my left foot, and pivoted with a move I'd learned a long time ago at the police academy, and kneed him as hard as I could in what Spike still insisted on calling his junk. I'd now bitten one Russian and kneed another and was generally folding the Marquis of Queensbury rules into a party hat.

He let go of me and fell to the floor on his side and rocked gently, while I pulled my gun out of my bag and pointed it at him.

"Hey," Lawton said. "*Hey.* Everybody calm down here."

"Him first," I said. "I've had a rough week," I said to the guy on the ground.

"Sunny," Lawton said, "you've got to calm down."

"The one with the gun," I said, "is generally quite calm."

"Let's you and I go somewhere and talk," Lawton said.

"You're in on this, aren't you?" I said to him.

"Downstairs," he said. "In the bar."

"Does this mean we're not going to play cards?" the bald man said.

I backed toward the door, nodding at Emily.

"I'll be in touch," I said.

"Don't count on it," she said. She shook her head and looked at me as if she'd finally identified the sucker in the room. "You think you're so fucking clever," she said. "And you don't even know what the game is, you stupid bitch."

Lawton opened the door. I walked out first. He followed me. We went down to the lobby and into the small bar next to it. There was only one occupied table in the dimly lit room, a couple leaning forward over glasses of white wine, close enough to kiss. Maybe they were the ones here for unbridled passion, the lucky ducks.

The only other customer was Gled, sitting alone at a table to the bartender's right.

Lawton asked if I wanted to sit at a table. I said the bar would be fine.

"You've got this all wrong," he said.

I told him I'd been hearing a lot of that lately.

FIFTY-SEVEN

The bartender, a young redheaded woman in a white shirt and a black vest, greeted Lawton as if he'd just returned safely from a tour in the Middle East. Lawton asked for a Johnnie Walker Blue, straight up. She had it in front of him in what I thought might be record time. When she asked what I wanted, I said I'd pass.

Lawton took a sip of his drink and angled his barstool so he was facing me. He kept his voice low.

"First off," he said. "What is it that you think I'm *in* on?"

"You, Eddie, Alex, poker, Emily, Russians," I said. "Did I miss anything?"

"I understand that you'd think a confluence like that suspicious," he said.

"No kidding," I said.

He drank.

"After COVID," he said, "actually, *during* COVID, I was about to go under here. The

325

bigger hotels downtown, they were always going to make it. Ritz. Four Seasons. Westin. Omni. But we're off the beaten path here, even though we're not that far from Kenmore Square. I'd finally gone through what I got from Alex when we split up. Stimulus money wasn't going to cut it. I needed somebody to throw me a life preserver."

"And Alex wasn't an option," I said.

"I couldn't make myself go begging to him," he said. "If I'd needed it now, maybe."

"Why now?"

"Things got better with us," he said. "Right before he died. He called me up and took me to dinner and said that he didn't have any family heirs and that even with everything that had gone down between us, that I was as close to family as he had, and he wanted me to be the trustee of the fund if anything ever happened to him."

"So you're inheriting the fund?"

"No," he said. "It's not like that. He basically wanted me to oversee its deconstruction. Paying out any outstanding financial obligations, unpaid bills, taxes, things like that."

"Where's the money go?" I said.

He grinned. "I asked him that," Lawton said. "He said he was going to surprise me.

Now there's a meeting at the bank in a few days to sort it all out."

He drank some scotch. I was starting to second-guess myself about not having ordered a drink of my own.

"So back when you needed an infusion of cash, you went to your old friend Eddie."

He nodded.

"Did you know when you did that Eddie was in business with Alex?" I said.

"I thought it was just the poker," he said. "I didn't know that Eddie was going to inherit some money when Alex did close down the fund."

"Explain closing down the fund," I said.

The bartender asked if Lawton wanted another. He said he did not. She asked if I'd changed my mind.

"Not about anything," I said.

"What a successful fund does at the end, if it's not completely crashing and burning, is transition to what is called a family office," Lawton said. "They don't make an announcement in the *Journal,* but the guy running the fund sends letters to his investors and the regulators. And what he basically tells them is that they're going to get their original buy-in back, plus one last big, fat return. And then the guy who's been managing their money — Alex, in this case

— is only going to manage his own money going forward."

"And that makes everybody happy?"

"Depends on what the returns have been," Lawton said. "Nobody ever questioned old Bernie Madoff because his returns were as regular as the tide. Until they weren't, of course. But, yeah, if the returns have been good, the investors walk away happy, as long as there's no fraud involved."

"Was there fraud involved with Alex?" I said.

"Not that anybody ever heard of," he said.

"But you don't know," he said.

"And frankly don't give a shit," he said. "I went to Eddie because I was the one who needed investors, even if they weren't people you'd see having lunch at the Harvard Club."

"Like your friends upstairs?" I said.

He shrugged, almost apologetically.

"And what was in it for Eddie," I said, "other than the chance to reconnect with an old college pal?"

"Some of The Carmody," Lawton said. "You want to know what I was in on? That's what I was in on. It's funny how these things work out. In the end, Eddie had a little piece of Alex and a little piece of me."

"And you both got to make new friends

from the Eastern Bloc."

"Old friends, in Eddie's case," Lawton said.

"Care to share some names?" I said.

Lawton gave me a long look.

"Not unless I want to end up like Alex," he said.

"You think it was a Russian who killed Alex?"

"Don't you?" Christopher Lawton said.

I looked past him. Gled was still at his table, studying his phone.

"Why did you lie to me?" I said to Lawton.

"I didn't think of it as lying," he said. "More self-interest. Or self-preservation."

"The financial aid you got from your Russians," I said. "What kind of strings were attached?"

"None that I couldn't live with," he said. "Put it that way."

"Do you have an NDA with them, Christopher?" I said. "Or was the NDA that you said you had with Alex Drysdale just more of your bullshit?"

"That was real."

"Why in the world should I believe any of this?" I said.

"There's an old line, Sunny, maybe you've heard it," he said. "From an old boxing promoter who got caught in a lie. When they called him on it he said, 'Yesterday I was lying. Today I'm telling the truth.' "

He finished his drink and threw a twenty on the bar, then stood up.

"Who was the guy I put on the ground?" I said.

"One of my investors," Lawton said.

"I'd like a name," I said.

"And I'd like to stay alive," he said. "If you're going to get his name, you're not getting it from me. I promised the guy privacy until you came walking through the goddamn door."

"Maybe I'll ask Emily," I said.

"Only if you can find her," he said.

Then I said to him what I'd said to Emily upstairs, that I'd be in touch.

"Only if you can find *me,*" he said, and walked back into the lobby and toward the elevators.

When the elevator doors opened, the guy with the accent was standing there. He stepped outside and let the doors close and nodded in the direction of the front door. He and Lawton left together. I was standing next to Gled by the time they were outside.

"You want to follow them?" Gled said.

I told him I tried to limit myself to one tail job a night, and walked outside myself and got into my car and drove back to River

Street Place. On the way home I called Spike and told him about the festivities at The Carmody.

By then I was passing Arlington Street.

"You ever read *Crime and Punishment*?" I said.

"College," he said.

"Same," I said. "Now I'm just trying to figure out in my version who's Raskolnikov."

"Beats the hell out of me," Spike said.

When I'd parked my car in my spot in back of the house and walked around to the front, I saw something taped to my front door.

FIFTY-EIGHT

I had just come around the corner and stopped about twenty yards away when I saw it, thinking that this was really where I'd come in, the envelope with the pictures of my father inside.

But this looked to be just a piece of paper, something written on it. I still wasn't close enough to see.

I pulled out the M&P9 for the second time tonight.

I walked over to the door and saw that it was a note.

From Jesse.

"I'm inside," it read, but then he'd always had a minimalist style. In just about everything.

He had a key because I'd given him one. When I'd told him I wanted him to have it he'd said, "Does this mean I have to give you my letter sweater?"

I told him that it was somehow comforting that occasionally his references were more dated than my own.

He was on the couch with Rosie, watching *The Godfather Part II.* He usually watched only westerns, but I knew he practically had the first two *Godfather* movies memorized. He liked to say that as bad as the cops were, he was surprised the Corleones didn't end up running the whole freaking world.

I saw a glass of club soda on the coffee table, a coaster underneath it, of course. He was as fastidious as my father. Richie was like that, too. If I mentioned that to Dr. Silverman, she'd probably treat it like she'd unearthed buried treasure.

I realized I still had the gun in my hand when he said, "I think it's safe to put that away."

"I thought you might be a Russian," I said.

"I never even liked vodka," he said.

He got up and came across the room and kissed me. I noted, and not for the first time, that for a professional tough guy he had very soft lips.

When I finally, and reluctantly, pulled back, still in his arms, I said, "To what do I owe the pleasure, Chief?"

"Had to see a guy about a case," he said. "And then I was closer to your place than my place."

"You impulsive devil."

He smiled the way he did, mostly with his eyes. "Not so much," he said.

We were still in the foyer, still holding on to each other.

"Would you like to hear about my day, dear?" I said.

"Always," Jesse Stone said.

I told him that first I needed a drink.

He was still smiling.

"Who doesn't?" he said.

I knew roughly how long he had been sober, once he'd gotten himself to rehab. And knew he knew the exact date, and how many days since his last drink. Recovering alcoholics knew things like that the way they knew their birthday.

I came back with a glass of Chardonnay and sat next to him. He had shut off the television. Rosie was now between us as I told him about The Carmody.

"You trust Lawton?" Jesse said when I finished.

"Thought I did," I said.

"Poker and hedge funds," he said. "Different games of skill and chance, connected by a bunch of assholes." He shrugged. "But what do I know?"

"A lot," I said.

He asked if I'd eaten. I told him I had not, I hadn't even eaten the apples I'd brought with me on stakeout duty. He suggested the Gourmet Dumpling House this time. The food, still hot, was delivered a half-hour later. We spread it all out on the coffee table and ate on the floor, like we did, and made gluttons of ourselves.

While we ate he asked questions about the scene at The Carmody, from the time I'd walked into the suite until Lawton left with the Russian.

"The one you kneed in the balls?" Jesse said.

"That be the one," I said.

He speared an oyster pancake off my plate. I said, "Hey!" And he told me he was a seasoned investigator and could tell I was full.

"I think Lee's niece knows a lot more than she's telling," he said.

"Even without me knowing how much of what she's told me is the truth," I said.

"But she remains the player who knows all the players," Jesse said. "Alive and dead."

"I plan to take one more run at her," I said. "Try to get her alone. Even though she keeps finding different ways to tell me to get lost."

"Maybe Lee should be the one to take a

run at her," Jesse said. "Or Belson. See how she likes being sweated as a person of interest, if Frank hasn't done that already."

We were both full by now, even though we'd overordered, as usual. He leaned back against the couch. I did the same. We both knew it was only a matter of time before we headed upstairs. But it was going to be a while. He was fully engaged now, bringing the full intensity of his curiosity and instincts and orderly mind to my case. By now I knew he was as good a cop as my father had been. As good as Belson. Or Lee Farrell. Probably better when you added it all up.

"You mind if I have another glass of wine?" I said.

He grinned. "Neither one of us is driving," he said.

When I came back from the kitchen he said, "You need to know more about Lawton, too. Just because he says he doesn't stand to make out now that Drysdale is gone doesn't mean he won't."

"You think *he's* some kind of gangster?" I said.

"I'm not saying he's Hyman Roth from *Godfather*," he said, nodding at the television. "You know, the Meyer Lansky character. But the subject of money laundering does seem to keep coming up."

"Rinse and repeat," I said.

"The illegal process of concealing the origins of money obtained illegally," he said, "by passing it through banking transfers and legitimate commercial transactions." He recited it like a schoolkid in glass. When he finished he grinned and said, "I looked up the exact definition."

"You deserve some sort of prize."

"Soon," he said.

"Didn't Lansky use casinos?" I said. "In real life, I mean."

"But he used hotels, too," Jesse said. "Even if it goes nowhere, it might be interesting to see if you can find out if Lawton actually owns that hotel free and clear."

I picked up my glass, but then put it back down.

"Like an LLC owns Eddie's brownstone," I said.

" 'Zackly," Jesse said.

"You're saying that Lawton might be the middleman for a lot of dirty money?" I said. "Or the head man?"

"All the way to Drysdale's hedge fund," Jesse said.

"Which is apparently about to be closed down," I said. "With him as trustee."

"Be nice to know what Drysdale knew," Jesse said. "At least before he got popped."

Something pinged on the periphery of memory then. I just didn't know why. Or where. Something there, and then not.

"What?" Jesse said, staring at me.

"I thought I had something," I said. "But then it was gone."

"Why don't you sleep on it?" he said.

I took his hand and pulled him up off the floor.

"When I'm tired," I said.

FIFTY-NINE

Richie called in the morning, after Jesse was on his way back to Paradise. I was pleased that I was alone, especially pleased that he hadn't tried to call about an hour earlier, when Jesse and I were back to tiring each other out before he left.

"I gave Jalen a couple days off, in case you were looking for him," Richie said. "I blame myself for him getting shot, and ordered him to take some vacay on me."

"You didn't get him shot."

"I got him into this," Richie said.

"Not nearly as much as I did," I said. "The vacay ought to be on me."

"I asked him what I could do and he told me he wouldn't say no to a little R&R with that Kerry lady. He talks about her like she's better-looking than Kerry Washington. I told him to pick a spot. He said he always wanted to check out South Beach."

"And you sent him to The Delano," I said.

We both knew he had taken me there one time.

"Get a good thing, stay with it," he said.

"Cool area," I said.

"Not that we saw much of it," Richie said.

There was an awkward pause.

"How's Richard?" I said.

"Safe," he said, "at home."

"Good."

"You stay safe."

"Trying."

"Try harder," Richie Burke said.

When I'd had some yogurt and showered and dressed and done my face and hair and essentially looked like everything a young businesswoman carrying a concealed weapon should, I drove over to One Financial Center to talk to Gina Patarelli, former assistant to Alex Drysdale, after having left her a voicemail that I was on my way.

When Jesse had fallen asleep last night and I had not, I remembered what had been just out of the reach of memory: Gina having suggested the first time I met her that she knew everything that her boss did.

She wasn't at her desk once I was off the elevator. There wasn't anything *on* her desk, including her computer and what had been her office phone. There didn't appear to be anybody around. No people, no phones ringing. Nothing. Her chair was still there. I went and sat down and started opening the drawers. Nothing there, either.

"Can I help you?"

The voice startled me. I looked up to see a tall African American guy, lot of hair, twist-out style, khakis, polo shirt. Dress-down day, at what was left of Sale Riche.

"I was looking for Gina," I said.

"By looking through her desk?" he said.

"If there's nothing in it or on it," I said, "is it still really hers?" I smiled. "Asking for a friend."

"Who are you?" he said, and I told him. He asked me for some ID. I showed him. I asked him for his name. He said Darrell Dawes. I didn't ask to see his driver's license.

"Where's Gina?" I said.

"She doesn't work here anymore," he said. "The last time I saw her she was practically sprinting through the lobby with a box of her stuff, practically like she was being chased."

"You talk to her?"

"I don't even think she saw me."

"It appears nobody works here, Darrell, except you," I said.

He smiled.

"Last days of the Roman Empire," he

said. "Or maybe I'm the last of the Mohi-cans. Take your pick."

I asked him what his job was, or had been, with Sale Riche. He told me he had been a trader until the decision had been made, after Alex Drysdale's death, to close down the fund.

"Whose decision?"

"What?"

"The decision to close down the fund," I said. "Who made that decision?"

"Alex's investors, I assume."

"Who are they?"

Other than the two of us, the entire floor was as quiet as the creep of time.

"Well, I don't actually know," he said fi-nally.

"Could you find out for me?"

"No," he said.

"You say you were a trader," I said.

"And operations manager," he said with pride.

"And you don't know who had money with Alex?"

"Maybe some of them higher up the food chain did," he said. "But you'd be amazed at how secretive guys like Alex are. Or were."

"So who told you that you no longer had a job here?" I said.

"Gina did, actually," he said. "She said

342

that Alex's prime broker had informed her that Alex had started a full liquidation before he got shot, and had provided a mechanism for all of us on the floor to get one last month of salary."

"Bonuses?"

He shook his head.

"We were entitled to them," he said. "But what were we going to do, take a dead guy to court?"

"Who's the prime broker?" I said.

"He's got a London office now," Darrell Dawes said. "He's Russian, actually. Feodore Pozdey. Alex referred to him as Fred."

I smiled.

Of course he was Russian. What else would he be, Chippewa?

"What's the name of his company?" I said.

"As far as I know, and I don't know much about the guy, the company is him."

He looked at his Apple Watch.

"Listen," he said, "good luck with whatever it is you're doing here, but I've got to go, I've got an interview over on State Street in about forty-five minutes. Another fund. It's been a while since I was between jobs."

"Just a couple more things," I said. "Did Alex ever have business meetings here?"

"Never," Dawes said. "Always out of office. He was very secretive that way, too."

He made a gesture that took in the expanse of empty cubicles.

"Now he's gone," he said. "It's all gone."

"Did he ever mention that he'd made his old friend Christopher Lawton the trustee of the fund?"

Dawes chuckled. "We didn't have that kind of relationship."

"Do you have contact info for Gina?"

He reached into his pocket for his phone, came out with it, tapped the screen a couple times, asked me for my number. I gave it to him, and he texted me her information.

"Anything else you can think of that might help me?" I said.

"Help you do what?"

"Find out who killed him," I said.

He shrugged. "I told you everything I know," he said. "Or don't know."

But then he held up a finger.

"Except for this," he said. "I just remembered it. It was a day or two before he died. I needed to ask him a question, and Gina wasn't at her desk. But before I got to his office, I heard him yelling, just not loud enough to make out what he was saying. When it stopped, I knocked on the door and went in. He was standing at his window, looking at that kick-ass view. I asked him if everything was all right. He didn't turn

344

around, just kept staring out the window. It was like he was talking to himself, saying, 'You never think you'll get this high. But once you do, all you start thinking about is what the fall would be like.' "

Then Darrell wished me luck and turned and walked toward the empty cubicles, and into the quiet. *Sale Riche.* Filthy rich. Not that it did Alex Drysdale a whole hell of a lot of good in the end.

I took the elevator back down to the street and was about to call Gina Patarelli when Frank Belson called.

"Didn't you tell me that Alex Drysdale's former partner was a guy named Lawton?" Belson said.

I had been walking to the Government Center lot, where I'd parked my car. I stopped then. Knowing what he was going to tell me before he did.

"Talk to me, Frank," I said.

"He ate a gun last night," he said.

"Jesus," I said.

"You didn't let me finish," he said.

"There's more?" I said.

"It was your gun," Frank Belson said.

SIXTY

Lawton had lived in what I knew was a cool section in Cambridge, on Garden Street, a few blocks away from Dr. Silverman's combination of home and office. I thought about popping in to see her on my way to meet with Frank Belson, just to maybe work through the fact that people attached to my case kept dying on me. If I could even think of it as a case, since I had no client.

I didn't know when Belson had caught the call, but the crime scene people were mostly gone by the time I arrived at the narrow three-decker on Garden. I saw Belson's car parked at an angle facing the house. He was seated on the steps leading up to the front door. He told me, without preliminaries, that the housekeeper had found Lawton a little after nine. He was at his desk, in his leather chair; my .38, *SR* on the handle, was on the rug next to him.

Belson patted the area next to him.

"Please come sit," he said. "I just wanted to thank you in person for almost single-handedly keeping me in the game."

I sat down.

"I'm just curious," Belson said. "Did the poor bastard tell you he was going to end it all and ask if you could loan him a gun?"

"I forgot to mention that the Russian took it off me when they took me for a ride that night," I said. "I didn't think to ask for it as I was diving out of the backseat."

"Forgot or withheld?" he said. "Such a fine line with you."

"Come on, Frank," I said. "As you recall, I downloaded you a lot of information when we had coffee the other day."

"The Russian you bit?" he said.

"Yup."

"He have a name?"

"Vadim," I said.

He took out his spiral notebook and wrote that down.

"First or last?"

"Don't know," I said. "All I *do* know is that he's one of Eddie Ross's troopers."

Belson took his cigar out of his mouth. "Vadim," he said. "Maybe a first name, maybe last. Hell, I've practically got him booked already."

"I don't understand how my gun ended

347

up in Lawton's hand," I said.

"Look at you," Belson said. "You're like a mind reader."

"You know there's an old line about being rude and sarcastic," I said.

"Yeah, yeah, yeah," he said. " 'I'm not always rude and sarcastic, sometimes I'm asleep.' "

"I don't think he killed himself," I said, "for what it's worth."

Belson said, "We've got a new mobile scanning system. The only fingerprints on the gun are his."

"It doesn't make sense," I said. "I was with him last night, before he left with one of the Russians from a poker game upstairs."

"What poker game?"

I told him about busting in on the game, and my drink with Lawton later, and him telling me about getting money from Russians, and repairing his relationship with Drysdale before he died.

"The Russian who walked Lawton out, he have a name?" Belson said.

I told him what Lawton had said when I asked the same question, about wanting to stay alive.

"So he thought that Russian, but not your Russian, was some kind of threat to him?" Belson said.

"I'm just telling you what he said."

"We'll pull the security video from his lobby, if they've got it," Belson said.

"Somebody wanted this to look like a suicide," I said.

"The ME will tell us if there was a blow to the head," Belson said. "Or the tox screen will tell us if somebody drugged him to set this shit up."

He asked me to take him through it again, from the time Eddie Ross came to my office. I did. I told him about how the poker games were a connection to Drysdale's hedge fund, and how Lawton had used the games to get investors for The Carmody. And how I couldn't turn around without running into a Russian. Belson said he'd gotten that sense, yes.

"You sure that all Lawton was looking for was investors?" Belson said.

"You think he lied about that?" I said.

"I think what you think," Belson said. "That somehow they keep trying to spin you around as a way of keeping you dizzy. Trying to get you to take your eye off the prize."

"Whatever the hell the prize is," I said.

Belson stood.

"We gotta stop meeting like this," he said.

"Tell me about it."

He asked me for Emily Barnes's address in Brighton. He wrote it down in his notebook as I gave it to him. Old school, all the way.

"I sent a car to Ross's brownstone," he said.

"I don't think he lives there, even though the dealer, Matt Dunn, told me he did," I said. "And the phone number Eddie gave me has been disconnected."

"My guys already went in," Belson said. "Probable cause. A beautiful thing. The only clothes they found in any of the closets were a woman's."

"Probably Emily's," I said.

"Girl gets around," he said.

"I needed a class schedule like hers when I was in college," I said.

I walked him to his car.

"You got into this because of Spike, who has his restaurant back," he said. "And from everything you've told me, the girl keeps giving you the middle finger."

"Your point?"

"My point is that I don't want the next body I find to be yours," Belson said. "And don't give me one of your smart remarks."

I didn't. Jesse always said that he'd never gotten into trouble keeping his mouth shut when he had nothing to say. Belson drove off. I got into my car and drove to the North End to see if I could find Gina Patarelli.

Preferably alive.

Just as a change of pace.

SIXTY-ONE

I loved everything about the North End.

Loved the people, loved walking the streets, loved the old-Boston feel of it, as if you'd entered some kind of time machine, just one that served what I considered the best Italian food this side of Little Italy. Or maybe including Little Italy.

The address I had for Gina Patarelli was on Hanover Street, in what turned out to be a third-floor walk-up over Bricco, a restaurant I knew, and Caffe Paradiso, whose pastries I knew far too well. Richie and I used to walk over here from his saloon and sit outside when the weather was warm enough and even sometimes when it wasn't, and eat cannoli and drink Italian espresso with maybe just a splash of Hennessy in it and watch the world go by.

On the ride over here from Cambridge, I'd tried the number Darrell Dawes had given me, but my calls kept going straight to voicemail. I left just one message, reminding her who I was and referencing our conversation at Sale Riche, and that I needed to talk to her as soon as possible. I didn't say it was urgent. Too much.

It was a red-brick building set in the middle of a busy block, full of people and chatter and life. I rang the buzzer for 3B. No response from the speaker. No click of the door. Rang it again. Same thing.

I sat then on the top step and considered my limited options, none great. I could sit here and wait and hope that if she was inside and simply not answering the buzzer, she'd eventually come outside. Or that if she'd gone out, on a job interview of her own or to do some shopping, she'd come back sooner or later.

Or maybe she was gone and was never coming back, because she really did know everything that Alex Drysdale had known, and I wasn't the only one she'd ever mentioned that to.

I was about to get up and ring the buzzer again when an elderly white-haired woman, small and sturdy, started up the stairs with a couple grocery bags from the Star Market I knew was on Causeway Street near North Station.

She looked a bit out of breath. I knew the

market was probably a mile away if you walked it.

"May I help you?" I said.

She smiled. *"May,"* she said. "Not *can* I help you. *May* I help you. I used to teach English. Still appreciate the finer points of the language."

She had periwinkle-blue eyes and a face full of lines that was somehow still beautiful.

"I'm Betty Cafaro," she said, handing me one of the bags as I introduced myself. It was heavy.

"That's a good walk from the Star," I said.

"I can go more than that if I have to," she said.

We were still at the bottom of the steps. I could see her discreetly trying to get her breathing under control.

"You waiting for somebody out here?" she said.

"I was hoping to see Gina Patarelli," I said. "But she doesn't appear to be home."

"Sure she is," Betty Cafaro said.

She started up the steps, pulling her key out of the side pocket of her windbreaker with her free hand.

"By the way," she said. "I could have managed those bags myself."

"I have no doubt," I said. "You said you

354

think she's here and just not answering?"

"Unless she left while I was out," she said. "She was coming up the stairs with a new suitcase when I went to do my shopping. A big one. The kind with roller skates on them? I asked her if she was going somewhere, and she said something odd back to me."

"What was that?"

"She said she was about to be quarantining again," the old woman said.

She narrowed her blue eyes.

"You got any idea what that might have meant?"

"Can I trust you, Betty?" I said, lowering my voice and trying to make it sound conspiratorial.

"Just because I'm older than water doesn't mean I'm some kind of busybody," she said.

"There's a possibility that Gina might be in some danger," I said.

She put down her bag. I did the same.

"You here to do something about that?" she said. "If you were with the police, I have a feeling you would have already shown me a badge."

"Private detective," I said.

"Well, no shit!" she said, so loudly it made me laugh, and led me inside, telling me as we climbed the stairs that she was in 3H.

When we got to the third floor, she walked over and banged on Gina's door with surprising force and yelled, "Gina, it's Betty Cafaro and I need your help."

It took only a few seconds for Gina Patarelli to open the door. When she did, she saw me standing next to Betty.

"Fuck," she said, then immediately said, "Sorry, Mrs. Cafaro."

"I'm eighty-seven years old, missy," she said. "I've heard worse. Now let this woman in, she makes it sound like you might be up to your ass in alligators."

SIXTY-TWO

She had no choice but to do what Betty Cafaro had just told her.

So she did. She wore a West Wing T-shirt and tight white jeans I was pretty sure were Athleta even without any branding on them. Nike running shoes with some miles on them. Maybe about to get more.

The new suitcase was near a door I assumed led to her bedroom.

"Going somewhere?" I said.

"You're the one who needs to go," she said. "You need to leave me alone and leave this alone."

She sounded like Emily Barnes, standing in the middle of the living room, arms crossed, having made no indication she wanted me to sit.

"Define *this*," I said.

"Alex's death, the hedge fund, *me*," she said. "I told your guy, the black guy, the

357

same thing. Just please leave me the fuck alone."

"What has you this scared?" I said. "Or who?"

"They . . . It doesn't matter," she said. "I just need to leave Boston for a while." She paused. "Maybe forever."

I wanted to keep my own voice calm, hoping it might do the same for her, if that were even possible.

"Gina," I said. "Who's *they*?"

"You know who they are!" she said. "It's not even a *they*! It's that Eddie Ross."

"He came to see you."

Now she seemed to be hugging herself.

"He thought I knew more about Alex's business than I do," she said. "I told him I didn't, that all's I did was talk a good game."

"Where was this?"

"The office, after Alex died," she said. "Then he told me that just to be sure, he was taking my computer. He had some big guy with him, never said a word, just stared at me the whole time. He took Alex's computer. The big guy. Eddie took mine. Out they went. When I got home later, the big guy was waiting for me outside. He pulled back his coat and showed me some little gun he had in his belt and told me we were going up to my apartment, he was here

358

to pick something up. I just kept looking at the gun. I asked him what he wanted. He said my laptop."

"That was it?"

"Before he left he said he had a message from Eddie," she said. "Told me that Eddie wanted him to tell me that if I knew what was good for me, I'd stay out of his business."

"Eddie came to my office one time and basically told me the same thing," I said.

"You have a gun?" Gina said.

"I do," I said. "I think the little one the big guy showed you might have been one he took from me and maybe used on Christopher Lawton."

"Alex's old partner?" she said. "He's dead, too?"

I nodded.

"Jesus, Mary, and Joseph," she said. She shook her head. "Just leave so I can leave, okay? I didn't sign up for any of this shit. I'm just a smartass girl from Revere whose old man owned a pizza place over by the beach."

"Did you know Alex had made Lawton the trustee of the fund?"

She shook her head, very quickly, side to side. I thought she might cry.

"I thought if anybody was going to be in

charge, it would be his prime broker, this guy Fred from London," she said. "Or maybe not even him. Alex was getting more and more tight-lipped lately, like he was scared of something."

"Obviously with good reason," I said.

"Listen," she said, "I'm telling you I don't know everything Alex was into, and whether or not it was what got him killed. I just know that I don't want it to get *me* killed, if that's just the same with you."

There was no telling her that at this point in the proceedings, I happened to feel the exact same way.

"Could there be something more going on here than just turning the fund into a family office?" I said.

"You know what that is?" she said.

"Barely," I said. "So could there be something more going on with Alex's money now that he's gone?"

"That's for you to find out and for me to no longer give a shit about," Gina said.

She walked over to the window and pulled back the draperies and looked down on Hanover Street as if afraid she were being watched. Probably wondering how she had ended up here. Not in her apartment. In what she had called "this." A few weeks ago her world had been Alex Drysdale's fee

360

structures and payouts and pairs trading and even the alpha and beta that Jalen Washington had told me about, all part of a language I was trying to learn on the fly.

Now she lived in fear of the same goon squad I did. But she was right about something. I had signed up for this. She hadn't.

"Where will you go?" I said.

"Somewhere they can't find me."

"Hard to do."

"Watch me."

Then: "Please leave now."

"You must have some idea about what might be about to go down," I said. "You're too smart not to."

She hesitated.

"I'm telling you I don't know," she said. "Alex knew. Didn't help him very much, did it?"

"I can help *you*," I said.

Somehow I did feel as if I were talking to Emily Barnes all over again, all the way back at the beginning, at Lee's place. Now Gina Patarelli didn't want my help, either. Sunny Randall, ace private eye. Starting to detect a pattern here.

I reached into my bag and came out with a pen and one of my cards and wrote my cell number on the back, and my address, and handed it to her.

"If you need anything," I said.

"Just to be left alone," she said.

She walked past me and opened her door. I didn't say anything. Neither did she. I walked toward the stairs. As I did, I was pretty sure I heard a door close at the other end of the hall. It was probably my friend Betty Cafaro.

At least she'd wanted my help.

Whatever happened to girl power?

SIXTY-THREE

I was back home and had walked Rosie and was prepping for a much-needed run when Jalen Washington called.

"How's the arm?" I said.

"The Sox think I can be ready by Opening Day," he said.

I asked how the vacation was going.

"Itching to get back up there and get back in the damn game," he said. "I like being a private eye."

"You'll get over it," I said.

He asked me to bring him up to date. I did, telling him about my conversations with Darrell Dawes and Gina Patarelli.

"She tell you more than she told me?" Jalen said.

"Hostile witness," I said, and told him she'd told me she was about to disappear, I just had no idea where.

"Sounds like Eddie and the boys got her attention," I said, "the way they got yours."

"Sounds like you don't know any more'n me about what they got going with old Alex's money," he said.

"But maybe getting closer," I said. "Let me do a little forensic sleuthing of my own and get back to you."

"Call you when I'm back."

"In the meantime," I said, "try not to get yourself shot down there."

"Only if someone at Joe's Stone Crabs is packing," he said.

I found myself wishing that I had a sit-down with Susan Silverman today. But I often felt that way. If she wasn't able to solve interior problems for me, she was always useful helping me organize my brain, especially when I was processing what felt like an overload of new information.

Like now.

Like finding out that Lawton and Alex Drysdale had mended fences before both of them had ended up dead, and left Eddie Ross the only Stanford guy still standing.

"You don't even know what the game is," Emily Barnes had said, before calling me a stupid bitch. Another reason why I wanted to see Dr. Silverman. She never called me stupid, though she had to have thought it from time to time.

I changed my mind about a run, because

sometimes it didn't take much to do that, and went upstairs to paint, hoping to clear my brain of everything except trying to capture the lighthouse in Paradise I had frozen in time. I needed to use all of the overhead lighting in the room today, because we'd just changed over to Daylight Savings Time, and the late-afternoon light that I loved up here was mostly gone by the time I got to my studio.

When I was done, after a good long session, I went to the window and stared out at the lights of Back Bay, watching darkness chase away what was left of the afternoon. Then I moved to the front window and looked down at the street, taking it on faith that Gled was out there somewhere, or someone working for him, even though I had never seen nor met any of his sidemen. Someone to watch over me. I smiled. I loved that song, particularly Ben Webster's version of it.

I could activate the sound system from anywhere in the house. I put on Ben Webster now as I cleaned my brushes and took off my Dodgers sweatshirt and went downstairs and poured myself a glass of wine and lit a fire and listened to Ben. It was the *See You at the Fair* album, the last one he recorded in the States before moving to

Europe.

I sat and stared at the fire and wondered all over again what secrets Alex Drysdale had died with, and now Lawton, two Stanford guys who were going to own the world.

Yesterday I was lying. Today I'm telling the truth.

Somebody ought to put *that* to music.

When I had first met Christopher Lawton we had sat and looked out at the ocean and he had talked about Drysdale as if they'd gone through a shitty divorce. But not long after, Drysdale had chosen Lawton to oversee his fund if something happened to him. Which something sure had. Then the same thing had happened to Lawton.

So who was the trustee now? The prime broker about whom Darrell Dawes had spoken might now be the executor himself, but it was the middle of the night in London even if I'd had his number, which I sure did not. Maybe Gina knew. Or could find out. Maybe I should have asked before she literally showed me the door.

The more I found out, the less I knew. Not the first time it had happened that way.

What secrets had Lawton died with? Belson said he might have the tox report in a couple days, to see if Lawton had been drugged before he died. *Could* he have killed himself, because of his secrets? Of course. I was no expert in depression. I had read enough stories about suicides to know how often even those closest to the victims said they had seen no signs. Was it as often as friends and family talked about all the signs they *had* seen? I had no way of knowing. Maybe Dr. Silverman would know that, too.

But I was a trained detective, even if I once again felt like one trying to find my way out of a deep and dark forest, and I had sat at the bar at The Carmody the night before he was found dead in his study on Garden Street. Not only had I not seen indicators of a possible and imminent suicide, I would have bet my own life that they didn't exist. This wasn't Richard Cory at the end of the poem, going home and putting a bullet in his head.

I drank wine and called Spike.

When he answered I could hear the restaurant in the background. He was still only using half of the old space while the other half was repaired. But customers were again coming through the door.

"Do you think I'm a stupid bitch?" I said.

He laughed. It sounded good. He was Spike again.

"Neither," he said. "Stupid, nor a bitch. Who said you were?"

"A mean girl," I said.

He asked if I wanted to come over and sit with him and talk things out.

"Not tonight," I said. "I just want to sit here and feel stupid."

"You know there's no talking to you when you're like this," Spike said. "You stupid bitch."

Now I laughed.

For some reason, I thought about calling Richie. I still felt that way sometimes, at this time of night, sitting in this room, listening to jazz and drinking wine and having a fire going, Rosie the dog next to me on the couch. But I didn't call Richie. Or Jesse. Sometimes the only companionship I needed was Rosie, even when things were going well with Jesse, the way they were now. But they had been going well with Richie until they weren't.

I had gotten into all of this to help out two friends. Now three people were dead. All of them shot, most likely by the same shooter. Perhaps the tall Russian I'd shot outside the Beacon Hill Hotel when all I was doing was picking up a pizza.

I had managed to live this long not knowing any Russians, not really, and yet now my life was crawling with them, like I was an election they wanted to hack.

I still wasn't sure if Eddie Ross was Raskolnikov.

Or what his real game was.

My doorbell rang. Rosie growled. I walked into the foyer and even knowing that the door was locked and that I didn't think someone intending me harm would ring the bell I still reached into the drawer of Melanie Joan's antique console table and took out my gun.

I slid back the opening to the peephole and saw Gina Patarelli.

When I opened the door she said, "There's something you need to look at."

Then she handed me a thumb drive.

"I took this when I left," she said.

SIXTY-FOUR

We sat at the kitchen table. I asked Gina if she wanted some wine. She said red if I had it. I told her I did, and opened a bottle of cabernet that Spike had given me, saying I could break it out the next time I cooked up a steak for him, if I ever did cook up another steak for him.

"I made it after he was murdered," Gina Patarelli said, the little flash drive next to my laptop. "But I didn't *really* go into it until after you left my apartment."

"I thought you didn't have a laptop," I said.

"Betty's old Dell," she said.

"Why did you copy his files?" I said. "You would have had to do it before Eddie showed up at the office, correct?"

"My boss had just gotten shot on the street where he lived," she said. "And there'd been a lot of general weirdness going on before that."

In her Boston accent, *lot* came out *lawt.*

"What kind of weirdness?"

"Like I said, he had started to act a little paranoid. Alex, I mean. I asked him one day if he was all right and he said, 'Never better.' But it was in that sarcastic way that made you think he meant the opposite."

She drank some of her wine.

"And I thought that maybe if I went through his shit I might finally know what he'd known. Or a lot more than I did."

Rosie sat at her feet. My dog didn't like all strangers. But maybe she sensed the same thing about Gina that I did. That she was real, and good.

"What changed your mind about me?" I said.

She looked at me and smiled for the first time since she'd come through the door. She still had a little too much hair and maybe a lot too much hair, and had gone heavier than she needed to on the eye makeup, and lipstick the color of a plum. None of that could hide how pretty she was. And the intelligence in the dark eyes.

"I come out of a pretty tough neighborhood in Revere," she said, "before Pop moved us over to Lynn. I have three older brothers and was raised not to take any shit. And the more I kept thinking about it, the more I decided that the reason they thought they could mess with me was because I was a girl."

"Happens to me all the time," I said.

Then I pointed at the drive and said, "So what you got going there, girl?"

She smiled again and plugged the drive into the side of my MacBook Air and took me through it, this young woman who sounded as street-smart as Jalen Washington did when he was trying to explain the world of money to me. It somehow made me happy, that the girl from Revere Beach and the street kid from Blue Hill seemed to know as much as the whiz-bang Stanford and Wharton boys.

Gina Patarelli tried to keep it simple, promising that she wouldn't take me too deep into the weeds. But the bottom line was that Alex Drysdale, as the general partner of Sale Riche — and the only partner on record — had essentially turned his fund into a trust.

"In this case," she said, "you can think of the trust as a will. Wills have beneficiaries. But that's the thing: There was no wife, no kids. He was an only child and, get this, his dead parents were only children. What're the odds? And as much money was involved, Alex kept things simple. He dealt with the investors directly. Bottom line, though? The guy hated paperwork, mostly because he didn't want to read any of it."

"No will?" I said.

"Like I said, the fund was the same as his will. One of the bank lawyers drew it up and he signed off on it."

"Who was his lawyer?"

"He didn't even have one when he died," she said. "Before that he went through them like Skittles." She sighed. "Even smart guys act like incredible dopes sometimes. Starting with this: They think they're going to live forever, and that they can work out the details later. He was like an old-fashioned bullshitter acting like he was running the whole thing out of his pocket."

"Even with big money at stake."

"Even with."

"So who got the money if something happened to him," I said, "the way something did?"

She paused just long enough to make me wait for it.

"You're gonna love this," Gina Patarelli said.

She waited.

"Wharton," she said.

"Wharton?" I said.

"Go figure."

Fig-ya.

"He used to talk about that MBA he got there the way guys talked about women they slept with," she said. "He told me once that it was football that got him into Stanford, but he got himself into Wharton on his own, whether he was the world's greatest student when he got there or not."

"And so they were going to get his money?"

"He would have changed stuff if he'd ever gotten married," she said. "Probably would've, whether he had a pre-nup or not. But it was still the school the day he died. As far as I know, the only trustee he ever had before this was his old man, who died about nine months ago. Heart attack. Alex put off naming another trustee until Lawton."

"But our Wharton guy was still going around shaking down people like my friend, and guys who owned gyms?" I said.

"He probably tried to keep it from the Alumni Association," Gina said.

Her glass was empty. I asked if she were driving. She said she'd taken an Uber. I poured more wine into her glass. Our relationship, clearly, had evolved exponentially across the course of the day. Now we were kicking back over a couple bottles of red and white.

"Are his investors listed on what you took off the drive?" I said.

"Every single one of them is a shell company, I checked," she said. "You know what those are, right?"

"I'm not a complete idiot about this stuff," I said.

She smiled and made a wavy motion with her hand.

"So he could've been fronting for Russians, even if their fingerprints weren't on the fund," I said.

"Maybe so," she said. "But good luck trying to find out."

"How much money are we talking about, by the way?" I said.

"Ballpark?"

Ball-pawk.

"Fifty million, give or take."

"All going to Wharton."

"That's fifty before the investors are paid off, provided they do get paid off," Gina said. "After that, there's just one question we need to get answered."

"You have my undivided attention," I said.

Gina Patarelli grinned.

"Who's the trustee now that Lawton is dead?" she said.

375

Spike came over to pick up Gina and drive her back to Hanover Street to pick up clothes and toiletries and other girl stuff. Then they were going back to his apartment, where she had agreed to stay for the next couple days.

"You think I'm not safe?" she said.

"I'd just rather know that you are," I said.

"Think of me as a gay superhero," Spike said, "just with no tights."

"To his everlasting chagrin," I said.

"We can even go over those files again," Spike said. "You can ask Sunny. I'm way better with numbers than I used to be."

It was after eleven when they left. I told Gina that I had some calls to make in the morning, and would check in with her after I did.

At the door she said, "I'm sorry I acted like an idiot before."

I said, "Now you know how I've been feeling lately."

Spike kissed me on the cheek.

"You think the balloon is about to go up?" he said.

The Americanization of Emily was one of our favorite all-time movies.

"Yeah," I said, "I do. Now I just have to figure out where."

"And with who."

"Whom."

He kissed me again. "Even better," he said.

They left. I put on my very cool L.L. Bean utility vest and walked Rosie. I looked around for Gled, or his men, and of course they weren't in sight. When this was over, I would ask him where their stakeout location had been, or if they changed it from day to day, night to night.

When Rosie had finished her oblations, we went back inside. I locked the door and set the alarm. Spoiled myself, because I deserved it, with a chocolate chip cookie and a glass of milk, before Rosie and I went upstairs to call it a night.

There was much to do in the morning, starting with a phone call to Wharton, without even knowing to whom I needed to speak about Alex Drysdale's trust, and if anyone had contacted them about it since his death. Maybe someone up there could complete the refresher course that Gina had started for me, and Jalen before her.

I still didn't know everything I wanted or needed to know. But I knew a lot more now than I had before Gina had appeared on my doorstep with her thumb drive.

Follow the money.

I was awakened in the night by my phone. I was afraid it might be Spike. The display said that it was 1:15 in the morning and that it was an unknown caller. Rosie was standing at the end of the bed, staring at me.

"They're going to kill me," the voice, female, said.

I sat up, fully awake now, the only real light in the room coming from my phone.

"Who is this?"

"Emily."

"Where are you?" I said.

"A friend's house, near Taft," she said, her voice sounding high-pitched, as if about to shatter. I had read somewhere that anxiety affected the throat area that way.

"Who's going to kill you?" I said.

"Who do you think?" she said. "Eddie. He killed them all and now he's going to kill me."

"Why now?"

"I found out something I wasn't supposed

to know," she said.

There was a pause and then she said. "I should have listened to you from the start."

Everybody was getting religion late in the church service tonight.

"They don't know about this place," she said. "My friend's out of town. Please come get me."

She gave me the address in Walford. I told her I was on my way.

Sunny Randall Investigations, I thought. We never close.

SIXTY-SIX

I thought about calling Spike, despite the hour. But I didn't want him to leave Gina. I still trusted that I had backup from Gled and the boys if I needed it, even though I couldn't spot anybody trailing me on the way out to Walford.

Whatever Emily Barnes had become — or perhaps had been all along — she was still Lee Farrell's niece. I'd promised him I'd find out what had happened to her. Now I kept finding out. And would do it one last time now.

I knew Lee was in Nantucket, chasing down a lead on the Carly Meme case, the lead being that she might be alive and had staged her disappearance.

"Imagine what it would do for her You-Tube channel," Lee had said.

But then the world was full of drama queens, and kings, lives played out on social media with moment-by-moment updates.

Maybe Emily Barnes, poker queen, had thought her life was some kind of drama. What was the movie about poker? *Molly's Game*? Maybe Emily had thought she was playing the Jessica Chastain part. Or that Jessica Chastain should have been playing her.

Only she had ended up in over her head. Way over.

He killed them all and now he's going to kill me.

The address she'd given me turned out to be a couple miles away from the Taft campus, and the reservoir where Emily had been attacked. Lee had told me once that off-campus housing was scattered all over the town of Walford, almost as if the whole town *was* the Taft campus.

Brick Kiln Lane was off Taft Drive, and 44 Brick Kiln was at the end of a cul-de-sac, a fair amount of distance between the house and the ones closest to it. I could see a faint light behind the drawn curtains on the first floor of the house. I parked in the driveway and took one last look behind me for Gled. If they were still with me, they were even better than I had originally thought.

I had brought the Glock with me. I took it out of my bag as I walked toward the front door of 44 Brick Kiln.

Yesterday I was lying. Today I'm telling the truth.

Which was it with Emily Barnes?

Lying tonight or telling the truth?

I knocked on the door and waited. No sound from inside. I tried the handle. Locked. If she was afraid for her life, it would be locked.

I knocked again.

"Emily?" I said.

Now I heard her.

"Sunny?" she said from the other side of the door.

I heard the bolt being released and saw the handle turning and when the door opened, Vadim had a gun pointed at me.

Presumably his own this time.

He motioned me into the front hall and put out his hand and I handed him my gun. Kind of our thing.

"They are waiting for you," he said, and motioned me toward the living room to my left.

Eddie Ross was standing in the middle of the room, wearing what looked like the same suit he'd been wearing that first day in my office. Emily Barnes, legs crossed, wearing an even shorter skirt on her than she'd been wearing at The Carmody and a

382

tight, scoop-necked T-shirt, was on the couch, a champagne flute on the coffee table in front of her.

Eddie looked at me and shook his head, as if I'd just broken curfew with Mom and Dad's car.

"You just wouldn't get the message," he said, "even though I did everything except hire a goddamn skywriter."

"Stupid bitch," Emily said to me again.

SIXTY-SEVEN

A very tall man was leaning against a wall to my right, behind Emily. He also had a gun pointed at me.

Eddie nodded at the tall man.

"Boyko thinks that he should be the one who gets to shoot you because you shot him, and he believes that is worse than you biting Vadim."

"I could leave," I said, "and you could work it out among yourselves."

"You don't get away this time," Eddie said.

"I intuited that," I said. I looked at Boyko. "That means I'd already figured that out."

"Хуй Тебе!" he said.

"Probs can figure that out, too," I said.

"Let me be of help," Boyko said. "Fuck you."

Keep talking. Keep everybody talking. And hope that the Russian cavalry was out there somewhere. I tried to tell myself I had been in tougher spots than this, but now I was the one lying.

I looked over at Emily. "You and Eddie make a cute couple," I said.

"Stupid, stupid, stupid," she said.

"We did everything we could not to have to kill you, Sunny Randall," Ross said. "We thought you would walk away after your friend got his restaurant back, even after poor Alex died."

"I might have, Eddie," I said. "I actually considered it. But then you had to go ahead and shoot poor Matt Dunn, too."

Eddie shook his head slowly again, side to side, then sighed.

"He was just a loose end," Eddie said, "at the table the night all of us met and this all started. Eventually he started to ask questions."

"Why'd you stuff the card in his mouth?"

He said, "We wanted you to keep thinking this was all about poker."

"And not Alex's fund," I said.

"And Kuznetzov, the big Russian, that was just another bluff, right?"

"The last time I checked, Mr. Kuznetzov was living the life with his latest wife in the Maldives."

"Never came to Boston to play poker," I said.

"Never been to Boston, far as I know,"

385

Eddie Ross said.

"So you were the one who ordered somebody to shoot at me and my friend Jalen," I said.

"Your last warning shots," Ross said.

"Fuck all this talking," Boyko said. "Let's get out of here and be getting this done."

Eddie turned to stare at him.

"Did I ask you?" he said.

He turned his attention back to me.

"We just needed a few more days," Ross said. "But you just would not leave this shit alone."

"I've got more questions," I said.

"This isn't the movies," Eddie said.

I had my Beretta in my boot. Wasn't sure if Vadim would have felt it if he'd patted me down. But I knew that if I went for it, Vadim and Boyko would both get their wish.

"At least answer me this," I said. "Who's the trustee now that Lawton's dead?"

He smiled at me. "It is of no further concern to you," he said.

"Me being the last loose end," I said.

"Not for much longer," Eddie said.

"Last question," I said, "I promise."

"For fuck's sake!" Boyko said.

I ignored him.

"Did you think Wharton isn't going to notice that you're trying to take their

386

money?" I said.

Something changed then in Eddie Ross's eyes, something reptilian in them now as he stared at me across the room.

"To the end," he said, "you still won't let shit go. From the start, Alex didn't understand the problem he'd made for us by bringing you into this."

"You're too kind," I said.

Ross nodded at Boyko, who limped toward the front door.

"Go around back and get the car," Eddie Ross said. "Enough talking."

I hadn't heard the door open. All I heard now was the sound of the first gunshot that spun Boyko around and put him down before he could raise his own gun.

Then I saw Gled leading the way into the room, a long gun in his hand.

Richie Burke was right behind him, yelling for me to get down.

SIXTY-EIGHT

Vadim had dropped to one knee and started firing in their direction. Richie shot him twice and he fell over backward and was still, his gun still in his hand. I crawled over and took it from him. The room was suddenly thick with the smell of the fired guns, sulfurous and metallic.

When I turned I saw Eddie Ross crouched near the other couch in the room, aiming his own gun at Gled.

"Gled!" I yelled, but I was a moment too late. Gled had put himself between Ross and me and Ross shot him now and Gled went down as Ross turned his gun on Richie.

I shot Eddie Ross with Vadim's bull-barreled gun and then Eddie was the one on his back, and the room was finally still. I looked around for Emily Barnes. But she was gone.

Richie was kneeling next to Gled, who was

bleeding in the hip area but very much alive. Richie called 911 and then went to find a towel to apply to Gled's upper leg.

When Richie came back I said, "Did Gled call you?"

He grinned.

"Jesse," he said. "We had the nice visit the other day before he went to see you, the lucky bastard. He thought your backup might eventually require backup."

"Clearly the beginning of a beautiful friendship," I said.

"Not bloody likely," Richie Burke said.

Then I heard Eddie Ross say, "Hey?" in a voice that sounded as if it were coming from another room.

His jacket had fallen open. I could see the blood spreading on the white shirt. Richie went and got another towel and brought it back and I pressed it to where I knew the wound was. But it had been a center-mass hit, the way Phil Randall had taught me before the academy had.

In the distance, I heard the first sirens.

"Was this all you?" I said.

He coughed. A crackling, wet, terrible sound.

"You want to hear the funniest part?" he said. "It was her idea. She played poker with us that night, and after Alex left she said,

'We can take this guy.' "

He waved me to get closer, trying to tell me something else before his eyes closed.

From across the room Gled said, "Ever notice how sooner or later everybody comes across somebody they shouldn't have fucked with?"

I couldn't help myself, despite everything around us in the room, everything that had just happened. I smiled at him.

"Eastwood?" I said.

He winced as he looked down at the towel in his hand.

"*Gran Torino,*" he said. "Except he was talking about himself. I was talking about you."

SIXTY-NINE

This was late the next afternoon, at the Pilgrim National Bank on State Street, a conference room on the fortieth floor. I had brought Gina Patarelli with me.

Ms. Dietrich, one of the bank's lawyers and also a notary public, was seated at one end of a long table. She had silver hair pulled back into a bun, thick black glasses at the end of her nose, and looked like every teacher I'd ever had who sat behind her desk and knew just by looking at me what I hadn't studied the night before. Next to her was a vice president from Wharton, Tim Fox. He had taken a commuter flight from Philadelphia that morning after I'd called him and told him what we thought was going on.

Now Gina and I were standing with our backs to the huge window at the opposite end of the room from Ms. Dietrich, a very sporty view of downtown Boston behind us.

Not as good as Alex's view of the water had been at One Financial Center. Just the city, looking like a brilliant black-and-white photograph against a gray sky. Maybe I'd paint it like that one day.

Ms. Dietrich opened up a folder and shuffled some papers inside it as if paper-shuffling were something she had learned at banker school.

"Are we ready to begin?" she said.

"Not quite yet," I said. "We're waiting on the star of the show."

She looked over her glasses at Gina and me as if she'd just noticed we were in the room. I smiled at her. She did not smile back.

"And you are?" she said.

"With the band," I said.

The meeting had been scheduled for four o'clock. It was only five past, but I could tell that Ms. Dietrich was the type who wanted the plane to pull back from the gate on time. She had been drumming her pen on top of her folder for the past five minutes. She kept checking her watch.

It was then that the door behind her opened, and Jalen Washington came walking in.

392

SEVENTY

He tried to stay cool, I had to give him that. I thought perhaps his arm might still be in a sling. It wasn't.

Just his ass.

"Heard you had some excitement last night," he said, as if we were still buds. "Heard also that our friend Eddie didn't make it."

Now I smiled at him.

"You heard wrong," I said.

He might have looked a couple degrees less cool now. Swift, subtle drop in temperature.

"That's what Richie told me," he said.

"Richie can be an even better liar than you are," I said.

Ms. Dietrich said, "As fascinating as this all sounds, can we get started here?"

"Not quite yet," I said again.

"May I ask who put you in charge of this meeting?" she said, putting some snap into her voice now, as if she were about to foreclose on the family farm.

"Since I represent the institution that is the beneficiary of Mr. Drysdale's fund," Tim Fox said, "I guess you could say I'm the one who put Ms. Randall in charge." He smiled. "It's the old one about the golden rule. He who has the gold, rules."

"But I'm the trustee now, soon as we get the paper Chris Lawton drew up before the poor man killed himself," Jalen Washington said. "Signed over his trustee rights to me. I got the right to distribute those funds however I want."

"Why?" I said.

"Why what?" Jalen said.

"Why would Lawton do something like that?" I said. "Unless somebody had a gun to his head."

"Got no idea what you're talking about," Jalen said. He patted his jacket where the inside pocket was. "All I got is that paper, waiting for me to sign it and this nice woman to notarize it."

"Yeah," I said. "Go with that."

"I'm here for my money, long story short."

"Not if Ms. Dietrich doesn't stamp that piece of paper in your pocket," Fox said.

"But I'm the trustee now," Jalen said.

"You don't listen, do you?" Tim Fox said.

"You're the trustee when Ms. Dietrich says you are. Until she does, what you think is your money is actually going to Wharton."

Gina Patarelli whispered to me, "Alex loved watching things get stamped. If they'd done this with a DocuSign, they might have gotten away with it."

Dawk-u-sign.

Jalen Washington, wearing what looked to be one of Eddie Ross's extra slim suits, was still standing, just inside the door, to Ms. Dietrich's right.

"Eddie gave you up, Jalen," I said. "And I'm pretty sure that when I explain to Ms. Dietrich how you really came into possession of that trust agreement, you can probably wait forever for her to go all notarial on you."

"This is bullshit," Jalen said.

Tim Fox leaned forward and tented his fingers under his chin.

"I'm curious," he said to Jalen. "Where'd you get *your* MBA, Mr. Washington?"

"Orchard Park Houses," I said to Tim Fox. "Eustis Street. Roxbury, Mass."

"You don't think I can't get me a fancy lawyer, when I tell them how much money's in play?" Jalen said. "Would've brought a couple today, thought I needed them."

"Mine are better," Tim Fox said.

"We'll see about that," Jalen said.

"When?" I said.

"What's that supposed to mean?" Jalen said.

I walked down to his end of the room then, his eyes on me the whole time, walked past him, walked past Ms. Dietrich, opened the conference room door.

"Check it out," I said.

There, bookended by two of his troopers, stood Desmond Burke.

Before Jalen Washington left, more than somewhat reluctantly, I told him to make sure and say hello to his girlfriend.

He turned to look at me one last time.

"Eddie really alive?" he said.

"Not even a little bit," I said. "But if it's any consolation, he was talking about you when he died."

SEVENTY-ONE

Before Tim Fox had left the conference room, I had explained the situation with the restaurant, and Victor Morozov's gym, and how technically I thought they might still belong to Alex Drysdale.

"I'll take care of it," he said.

"How?" I asked.

He smiled. "Don't worry your pretty little head about it," he said, then quickly added, *"Kidding!"*

The next night I was sitting next to Spike, at Spike's, at the head of a long table he'd had set up in the back room. The front room was still a work in progress, because of the bombing. But the new front window had been installed, the bar had proved that it might be able to survive a nuclear attack, and the back room had needed far less repairs, and painting, than the front. Best of all? The dominant smell was food again, and not bomb.

Gled was there, still needing a cane to get around. Gina Patarelli was sitting next to Gled, as Gled had requested. Jesse was sitting next to me. Richie was across from Jesse. I'd thought about sitting between them, but decided against it. I didn't want to feel like Switzerland, even with them engaged in what I imagined as an armed truce.

"All along I thought of it as *Crime and Punishment,*" I said. "And what it really turned out to be was *The Grifters.*"

"They were all lying," Jesse said.

"Out the ass," Richie Burke said.

Richie knew a lot of it, mostly because, as he said, Jalen Washington had been more than forthcoming once he'd gotten to Desmond's house, about everything that had begun after a poker game at Eddie's brownstone one night about six months ago.

"How did Jalen get a seat?" I said to Richie.

"You know that lady friend of his that Jalen talked about? Kerry?" Richie said. "Turns out her place of employment was, no shit, one of Tony Marcus's high-end escort services. And Alex was one of *her* friends. She was the one who put them together. Or maybe it was destiny."

When the game was over that night, Eddie and Jalen and Emily went for a drink. It really was Emily who told them, "You can take this guy for everything."

Meaning the late Alex "Ace" Drysdale.

That was how it began.

It was a lot of talking from Richie, but he took us through the rest of it as quickly as he could. How old Russian friends of Eddie's father *had* been using Drysdale's fund to launder money, some of it from arms sales in Africa, more in lithium, which Richie said was big on the black market these days. The cash kept Drysdale afloat at the same time. But Eddie and Jalen convinced Drysdale that they could get him out from under the Russians once and for all. Clean out the fund and split up the money before all of them rode off into the sunset.

"Eddie's Russian himself," I said. "He thought they could get away with that?"

Richie said, "He and Jalen had something in common: They *both* thought they were the smartest ones in the game."

"So Alex was in on it," I said.

"Till he wasn't," Richie said. "He's in bed one night with this Kerry, and he runs his mouth, not knowing she's Jalen's lady." He shrugged. "That was that. They were about to have control of the fund, they didn't need him anymore. Eddie had him taken out.

Now there were only two people cutting up the pie. They just had to speed up the process. Lawton told Jalen about the meeting at the bank before he died."

"They were never going to let Drysdale live," Jesse said.

"It wasn't just him opening his big mouth to Kerry," Richie said. "By then he'd brought you into their lives."

Jalen and Boyko went to Lawton's house and told him that if he didn't sign over his trustee rights, they were going to kill him. If he did sign, they'd let him live, maybe even give him a cut.

"He bought that?" I said.

Jesse said, "Sounds like he didn't have much choice at the time."

"Then they drugged him and made it look like a suicide, just to buy themselves the last bit of time they needed to get to the bank," Richie said.

Belson had told me that morning that they'd gotten the tox results back on Lawton, and found chloral hydrate in his system, and that Lawton's death was now being classified as a homicide.

Just not for long.

"They were banking, pardon the pun, on Wharton, being Wharton, not wanting to rush in with their hand out so soon after

400

Drysdale died," Richie said. "But they knew the power a trustee has. The document Jalen had Lawton sign mirrored the one Drysdale and Lawton signed."

He paused.

"And, not for nothing?" he said. "Jalen believes that Lawton would have done the same thing he tried to do if he'd gotten the chance."

"Walk into the bank and walk out with the money," I said. "Like one more grifter."

Gina smiled.

"But only if they could get the sucker notarized," she said.

Suck-ah.

"Who shot him in the arm?" I said.

"One of the Russians," Richie said. "I can't keep them straight."

"I gotta hand it to him," Jesse said, "he was smart enough to nearly pull this off. But there's an old-school cop word for guys like him. He's a 'skell.' And being one caught up with him in the end."

"I still don't understand why they didn't try to kill me sooner," I said.

"They really did do it as a last resort, at least according to what Jalen told Desmond," Richie said. "I told you one time that the only thing that scared Jalen was my father. He apparently kept telling Eddie that

401

he didn't want to be rich and happy on a beach somewhere and have me or my father's men come looking for him."

Richie smiled again. "Go figure," he said. "He still loves you like a daughter."

We drank to Gled then, and to Gina Patarelli, and to Spike having Spike's back, free and clear. Jesse was having club soda with a twist. When the toast was over, he looked over at Richie.

"Where's Jalen now?" Jesse said. "Or do I not want to know?"

"Not dead," Richie said, "if that's what you're asking. What happens from here is between him and my father."

"That doesn't sound good," I said.

"Probably so," Richie said.

I took a small sip of champagne from one of the bottles Spike had just ordered up for the table.

"I was all that was standing between him and fifty million dollars," I said.

"Well, yeah," Gina said, "before taxes."

SEVENTY-TWO

A few minutes later I got a call from Lee Farrell, who had indeed found the unsinkable Carly Meme alive, even if he said he now wanted to murder her himself.

"Emily called," he said.

I told him to hold on, and walked over to the small hallway where the restrooms were located.

"Where is she?" I said.

"She called on a burner," Lee said. "Told me that this was goodbye, she'd already told her mother the same thing, she was about to disappear."

"Vegas?"

"She didn't say," he said.

"That was it?"

"Not quite," Lee said. "She asked if I'd be talking to you, and I said I would, and then she told me to give you a message."

"That doesn't sound welcoming," I said.

"Not so much," Lee Farrell said. "She told

me to tell you that it wasn't over between the two of you."

"Tony Marcus has said the same thing to me, on more than one occasion," I said.

"And yet here you are," Lee said.

He said that if he did hear from her again, even though he didn't expect to, he'd let me know.

"I know how you hate loose ends," he said.

"I just don't shoot mine," I said.

I ended the call. Came out from the hallway, stopped and looked across the room at our table. I smiled as I saw the way Gled was looking at Gina Patarelli. Jesse and Richie weren't smiling at each other, but they seemed to be engaged in polite conversation. The two men in my life. I kept wanting it to be just one, as a way of untangling things. But I knew it would always be two. And things would always be complicated as hell, having both of them prominently in my life. Which both of them had just had a hand in saving. Somehow, as hard as I tried to make it otherwise, I was still living in a man's world.

So often theirs.

They didn't overanalyze things the way I did, whether in Susan Silverman's office or not. Jesse's life was hardly uncomplicated, as he continued to try to stay sober a day at a time. But when the two of them confronted a problem, they were generally about as uncomplicated as a punch in the mouth.

Now here the three of us were, in the same loud room at Spike's.

Spike got out of his chair now and walked over to me and said, "How come you look like you've lost your best friend?"

"You're my best friend," I said.

He put his arm around me and squeezed. "You saved me, friend," he said.

"You've saved me plenty of times," I said.

"Kind of our deal," he said.

I went back with him to the table. Jesse and Richie stopped talking.

"Think I'm gonna call it a night," I said.

They both looked up at me.

I smiled. "Sometimes I just need to be alone."

"I know," they both said at the same time, and the three of us laughed.

I was just tired of talking about it all. Tired, period. I just wanted to see Rosie the dog. She didn't need to worry about having me all to herself because she already did. I still wasn't sure why Eddie Ross had given Jalen up before he died. Maybe if he couldn't have the money, he didn't want anybody to have it.

I parked my car in my space behind the house and was coming around the corner when Emily Barnes stepped out into the light, pointing a gun at me.

Of course, I thought.

Who wasn't these days?

"Where's Jalen?" she said.

"Put the gun away, Emily," I said, keeping my voice calm.

"After you tell me where Jalen is," she said.

"I don't know," I said.

I kept my focus on the gun. There was a slight tremor to her hand, but at this distance she wasn't going to miss if she fired. Maybe she thought I was *her* last loose end.

"You ruined everything, you stupid, *stupid* bitch," she said. "And now I want my money."

Love or money.

"Jalen's not getting the money," I said. "You probably heard."

"He and Eddie had figured out a way to skim money off the Russians, a little bit at a time," she said.

"Before they screwed them on the back end," I said.

She offered a tight smile. "No honor among thieves," she said. "Now I want my cut."

"And Jalen's just going to hand it over?"

"I got him to tell me how he killed Chris Lawton," she said. "I taped him."

"Of course you did," I said.

She made a tiny forward gesture with the gun.

"Jalen taught me how to use this thing," she said.

"I'm sure he did."

"Tell me where he is or I swear, I *will* shoot you," she said.

"For the last time," I said, "I don't know."

"For the last time," she said, *"don't lie to me!"*

Her voice had gotten louder. Just not loud enough for any neighbors to hear. Just the two of us. No bodyguards any longer.

I turned my head to the left then, as if I'd heard something. It was enough for her to take her eyes off me, and distract her, as I stepped in and just slightly to the side and hit her with the hardest punch I'd ever thrown in my life. It was the one Henry Cimoli had taught me how to throw. One Jesse had joked he never wanted to see, but had just put Emily Barnes on her back.

Down and nearly out.

Maybe guys had it figured out. Maybe sometimes the way to solve the problem was a punch in the mouth.

It felt awesome.

I reached down and picked up the gun that had fallen next to her and said, "Now we're done."

ACKNOWLEDGMENTS

I have been given the high privilege of writing Sunny Randall and now Jesse Stone by Daniel and David Parker.

The great Esther Newberg told me to write a sample chapter one day, which is how I came to work with — and for — Ivan Held and Sara Minnich.

I am grateful to all of them, and finally to my pal Peter Gethers, who taught me everything about poker except how to beat him.

ABOUT THE AUTHOR

Robert B. Parker was the author of seventy books, including the legendary Spenser detective series, the novels featuring police chief Jesse Stone, and the acclaimed Virgil Cole/Everett Hitch westerns, as well as the Sunny Randall novels. Winner of the Mystery Writers of America Grand Master Award and long considered the undisputed dean of American crime fiction, he died in January 2010. **Mike Lupica** is a prominent sports journalist and the *New York Times*-bestselling author of more than forty works of fiction and nonfiction. A longtime friend to Robert B. Parker, he was selected by the Parker estate to continue the Sunny Randall series.